MW01222677

Within The Veil:
An Adventure In Time

Within The Veil:
An Adventure In Time

A Book by Ruth Lee
That Teaches in a Novel Way

LeeWay Publishing
Pittsburgh, Pennsylvania, USA

LeeWay Publishing

Books That Teach in Novel Ways

For a free catalog or ordering information, write:
LeeWay Publishing
4885-A McKnight Rd., Suite 406
Pittsburgh, PA 15237 USA
(412) 367-1746   Fax: (412) 369-8936

Copyright © 1996 by Ruth Lee

All rights reserved. No part of this book may be reproduced by any means or in any form whatsoever without written permission from the publisher, except for brief quotations embodied in literary articles or reviews.

Cover Illustrations: Julie Hart

Published by LeeWay Publishing
4885-A McKnight Rd., Suite 406
Pittsburgh, PA 15237 USA

ISBN 1-888988-05-3

Library of Congress Catalog Card Number: 96-94779

This book was manufactured in the United States of America.

In Memory of
My first and wisest teacher—this life,
My Mother

Contents

TIME OUT!

WITHIN THE VEIL

AN

ADVENTURE

IN TIME

Time Shifts

"Things are never what they seem after you meditate. You either feel you know everything, or you feel like you are nothing—which is how I felt the other day.

"I was just sitting out front on the curb when a horse pulling a carriage came swinging by me at a fast canter—not exactly a gallop. It appeared to be out of mid-century London—18th century, that is. I saw myself as a boy of about ten or twelve. It was weird. I felt like I was lost in time. When the carriage got to the red light at the corner, it disappeared!

"Right. I know. You think I'm cracking up and acting like an idiotic woman who has lost her mind and can't find it; but believe me, it happened.

"I just sat there staring into space when all of a sudden an old-fashioned lady approached me. She was dressed in an elegant empire-style gown with a hat that sort of perched on her head and was tied under her chin with a wide velvet ribbon that ended in a big bow at her left ear. I immediately thought of Jane Austen; but why would anyone parade around dressed like her? Before I could get a handle on it, she was gone, too.

"I have to admit this has happened to me before—from time to time, and I always figured it was due to an over-active imagination, but lately something is wrong—maybe different or way out describes it better. Anyway, lately I feel, rather than see, strange things happening all around me. I discern weird beings sitting around watching me. I can almost touch them, but they're not really there. Anyway, believe me when I say: 'Strange things are happening!'

"Another example: When I got dressed today, there was a stranger in the mirror. Yeah, I know it sounds psychotic at best, but I saw a woman in the mirror who looked nothing like me. She had a deep blue scarf wrapped around her neck and a pin—maybe a cameo—was her only jewelry. It looked like she

I

was wearing some kind of suit. Actually, she looked like an actress made up to play an old-fashioned shop girl from the turn or the century. Weird.

"What does all this mean? I don't know. You're a scientist. You know everything, so tell me. What is happening?"

"Well, I sort of think maybe you've had a deep disturbance in your time warp and are having trouble concentrating on this one—and if you don't get back in it now, you may be wandering about in time for the rest of eternity. You're supposed to be here and now!"

"What?? Are you saying I'm turning into some kind of *time traveler* or something?"

"Could be, but I kind of think you're just experimenting, but not fully aware of it."

"Right! I sit down and drift off to la-la land and sort of experiment with out-of-body work which takes me into other times while I'm wide awake?"

"Yeah, something like that."

"You've got to be kidding! I may meditate, but I'm no New Age whiz kid. I don't stand around on my head for hours or indulge in angst encounters. I'm just a happy-go-lucky nobody."

"There! You said it. Now you know why you've been chosen."

"Chosen?? For what? And why would I be chosen for anything? You're not making sense."

"Oh, yes, I am, and you know it. Think! Concentrate on YOU. React if you must, but you know. Your mind is always full of ideas and ideals waiting for their time, and you know you have enough energy for three people but never figured out why. It's simple! You're one of the chosen."

"Wait a minute! You think that because I'm happy and full of spirit I've been picked to do something really weird?"

"Not really, but now that you mention it, maybe so."

"Why weren't you picked, instead of me?"

"I'm not happy—and I don't like to work. You do."

"Whatever happened to the work you were doing on that thing about space? Did you ever finish it?"

"No, I dropped it when the degree of intelligence required surpassed the degree of intellect I possess."

"What?"

"You heard me. I got tired of the work. I couldn't hold it together. I felt like it wasn't my time....All right, all ready, I fell in love and forgot myself. Are you satisfied now?"

"Sort of, but you never should have fallen in love. You know it messes up everything."

"Now you tell me, but then you got all rosy and said, 'I think you're awfully cute, too'."

"What? You fell for ME? I don't believe it. It never happened. You're joking."

"I would like to agree with you; but for the first time ever, I'm going to tell you, I really loved you, and if I thought there would ever be a chance, I would change that from past to present tense immediately, but I know it won't happen. Right?"

"Oh, dear, I wish I could see that far into the future."

"Oh, no, don't tell me that. It's hard enough declaring out loud something you only whisper to yourself, but to hear it go down the drain in a swish and a glop isn't pretty."

"I'm sorry. I can be so insensitive at times. I'm almost inhuman. I hate that about me. I get so detached. I can't seem to feel the depth of emotion others roll around in and moan about. I love people—en masse—but hardly ever individually."

"You can say that again."

"What part are you referring to?"

"The part where you said you're almost inhuman. I can't place you, which is part of the fascination."

"The entire fascination—believe me. You have to get going on the work you came here to do and then you will feel like me. Honest!"

"I'm working on it, but I get tired."

"You will never get tired of your real work. You just haven't found it yet—believe me."

"Would you stop saying, 'believe me'!"

"No, that's what is wrong. You don't really believe in anything—not God, not You, not anything. How can you? You're so sure your scientific pursuits will give you all the answers you seek, and they can't. You're not even close!"

"You think you're so great because nothing ever gets you down—even stuff that knocks everybody else off their feet."

"Now, now, we're getting a bit testy. You better watch those raging hormones or you'll end up with some kind of male monthly problem that will hang around for days afterward—like a shiner, or a case of VD, or whatever things men get themselves into when they are all pumped up with Father Nature."

"Go ahead and laugh. You think you are very funny. Don't you? The trouble is, you are. You say such outrageous, deep-cutting—really mean things—and always get away with it. How do you do it?"

"I don't care. I just don't care, and I won't accept anybody else's anger, either. I have my own load to pull and don't need yours, too—nothing personal, you know."

"Yeah, I know."

"Oh, come on, you're okay. You just set yourself up for another disappointment and got it—that should make you feel better."

"You know, someday I really am going to punch out your lights."

"There you go, the last of the erudite lovers. Ready at the first sign of conflict to bare arms. That's 'b-a-r-e' not 'b-e-a-r', in case you missed the pun."

"No one can miss your puns. They're all lousy."

"There, there, I see I've ruffled your feathers, and all I wanted to do was bounce off a few far-out ideas. If I can't talk to you, who can I talk to?"

"I don't know. There are so few of us left who are smart, witty, and totally open minded about everything."

"My, my, aren't we straining our triceps a bit much patting ourself on the back?"

"Oh, so you noticed I've been working out?"

"Well—not really, but now that you mention it, I see you have. Why?"

"Why? Why, the woman asks. What are you doing with your life? Don't you know there is a cultural revolution going on? Everyone is trying to keep up their youthful looks by exercising. Everyone but you, of course. But then you don't have to."

"I wouldn't say that, but you're all going about it the wrong way."

"Oh, yes, I know. We're supposed to do yoga or meditate and our bodies will mold themselves into visions of wonder while we do literally nothing."

"Why is that so hard to believe? Oh, yes, I keep forgetting—you don't believe in anything. You're a scientist. You have no room for unformulated material that develops nothing into something. You can't mix black and white and come up with anything but muddy shades of gray or whatever it is you rattle off about whenever anyone comes too close to your sore spot."

"Now look who's getting sore. You are! I can't believe it."

"I'm not mad. I'm just frustrated because every man you meet has to bring out an endless array of artillery—that shoots nothing but blanks. You can't even have a good argument any more—with anyone! No one wants to have a real conversation—not even you."

"Well! I've never been so upset in all my life."

"Oh, knock it off. Sounding like your Aunt Kate doesn't get you off the hot seat. You know you're not doing your work—your real work, and I'm not letting you forget it until you do."

"I guess I better take a nice long, extended vacation if I want to get away from the Great White Wag. Notice I didn't say 'nag'."

"Doesn't matter. You're right. It's your life. You do what you want. I don't have time to barge into your business and help you. If I did, I'd find myself in a big mess—just to teach me a lesson. No, you do what you do, and I'll help if you need me—otherwise, I'm out of here."

"Wait a minute! Wait a minute! Before we got off the track, you started to tell me about this vision thing, and now I'm really interested in what happened."

"I can't remember."

"There you go again. You can't remember. Why do you do that all the time?"

"Because I don't hold onto the past. It's useless—once you know. Do you see?"

"See what? We never discussed it—or your daydreams. We just sort of kidded about it and then you let me redirect the conversation down the same old familiar path, but we never settled anything."

"Oh, yes, we did. You helped me a lot—and I thank you for that."

"How? I didn't say anything. I just sat there with my usual look of stupid adoration while you told me some weird story about how you're feeling out of step with time, then we went through our usual Saturday morning wrangle. How, when, and where did I help you?"

"The same way you always help me. You just listen. You don't really care, but you listen anyway. You let me say what is on my mind, and when I hear myself thinking out loud, the answers come into my mind and then—*I just know.*"

"Wow! You are some crazy chick!"

"Better watch your language, your age is showing."

"Yeah, it's a drag when I'm trying to pick up 30-year-old kids."

"No wonder you're getting nowhere with young women. You're too old."

"Too old? Why I have the body of Adonis! I work out four times a week at the gym and run three miles a day."

"Yeah, and women are falling all over you."

"So, what is your point?"

"You're too punctilious."

"Punctilious? What does the application of the scientific method to everyday life have to do with my scoring with chicks?"

"Forget it. You are absolutely wonderful just the way you are. You chose to come back as an engineer. Nobody said you had to."

"There, I agree. Now we're getting somewhere. The one thing you ever said that made sense to me was when you went into that strange dream thing and

told me you saw us together in Rome—back in the golden times—not on a 17-day tour. Remember? You said I was an engineer then and built or designed the major roads leading out of Rome toward the northwest. That makes sense to me somehow, and I think there are lots of Romans around now. That's why we're paving over the Earth—at last we've got the technology to do it!"

"Did you ever stop to wonder why so many highway contractors are Italian, and why they go to Italy to bring back boatloads of masons and concrete finishers when they need them?"

"Yeah, I actually have. . .See, I am getting New Agey in my old age."

"Not really, but you'll pass—but only if you get going on your work."

"Work! Work! Work! That's all you care about. Why not lay off and let the grass grow for once."

"You know, you really are one of my Guides. I can tell."

"Now there you go again with that Guide nonsense. You lose me every time you do that. What are you saying now?"

"I'm saying that you say things which lead me to my best conclusions, which in turn lead me further into the current that carries me along so efficiently and joyously that I can't believe it's life."

"Translation please. What's going on in that head of yours now? Why are you looking like that? Where are you going this time?"

"See, you are psychic! You *know* I've just decided to take a trip."

"Anybody who knows you knows when wanderlust has struck again. It's printed all over your face."

"For shame! and everybody says you're stupid—when it comes to reading people!"

"What? Now don't you start laughing, that is a really low blow and I don't deserve it."

"You're right. You deserve far worse, but enough for now. I've got work to do if I'm going on a trip."

The Adventure Begins

When you seek, you look, but you may not see what you are seeking until it is in front of you; and do you ever really know what you want until you see it? I didn't.

I thought I wanted a cottage in the suburbs with 2.5 kids and a handsome husband who left the house every morning with his briefcase—bound to do something, somewhere, and would be gone until 5:30 PM—during which time I would be free to be me. I dreamed of a sheltered life away from the grime and crime of the city, where I would be able to pursue—whatever. Instead, I married an idiot, woke up ten years later, divorced, and have stayed happily single ever since.

What if you had gotten your childhood dream, would it have been that great? I doubt it, but then I'm sort of sardonic and sarcastic in my older youth. I see things a lot different from when I was running around in high school and college. Then I thought I knew everything and everyone was my friend. It took a few years of working to convince me that most people don't want to be friends or don't know how. So when I divorced, I became my own companion and have never regretted it—not even once.

When you see yourself divorced, you think everyone will brand you a failure. What egos we have! You really believe others care, and when you finally realize your life's 'tragedy' amounted to one morning's coffee break gossip, it is deflating to say the least; but there you have it. So, if you are staying married for all the wrong reasons, don't bother. Nobody cares what you do! They assume you must be happy and making it or you would change your life.

Whether or not I say what I mean doesn't mean anything either. It just feels good. If you stand around everyday kibitzing over nothing with the gang in the office—never letting them know who you really are, you have it made. You can feel smug when others think they know you—but haven't got a clue. But eventually, even that wears thin. You get tired of being second-guessed and over-looked for promotions or whatever, so you decide to leave, and so on. It gets worse, but you get the picture.

I got bored with jobs I was most suited for and couldn't stand the people who thought they liked me. I say 'thought', not because they were hypocrites or anything like that, but because I never was myself around them; so how could they know me?

When I went out at night, I saw the same old tired faces, and they got tired earlier and earlier every year, until I just stayed home. It was less of a hassle. You didn't have to talk over or around loud, insane music played by guys, and sometimes even girls, who looked like you felt—lousy.

When the time comes to cash in your chips, as the old-timers say, I want to cash in BIG! I want stacks and stacks of chips on the table and hear St. Pete say, "Wow! You really made it BIG!" But now I kind of doubt it will ever happen, and more and more often—I don't even care. It's getting to the point where I could sum up life as a pair of pantyhose—one run and you're done.

This kind of talk gets me nowhere—which also bores me, so I'm heading out to Merida in the Yucatan to see what adventure awaits me there. If I'm not back by the time you get to the end of this letter, you don't have to call, I'll drop you a line or two then.

These are not the best of times to travel, no matter what the ads say. You think you have the entire routine down pat, then they cancel the flight; or they tell you they are having mechanical difficulties—when what they mean is: the flight crew hasn't shown up yet. It's a crisis in credibility. If the company has no integrity, how can you trust them to get you anywhere on time or in one piece? Anyway, I don't mind the flying part, but the waiting gets me down.

By the time the plane arrived, I was beginning to feel weird. I had this prickly feeling along my hairline like something wasn't quite right or someone was watching me—not exactly paranoia, but kind of insecure.

I counted seven different kinds of people waiting for the plane, you know what I mean—the usual: the friendly, the nervous, the idiotic, the strange, the sublime, the genteel, and the definitely weird. As we all sat around the waiting area knee-deep in popcorn boxes and candy wrappers, no one looked directly at anyone else, instead we watched the empty seats.

People looked cold or rebellious if compelled to condense their mountains of carry-on-luggage to block fewer seats in order to accommodate a newcomer, but they always complied. The interloper would be given a minute or two to settle in, then everyone, plus the new one, watched the next seat likely to be filled. Boredom has few charms.

When you sit and stare at people, you usually find negativity. They hate you right away, so I learned as a kid to prop a book up and stare at the pages while watching people out of the sides of my eyes. My right eye has better vision than the left, but the left can spot a freckle on a zebra's hind end at 20 paces.

When I was just about to give up watching the crowd, a fellow came in who looked downright romantic. I mean it! He looked like the classic portrait of a reporter or spy seeking the heat source—James Bond incognito.

Now remember, whatever you say about me later, you will never be able to say I cared that much about men. Actually, I like them all too much to chase after one of them. I don't need to land one, hook one, or even lie around on Saturday morning with one anymore. I just want to talk to one man who isn't trying to get me into bed before he has to move on to the next whatever. It isn't easy, but it keeps me going.

When this guy sat down opposite me, I saw he was doing the same thing as me. He wasn't reading his newspaper or even trying. He was scanning the crowd. He glanced at me, I know he did, but I made sure I was reading just then. Let me tell you, I did get a little high knowing he found me to be the most attractive of the women present. You know, you can tell. Anyway, I sort of watched him as he watched and got interested.

He looks young, but isn't. I'm not sure if he will ask me for the time or what, but I know he will say something to me. But, he isn't. He's really cool!

A skinny, young woman arrived with a baby in arms and a little girl who charmed all the elderly. She spoke no English, but had a fair knowledge of what was being said. She thrived on all the attention and they loved her for it, so when the trio converged upon the row of seats across from me and beside this guy, men gladly moved and their ladies sort of scrunched up their bodies and junk in order to accommodate them.

It shouldn't be long before the plane takes off, but still no sight of the ground personnel who open doors and clank around as they talk confidential-like about the loves of their lives or whatever turns them on.

When this great guy finally made his move, he asked if I cared to read his paper. I said, 'sure', but didn't. Instead, I checked out the section he had been scanning and found it was *News In Brief From Around The World.* Not surprising. He looked more and more like a very busy, self-made businessman—or a spy. Based on my previous record, however, I have to be ten miles wide of what he really does. I can never tell about men.

What is it about a guy with dark, dark eyes and very fair hair that makes me tingle? Thinking about all the guys I have ever dated, this guy has to be the best looking one ever. He really has something, but not classic looks. He stands out, but maybe it's this crowd that makes it so easy to star. Anyway, I was half-way to falling in love by the time the plane took off for Houston.

When you fly to Merida, your best bet is to take whatever gets you to Houston the cheapest and then hop on a Mexican airline. They have comfortable planes, great service, and even the food is delicious—if the flight originates in Mexico. You think you are back in the 60's again. They haven't caught up with the US on ways to short-change the flyer yet.

I took AeroMexico because I have one of their Premiere Club cards, and sometimes they will bump you up to first class if there is room. This being my lucky day, I got on the plane after only a minimal wait and the stewardess came back and asked if I would like to move up front.

They have a much better way than just upgrading your ticket at the counter. They escorted me from steerage to first class with the attendants carrying my luggage over their heads like Indian bearers while all the other economy passengers looked on with envy.

Yes, this is definitely going to be a great trip. I can tell already.

As I sat down in the big leather easy chair of a seat, I noticed a man's hand peeking out from beneath a tented newspaper beside me. I couldn't see much more, but his khaki legs looked kind of familiar. In the rush to accept a drink and something to nibble on while the plane finished its whatever, I forgot about my seatmate.

As we took off I felt that strong urge to stretch my wings and fly. I always get it when we lift off the ground. It's such an exhilarating feeling, but the rest of the flight leaves me flat. I might as well be riding a bus.

After we reached the leveling off stage, the hand beside me withdrew into the paper. I watched surreptitiously while he folded the paper carefully—just like someone else. Yes, it was the guy from the airport. Can you believe my luck?

He stretched his shoulders, but not his arms and said, "How's it going?"

"Great! Didn't I see you at JFK?"

"I was there, but I guess I missed you."

"Oh, sure, that's why you gave me your paper to read."

"Just kidding. Of course, I remember you. Did you finish the paper? You can have this one if you like."

"No thanks, I'm getting ready to land."

"We still have a couple of hours. Were you planning to jump out en route?"

"No, I just like to get acculturated a bit before I land in a strange country."

"Mexico is not strange. You've been there before."

"How did you know that?"

"You have an AeroMexico ID on your carry-on. I noticed it at the airport."

"You don't miss much. Do you?"

"Not if the one I love to watch is sitting nearby."

"Whoa! 'The one you love to watch' sounds like a line to me. Don't tell me you don't tell that to all the girls."

"I don't."

The attendant interjected her menu selections into the conversation at this point and gave us both a chance to cool down. Frankly, he was moving too fast for me. I like to enjoy the ride. I like to take things easy and drag the preliminaries out as long as possible, then jump into the middle, but this conversation was getting out of hand. Next thing you know, I would be having dinner with him—and who knows what for dessert. I'm too old for this stuff. This is what gets you totally off track and is guaranteed to make you miserable for weeks—maybe even months, afterwards.

No, I'm putting on the brakes. It's going too fast for me.

We both ordered the same thing, almost simultaneously, then he noticeably retreated from his forward attack. We both just sat there saying nothing. It is what I want, but I want to be the one to do it, so when he looks at me again, I'll introduce myself and find out why he is no longer interested.

I'm telling you, the Mexicans know how to treat you right. The hors d'oeuvres really look appetizing, so I might as well just say what is on my mind.

"I guess I should introduce myself if we are both going to be here for awhile. It's a lot easier than saying, 'Hey, you'.."

"Forgive me. My name is Charles Randolph, but my friends call me Chip."

"Really? I always thought men got names like Chip because their real names were Archibald, Alfonso, Aloysius, or something like that."

"That is interesting. I never thought about it before—and I pride myself on being observant. But, I must admit I know your name."

"Really?"

"It was on that damned tag you have on your bag. You know you really shouldn't do that. You never know who will pick it up."

"What? My name or my bag?"

"Sorry. I just meant you should be careful. This is still the dark ages in Mexico. Men there aren't likely to believe a beautiful woman traveling alone is less than an easy target for their macho designs. You have to watch your step."

"Thanks! I guess you're right. I hate to admit it, but it is the one thing I dislike about Mexico. Single women do have to be on their toes. But then again, we should be regardless of where we are."

"So, Amanda Sheridan, where do you hail from? At least you don't display your address on the tag."

"My friends call me Mandy and I'm from Pittsburgh originally, but a half-dozen ports since then. What about yourself?"

"I'm from New York."

"Just New York? Not some place special in New York?"

"No, *just* New York."

"You don't sound or look like a native New Yorker."

"Looks are deceiving."

The arrival of the entree ended our exciting repartee and allowed each of us time to peripherally size up the other on the sly. We were well into dessert before he said anything of real interest.

"I'm traveling on business, but you don't look the type to be doing business in Mexico."

"What makes you jump to that conclusion. Don't I look professional enough?"

"You look too professional. Women who come down from the States to do business in Mexico usually look anything but business-like. Most aren't in the realm of what we normally refer to as business, if you know what I mean?"

"Yeah, I guess I know. Many were entertainers of one sort or another; but times are changing."

"You never said why you are going to Mexico?"

"Me? Oh, I'm looking for adventure."

"What? You're kidding!"

"No, I'm not. What's wrong with that?"

"Aren't you a little old to be backpacking and stuff like that? I thought that went out with the hippies in the 60's?"

"Looking for adventure? It never goes out of style. What you mean is, women aren't supposed to be running around with no other purpose than to find out about life in a foreign country—that's men's prerogative. Isn't it?"

"I stand corrected. You're right. I just don't come across women traveling alone who aren't headed for the brightest resort around in hopes of filling their vacation with glamour and/or love affairs."

"You haven't met many women—have you?"

"I wouldn't say that, but you may be right. Usually, I'm very busy. It's most unusual for me to notice any woman as much as I have you."

"That groan is to let you know you are going too far. I can't stand being BSed. Promise you won't do it again or I'll ask them to put Prozac in your tea."

"It's a deal. I'm really a nice guy, I just relapsed into the 70's. Funny how absent-minded you become, the older you get."

"You're right about that. I can't seem to keep track of time anymore."

"Good for you. It shows you're on the right track; but that being the case, let me inform you that we are now about to land."

"So soon?"

"We'll have to get together in Merida."

"Yes, that would be nice, but how did you know I would be in Merida?"

"Where else would you go? It's the home base for all adventuresome females seeking to know more about the Mayans."

"Is that so?"

"Probably not, but it was a good guess. It's where I'd go if I were you. Let's count on meeting at the Zocalo on Sunday."

"Sure. It's a date."

The Time to Begin is Now

Whatever happened to the time when you could do whatever you wanted to do, but felt you should wait? Why? Why did I wait? Why didn't I just do it? I would sit and stare into space and think, but actually did nothing. I would muse about someone else doing it for me or helping me so I would be given credit—I guess, but no more!

Now is the time when I take charge! No more sitting around and letting others tell me what to do. I'm on my own in Merida and I know what I want—ADVENTURE, and I shall have it!

Wow! The smoke and exhaust fumes from these junky old cars and trucks are terrible, and the motorbikes are just as bad—but noisier. Only a sick world would introduce such pollution to a city of so much charm and culture. The bus driver said all the gas here has lead added. So not only is the smoke filthy, it's also poisonous. What a shame that our contributions to the world are so often lethal, yet we Americans excuse ourselves because it's legal, and besides, 'they asked for it'.

Anyway, do you remember the time you and I went by train to New York and these three state troopers tried to pick us up? Remember? It's like that everywhere you go down here, but the Maya men aren't nearly as bad as other Mexicans. Thank God! You can easily spot the Maya. They're very short, in fact, absolutely tiny, but not for much longer. The kids have huge feet. They are growing into giants compared to their parents. The Mayan explanation: better nutrition.

When you get down here, ask for me at the Hotel Astaria under the name of Amanda Brown. I thought it would add excitement if I assumed an alias. After all, it's harmless and I already feel like another person.

I'm going to fly over to Cozumel one day, but I'll wait until you get here. We can decide if we'll go diving or not. There is a shrine on the island which every Maya woman is supposed to visit at least once in her life—to insure fertility or something, but you and I can go anyway. I feel strangely drawn there and want to explore it.

Let me know for sure when you will arrive and I'll get you a room here. It is really quite nice for being so cheap but there may be something better, so I'll look around a little more before I talk to the desk clerk. Furthermore, I don't believe you will actually arrive while I'm still here. Write when you get a chance. My address is: Hotel Astaria, Cinco Madrid Avenue, Merida, Yucatan, Mexico.

Mandy 'Brown'

I hope this isn't a waste of postage. They say mail may or may not get through, especially post cards, but what the hey, my mail will. It has to! If I stay down here too long—totally on my own, I may never go back and I think God has better plans for me. But what are they? I'm still waiting to find out.

There is supposed to be a crowd that collects in the Astaria's lobby for cocktails every afternoon around four to enable Americans to catch up on the news and find out where the action will be that night, so I think I'll check in with them every other day or so. That way I won't look lonely or in need of company but can keep my ear to the ground in case something interesting comes up further afield than just around here. Maybe I can even link up with others to explore the local archeological sites rather than chance it on my own. There I go again—not really confident I can do it all on my own.

This afternoon is about the same as any other afternoon, only today I'm ambling around a strange city in a foreign country and the people are all too polite to stare—but I'm not. Some are curious, but most ignore me. The perfect atmosphere for a game. I'll stand and stare at something that looks interesting and see if anyone tells me about it.

No one appears willing to play with me. I've stared at this statue for ten minutes, yet no one has said a word. Maybe everyone is too polite, or maybe they think I'm lost in rapture? Which means: I must adapt!

Step Two, look at my guidebook. I must have it somewhere. Ahhh, it's working already. I can see out of the corner of my eye a woman sidling up to me. She looks poor.

"Chicklets? Do you wanna buy Chicklets?"

Oh, no, a beggar. What now?

"I have no change. I want no Chicklets." There I've done it. They'll probably stone me for turning her down, but it should get a reaction out of somebody.

As she shuffled away, a throat cleared close by and a handsome 'tall' Maya appeared as if by magic and said, "That was wise Senora. We do not condone the behaviour of beggars. We do not want them to reap a harvest from the streets. It teaches all the wrong lessons of life—to them and the young. You are wise."

He means: 'for an American'. I can hear it in his voice, but what the hey, he looks nice—and speaks perfect English.

"Thanks for recognizing I'm neither cheap nor mean. I just don't give to beggars unless I feel a certain urge to do so, and I felt nothing for this woman."

"Oh, so you are spiritual?"

Taken by surprise, I suddenly felt weird inside, but managed to say casually, "Not exactly spiritual, but I guess it sounds that way. Doesn't it?"

"You sound only as the heart amplifies the spirit. You must be spiritual or you would not have come. We know. We watch for you—and others like you who come seeking."

Oh, oh, he means, they watch for suckers like me. This is not a great game. He seems intent on staring my eyes out. I wonder how I can get rid of him nicely.

"You need not fear us, Senora. We are not watching in order to take advantage of you. We, too, wait for a feeling or image to appear and direct our steps. That way, we are never wrong. We identify those who are here to seek answers to their lives' questions, and you are one of them. You have come to Merida to seek the truth and let it find you, and I am here to announce that your journey is beginning now and we will go together."

What? I can't follow this guy. I have to be out of my mind. This is not a smart thing for a single, American woman to do anywhere—let alone in Mexico. But he seems so very reasonable and sane, and I like him—even though I haven't a clue about him. I don't even know his name.

"My name is Jorge, and I am your guide today."

Oh, I get it. He is one of the government's licensed guides and watches for tourists and steers them to the right places. Yes, he does have the look of a man on a mission. I'll just take it easy for now and see where he leads me before I start dragging my feet or baling out.

"My name is Amanda Brown, and I'm here on vacation. My friends are joining me later." That should warn him I'm not alone or without friends to rescue me—just in case he has any big ideas.

"Welcome, Mandy—that is the name that comes to me now. You do not seem like Amanda Brown to me. I do not know why, but you don't. Perhaps you have only recently changed your name?"

"Wh-h-a-at do you mean?"

"I'm sorry, Amanda, but I just felt perhaps you recently got married or the reverse because the name somehow does not suit you—at least not yet."

"Oh, I see. You're right. I usually go by Mandy and seldom ever use my last name. I come from a small town where it's not necessary—everybody knows me."

He laughed good-naturedly and said, "If you call your home base a small town, what must our city look like to you?"

This guy is amazing. I wonder how he does it?

"Why do you think I come from a big city?"

"All the great visionaries do. You have many vibrations clinging to you, and they are not universal—rather more local. You have managed to escape just in time. Very much longer and your whole mind and body would have been warped beyond recognition and have to be returned to a resting state before being able to go forward."

"Hmmm, I don't understand, but it sounds interesting."

"If you do not understand, then it cannot be interesting. You cannot be interested in what you know nothing about or care nothing for, but you are always interested in what affects your own life. . . You have been close to death several times and it has caused you to decide that this life is to be the last time you encounter certain people and events—but more of that tomorrow."

All the time we walked, he was leading me back to my hotel, but I did not notice since it was a different route from what I had followed in my earlier excursions. He was not shy nor forward, but he acted like he had known me for years. It was uncanny, but I felt like we were supposed to meet today—and he knows why, but I'm still in a coma or something and haven't figured out yet why I'm here or what I'm supposed to do.

"Thanks for leading me back to my hotel, but how did you know I wanted to return here at this time?"

He continued to smile cheerfully and said, "It's four o'clock. All Americans gather at the Hotel Astaria on their first day in Merida."

"Oh. How did you know it was my first day?"

"I would have found you before this if it had not been."

"Oh, how nice. Well, thanks for showing me another route to my hotel. I hope we'll meet again."

"We shall. I will be back at seven o'clock to escort you about town. It is not the wisest thing for a beautiful American woman to walk unescorted through the streets of any city—even ours. It is regrettable that the ways of the world have encroached on our lives and values so very far, but it is a fact of life which we permit. You will be perfectly safe with me or any of your guides. Have a good time now at your party. You will meet other seekers but not recognize them."

Feeling dazed, but not confused, I said without emotion, "See you in the lobby at seven."

He nodded then walked away but apparently felt my eyes on the back of his head because he paused at the corner and looked back at me. After only a slight hesitation, he smiled and doffed his panama hat to reveal a lustrous mop of black curly, not straight, hair.

I went inside then to find an odd assortment of people who might or might not be Americans. The din might be considered extraordinary if the room was not populated by Americans. You know how loud we are compared to everyone else in the world; but why do the loudest have to be the rudest?

"The only time to tip these people is if they get off their fat cans and do something for you." The ugliness of this remark matched the face of the stout, red-faced man who uttered it.

"You're calling these people fat? There isn't a fat Mayan anywhere. These people are as thin as you get. I think the Chinese are the only ones who could give them a run for their money—in my opinion."

"I don't mean it literally, but Mexicans are all the same. They don't want to move unless you pay them."

"Oh, Regis! You lie! You've got the worst possible attitude of anyone I've ever met—while traveling abroad. Why don't you go home if you can't stand it here?"

"I would—in a flash, but I've got work to do. I'm not some stupid tourist, you know. If I weren't still working on my first million, I'd be out of here or have someone else take my place, but right now I have to put up with all this." He motioned toward the crowd standing around the bar.

"And they have to put up with you."

"Now, now, Cathy, you're getting catty again. I'm allowed to voice my opinion, and just because I'm not overworking my imagination to see things in these people that don't exist doesn't mean I'm a terrible person. I am no ugly American!"

Amanda thought, he better look in the mirror. He is just about the ugliest American I've ever seen or heard. Wouldn't you know he would be staying in my hotel—probably right next door to me, if I know my luck. Oh, no, he caught me.

"Welcome! Welcome! My name is Regis and I am an American. You have to say it just like at AA meetings. If you get it out in the open right away, it's a lot easier on everybody. The rest of these freaks will try to convince you they're not Americans or that they're enlightened beings or aliens or whatever; but no one but a stupid American would come to this dump at four o'clock in the afternoon."

"Thanks for the welcome, Regis. My name is Amanda Brown."

"Amanda Brown? Suits you to a tee. It's amazing how people look like their names. Isn't it?'

"I hadn't noticed. I'm so used to it that I forget my name until I enter a group like this."

A young blondish, overgrown boy of a man joined in, "You're about to enter the Twilight Zone—not a group encounter. The people who come to this hotel are all losers. You have to be, otherwise you're thrown out after the third night. We don't want any winners! We drown them if we can. Right, Harriet?"

"Don't include me in your loser speech. I'm tired of it, Frank. You're a loser, but you're not enlisting me or anyone else in your club. All of us have interesting—no fascinating tales to tell each afternoon, Amanda. Hopefully you will, too, but it may take you awhile to meet any of the natives. They're not particularly forthcoming or welcoming to most Americans—especially women. It's their macho government, you know, always trying to keep women down."

"Oh, shut off the faucet, Harriet. We're all tired of your women's lib crap!"

"I will not shut up! This world has to be converted to the realization and acceptance of the goddess within each woman before it can go forward."

"You're no goddess! Take my word for it."

"Oh, shut up, Regis. You're the most obnoxious man I know—and I know a lot, so just stay clear of me; and we'll get along a lot better in the future."

"Believe me, honey, we have no future. You're a loser. You're hunting for men with the wrong bait—or maybe you're hunting for women. Better watch your step *Ms.* Amanda Brown. She may go after you."

Weighing her words, Amanda thought: how repulsive, but said, "I was just wondering if I have to order my drink at the bar or are you served at the table?"

"They serve you, but it takes them until at least four-twenty before they ever come near you."

"That's okay. I'm in no rush. I'm on vacation. I'm here to relax and enjoy myself and might as well get used to Mexican time now."

"You've got the right attitude if you're going to enjoy Mexico. Don't rush. Let time take you. Everything works out fine if you do, otherwise it can be a disaster." The man speaking looked different from the rest. More peaceful, less attentive, but not distant.

It was not easy to size him up and figure out his angle because he looked- deep into your eyes while talking. His gaze forced you to look back into his eyes just as intently. A truly hypnotic stare yet not quite a stare—just penetrating. I did not intend to talk to anyone, but could not stop myself from speaking to him.

"You sound like you've lived here for quite awhile."

"All my life."

"Really?"

"No, not actually, but it's my life now and the only one I know or care about. I live NOW. I refuse to dwell in the past or where I'm not. It takes too much energy."

"I see." I bet he's one of the seekers. He has to be. His looks and talk are so 'evolved' or something.

"I'll see you later. I just stopped by to see if anyone I knew was here."

His warmth of manner collided with a cold shout from across the table. "Oh, sure, you did. You stopped by to check out the chicks. Always on the move, our own little Don Juan."

"Someday Regis, someone is going to knock you right back to today, but I can't be bothered now, so just hang. Well, folks, I have to shove off. See you later."

'Bye Kirk' and 'See ya', echoed from around the room.

Kirk. What a phony name! It has to be an alias. I should know since I have one—but Kirk. It sounds inhuman—like a love machine or something.

"Penny for your thoughts."

Oh, no, not another one. I'm going to strangle the next guy who can't start a civil conversation with a woman in anything other than drivel. Oh, well. "Hi! I'm not thinking. I'm waiting—for a drink."

"What's your favor? I'll go and get it."

"No, that's okay. I'm in no hurry—just enjoying the camaraderie."

"Right! Great group of people, isn't it?"

He sounds like he means it! "I don't know them yet, but I'm sure they all have something interesting to say."

Obviously not interested, he said to the air above my head, "Oh, yeah, well, anyway, I have to go. I like to get to know everyone, so I'll check back with you later to see how it's going. It was real nice talking to you."

Right. If this is any sample of how these sessions go, I won't be back.

"Hi! Hope you haven't been waiting too long, but Jorge told me you might need rescuing about now."

"Jorge?" Now who is this? He's cute. Maybe he's Jorge's brother? "Oh, yes, Jorge. How wise of him."

"He is very psychic, you know."

"Yes, I can see that now. He seems nice. How well do you know him?"

"I don't. He just asked me to deliver you from evil."

"Oh." That is a strange thing to say, but then time will tell.

"See you around, Amanda."

See you? He just got here. "Yeah, see you."

He called me Amanda. Jorge told him my name was Amanda, even though he calls me Mandy. What is going on? If this guy is supposed to be rescuing me, why did he leave? Weird, but I might as well take the opportunity to drop this bunch.

The Race Against Time

When I got back to my room, I found a note stuck in the door jamb right above the lock. It was slightly crumpled and smudgy, but legible. It simply said: 'Hope to see you at seven'. No name.

It must be Jorge, the mysterious Maya! I don't know anyone else who would leave such a note. But why bother when I have already confirmed? It wouldn't be Chip's style, I'm sure. Anyway, he doesn't know where I'm staying. Hmmm, I wonder what Chip is up to? I bet he's busy.

I tried to sleep but kept tuning in on the muted conversations floating up and down the hall or I'd hear a car unloading outside. Unable to drift off, I finally decided to get up and meditate.

Meditation is where it is if you are alone or in a strange country and don't know anyone. You are within yourself as always but can see all you are and all you will be, maybe even travel a bit; but this time I couldn't delve deeply within me. I don't know why. Instead, I continued to remain somewhat alert and tuned into passing conversations.

The sound or sense of someone standing outside my door, possibly listening, aroused me from my reverie. I could not hear any actual sound but sensed someone there. I zeroed in on the spot, but did not make a move. Just then a voice echoed down the corridor from the far end and I know I heard feet shuffle across the tiled floor outside my room, perhaps headed for the nearby stairs leading to the back patio. On a conscious level, I can't be sure anyone was there—I just *know* it!

When it got to be six-thirty, I dressed hurriedly since that is the only way I know to get ready and prepared to go down to the lobby early to await my 'date'. Once again I had the feeling someone was standing outside my door, so this time I strode rapidly to the door and flung it open. I sensed more than saw a figure fleeing down the back steps; however, there was no sound.

"I refuse to be spooked. I refuse to be bothered. I refuse to be upset."

I kept repeating my affirmation until it took hold in my mind and I believed it, then left the room and took the back stairs down to the inner courtyard where I intended to kill time waiting for Jorge to arrive. To my surprise, Jorge was sitting there waiting for me with the appearance of one who is accustomed to waiting for latecomers. He nodded in my direction and signaled the waiter to bring an earthenware pitcher and two glasses over to the table. The waiter and I arrived simultaneously at the table and he pulled out a chair for me as Jorge rose gracefully and bowed slightly.

"I see you're an early bird, too."

"An early bird? What is that?"

"Nothing—really, just that we who tend to be early wherever we go like to believe we get the best of what is available, thus Americans have a saying, 'The early bird catches the worm'."

"Ahh, I see. That is most appropriate. I will remember it."

"No need, it's not really worth the effort."

"Nothing in life is worth the effort or all things are. It is all in how you believe—or perhaps perceive."

"Yes, I agree. I'm always saying, 'Nothing is by accident', which is more of the same."

"We are much more alike than we are different. You will see. Now, do you have any special desires you would like considered before we begin our First Night Celebration?"

"Celebration? How nice! It makes me feel welcome."

"Of course, you are welcome. Can there be any doubt?"

"Frankly—yes."

Appearing shocked by my words, he asked quickly, "What do you mean? Has something happened?"

"Not really—not exactly, but something is strange. This afternoon I kept feeling like someone was prowling around outside my room—watching me. I don't have any proof. I just know."

"That is all the proof anyone needs." He looked carefully into the pitcher as though it contained a genie, then handed me a bowl of corn chips and said, "Do you know anyone here in Merida? Anyone who would be interested in your arrival?"

Perhaps foolish, but then that is my way, I answered honestly that I knew no one and had no plans to meet with anyone. As I finished, I thought for just a second about my arrangements to meet Chip on Sunday at the Zocalo. He seemed able to pick up on my second thoughts. This mysterious Maya of mine is very quick and obviously perceptive; but should I trust him so much?

"I will ask the owner to check out the hallway often to make sure no one is lurking about. Most likely it is a child playing or one of the maids. Our young people remain intrigued by American women."

"Oh—so the men aren't?"

"Not so much as they once were. They have learned that what is seen as 'typical American behaviour' in the movies does not translate to the way most American women act or wish to be treated in person. We are not savages. It takes only a hint for us to figure out the boundaries."

"Oh, I hope you don't think I'm indifferent to your intellectual abilities and social skills. I've been treated with only respect since I arrived—except by some ugly Americans."

"Americans are seldom ugly—more like teenagers away from home—but not ugly—as in mean or despicable or lacking charm."

"Teenagers!! There you have it! That is the most appropriate description I've ever heard, but teenagers *aren't* my favorite sub-adults."

"Why? They are merely children learning to be adults. They mean no harm. They are awkward, lack confidence and use inappropriate behaviours until they learn what works best for them, but they generally mean no harm."

"You haven't been reading our papers lately."

"No, I do not read newspapers as a rule. I find them too condensed and full of negativity for me to digest well. I prefer to wait until those who process words, I call them WP's, work out all the wrinkles and put it all together in some sort of narrative form."

"That's a great idea, but in America you would wait a long time before hearing anything of depth in everyday conversation—outside your own home. Everyone just listens, watches, and probably reports to someone; but they don't say much to those around them in public or at work as a general rule—only if an event or person makes them extremely anxious."

"You are very astute. I can see why you have been chosen."

What is he talking about? What is going on? He must have me confused with some professor or anthropologist—or somebody. "What do you mean? I'm not here at the request of anyone. I'm here to visit the ancient sites and take in the sociological aspects of your world. I love people, but I don't know anyone here well enough to be chosen to do anything."

An almost smug look passed over his face then, but he let it melt into a broad smile as he said, "It's okay. Many are chosen, but few are accepted. You will not worry about a silly Guide's inability to express himself well in English."

Nonsense! This guy speaks better English than two-thirds of New York. What is he up to? "On the contrare, my friend, you speak perfect English. You also know something you're unwilling to share with me. But if you would, I could save you many steps and a lot of time. I'm not here to meet anyone or do anything—but have fun. Honest."

He chuckled, then said, "You are obviously honest, of that no one has any doubt. The only doubt in some men's minds is: Why a woman? But they will learn. Men's egos hold them back. Women's egos are not so large—even in America and that is probably why more women than men are, eh, what you call in America 'psychic'."

Psychic? What is he talking about now? The only psychic I know charges $125 an hour to read tarot cards as she talks about things for which she has not one original idea. Oh, Oh, now I know. He has me mistaken for a 'moon beam' or whatever they call them. He thinks I can be taken advantage of by flattering me and telling me how 'spiritual' I am. Apparently, there are more than just the old ways to lure New Age ladies to their beds.

"I see I have made you angry. I didn't intend to. I simply meant that some of the lesser shamen think only men are suitable for exceptional growth, but no one who is wise thinks that way."

"I-I'm not angry!" Oops, said that a bit too loudly for someone who is not angry. "When do you plan to get started on our First Night Celebration?"

He chuckled unexpectedly, then said, "We have already begun! You are not aware of it?"

"Oh, sorry, of course, I just meant, what do you have planned, if I may ask?"

"Nothing is left to accident, but nothing is planned. We will go now. You will see."

He rose with a single fluid motion and seemed to float before me. I've never seen a man exit more gracefully than this mysterious man—not even the greatest flamenco dancer of them all, Jose Greco, could do it better.

Occasionally glancing over his shoulder, he led me out of the now-filled lobby and onto the crowded street. He said nothing as he walked down the center of the sidewalk. Everyone made way for him. Many Maya nodded respectfully, but the young showed no signs of recognition.

Who is this guy? I *know* I'm safe. I can tell by everyone's reaction to him that he must be somebody, but who? We walked for blocks into the shadowy streets leading away from the center of town before he stopped and let me catch up and stroll beside him. Funny, but his behaviour did not offend me. Obviously, he is a born leader and, frankly, I am a follower.

"We will soon arrive at our first destination. You can eat and drink whatever you like. You will not be asked to participate, but you would be wise to listen to what is said. It will be of the utmost importance to you one day. In fact, your life may depend upon it."

"Oh, sure, I'll listen. My mother taught me to take advantage of every class or lesson in life, because you will need the information sometime or other—or it wouldn't be given to you."

"Ahh, that explains much!"

"What?"

"Your mother. She was a great teacher. You have been chosen, and now she is opening the way."

"I think you're wrong there. She's been gone for 15 years."

"Not gone—just not here."

"Right. I know that, but in America you usually don't discuss such things with strangers."

"We are not strangers. We are reuniting after a brief time apart. We have been friends for a long, long time—many lives."

Here we go again—another New Age Casanova. I can't stand them! Why do they use women's spiritual inclinations and hidden beliefs to try to seduce us? Probably because it works. Oh, well, I'm on to him anyway and can't wait to see what his next move will be. What else can go wrong?

"You are anxious to know what our next step will be. No?"

Whoa! This guy is creepy. I better watch myself, Amanda thought but said, "Oh, sure. Wouldn't anybody?"

"Yes, of course, I am sorry to appear so mysterious about our evening's entertainment, but I want it all to be a surprise."

"Listen, Jorge, all of Merida is a surprise. Anything you do is a surprise. I haven't been around here before, you know."

"Oh, but you have."

Oh, no, not back to that again. He definitely has me tagged as somebody else. But whom? I'm not going to worry about it now. I've tried to tell him he is wasting his time and money on the wrong girl, but he won't listen, so I'm just going to enjoy it all—and I don't intend to pay him back later.

We stopped at a large wooden door or gate deeply recessed in a high wall in the middle of a block on some dark street somewhere in Merida, but no way could I ever find it again. He yanked a new rope attached to an old, old bell to announce our arrival, then pushed open the gate. I followed him in and saw only shadows and dark spots where flower beds probably lay. We followed a stone walkway directly to another door, but this one opened to a house.

Just as we got to the door, it swung open, startling me, but it was okay. A beautiful young girl stood there smiling up at Jorge while welcoming both of us. We were definitely expected, but I couldn't understand what she said to Jorge because they spoke in Mayan and I barely know Spanish.

"Welcome Senorita! Welcome to our casa. We are all well and awaiting you. You will enjoy yourself. No?"

"Yes, I'm sure I will."

Within minutes, the house became a blur to me. Too many people, too many aromas, too much Mayan talk, and too many unknown sensations for me to be able to concentrate on any one thing. I felt like I was entering a whirlpool or a really deep meditation—very weird and like I knew everyone there and didn't need to be introduced. Maybe that is why I wasn't.

The meal was served in a large lantern-lit dining room. Everyone wandered in and out and about picking out what they wanted to eat. No one seemed to care that most of the food was not eaten, because there was so much talk. The level of noise was not that high, but the intensity of feeling or energy was the highest I have ever connected with in a social gathering of this type.

I picked around at the fruit and exotic-to-me dishes, but was glad I wasn't expected to eat much. Frankly, I don't have any appetite when I am anxious, and I was quite anxious at some base level. It must have shown because no one bothered me except to ask politely about my health or my accommodations. They all seemed disinterested in me as a person—even though I was the only 'alien' in the room. In fact, I was far more curious about them than they were about me.

After about half an hour a teeny, tiny old woman requested me to follow her into another room where I found Jorge and several men talking most seriously in very quiet tones. All looked up, but only Jorge welcomed me with a smile. I felt like I was barging into a stag smoker.

"Welcome, Mandy. We were just talking about personal affairs and items of business, but are now ready to entertain you. Aren't we, Fernandez?"

A slightly younger version of Jorge nodded stiffly in my direction, but would not look into my eyes. Obviously, Fernandez was not happy to see me. Why?

In short order I met the others and we all chatted stiffly about nonsensical things. I mean it! Nothing made any sense. We talked in riddles or something, but they all eased up as I talked. I did not know why.

"We will have to leave our hosts soon, Mandy, for we have other places to go and more people for you to meet. I hope you have enjoyed your 'tapas' and saved room for dinner."

Jorge smiled at my shocked reaction to his mention of more food.

Addressing the group, I said in my best Spanish—which is very poor, "I'm sorry we have to leave before I have met everyone, but perhaps another time we can get to know each other."

The circle of men looked at me somewhat puzzled until Jorge said a few soft words, then they all laughed. Whatever was going on, I wished somebody would let me in on the secret. I could tell they thought they knew me already. Call me ridiculous, but I *know* that is what they thought!

Jorge turned to me and said, "We have to hurry if we are to get to your next meeting on time." As he shook each man's hand, they nodded in my direction. Apparently his peers, maybe even fellow guides, but Jorge seemed to be the most respected—or I have lost my ability to judge such things.

Upon leaving the house, I asked, "Where are we going?"

"If I were to tell you, would you know?"

I laughed to cover my annoyance at this folk wisdom but being led around and not knowing what was planned was losing its charm—fast. I decided to stick around for dinner, but then it would be adios.

As we moved quickly down the street away from the walled house, Jorge motioned for me to listen. I did not hear anything unusual, but obviously he did, and he grabbed my arm above the elbow and steered me around a corner and into a dark storefront. I could not see or hear anything, but Jorge remained still—not exactly tense, but very alert.

It was several minutes before he whispered, "We will attract less attention if we walk on the main street now."

I could not help thinking: What's up? Why would we attract attention now if we didn't attract it earlier? Something was wrong, but I did not say a word.

"Nothing is wrong, Mandy. We just have to be careful. Merida is like any other capital city—not all its citizens are likable or sociable, so we will always be careful when we travel at night."

Does he think we are going to repeat this business? I've got news for him. Unless this turns out to be a lot more fun than it has so far, we are not going anywhere—or at least not very far again. However, with only one acquaintance I don't have the luxury of casting him off quite so quickly as I would if at home. Lost in my thoughts, it did not register for quite a while that we were rapidly covering ground. We continually wove our way across town as though trying to lose someone.

After about ten minutes of silence, Jorge said, "At our next stop, you may wish to wash up. We will eat there, then go on to the home of an old story-teller. You will enjoy the food—and enjoy his stories even more. I promise."

It sounded promising; but what was really going on?

Jorge must have noticed something or someone posing a threat to us because he quickly led me through an arcade of shops and walked deliberately to the other end and exited to a dark alley where we climbed into a waiting taxi. It seemed prearranged.

"We are in a hurry. Take us to the Casa Grande pronto!"

"Yes, Senor."

As the cab took off, the irony of the driver acting like Jorge was an Anglo rather than a fellow Maya registered in my mind, but I don't know why I noticed it. I started to speak, but Jorge didn't look like a Maya anymore. His Panama hat was pulled down over his forehead somewhat jauntily, but with an air Maya don't assume—at least none I had observed so far. In fact, if I hadn't known, I would have said he was a Castillian.

We traveled about four blocks when Jorge leaned over and stuck a few bills into the cabby's shirt pocket and asked him to stop right in the middle of a seemingly empty block. We got out quickly and immediately blended into the shadows. Tall poincianas draped their branches low across the sidewalks, blocking out whatever street light there was. We walked in and out of the shadows for another block or two before we saw two figures in front of us. I could not make out who they were—most probably males, but unable to be sure.

Jorge gripped my arm again, only much stronger this time. I winced, but said nothing as he maneuvered me into an alcove of one of the walled houses. We stood still until we heard the footsteps of two people turning the corner beyond us and going off in the direction of downtown. Motioning for me to stay where I was, Jorge poked his head—minus his hat, around the corner for a brief peek. When satisfied, he pulled me after him and we continued to walk down the street as though nothing unusual had happened.

"Is something wrong? There seems to be more to this than just dodging muggers. I've lived in New York for years and usually just avoid certain areas, and if I do spot something unattractive, I clear out immediately and I'm not troubled anymore—until the next time."

"Oh, no, Mandy, nothing is wrong. I am just being cautious. Where we go they live a very quiet life. Time means nothing to them, but the world is always trying to capture them. I do not wish to bring them any static or negativity from the outside world tonight—only you."

Huh? What is that all about?

As though he heard my thoughts, Jorge said reassuringly, "You will see when we get there that all this mystery and racing about is well worth it, but we have to hurry because—even though our hosts do not recognize time—we are late."

"Gotcha! I hate to be late. Let's put on our running shoes and make tracks."

Jorge smiled, then laughed as we scurried into the night.

Tales of Time

There were seven men left at the table when we finished eating dinner. Everyone else cleared out as I sat digesting what was going on all around me. I felt like I knew everyone very well, but actually knew almost nothing about anyone since mostly Mayan was spoken. The few times I was deferred to during the course of the long meal English was used, otherwise, they lapsed immediately back into their own dialect. In fact, I suspect there were several dialects in use, because the kids could not understand what some of the elders said.

The lights seemed to have dimmed of their own accord. No one had adjusted them in any way, but it was no longer as bright within the room once all the other women and the children left it. I had motioned to Jorge earlier if I was supposed to leave with the women, but he shook his head quite curtly, so I stayed. I think I offended him. But how? I don't know what is going on now, but obviously something important is about to begin.

The high-backed chair beside me blocked my vision to the right and shielded me from my neighbor, so I could not catch a straight-forward look at him, then he deliberately moved his chair to include me within the elite circle of elders. I wondered why?

"How are you, Senorita Amandy?"

My neighbor looked more wizened than wise, if that is possible. I have never seen anyone who looked more truly like a Wise Man—a Maya Magus. My mouth was so dry I could barely speak, but from somewhere deep within me I heard myself almost croak, "Fine." Nothing else came forth. I felt like a mute must, so much to say but no way to express it in words.

The old man nodded thoughtfully in my direction and I got the feeling he had passed judgment on me in that fleeting conversation and I had made it over the first hurdle.

"What do you think of the war in the world? Do you think it will ever end?"

When the elderly man across the table spoke, I thought he was addressing the room at large but his eyes rested on me and demanded an answer. What a way to begin!

"The war of the world will be there as long as men and women are. They have to have conflict to fill their lives and vanquish their fear of living. If there were no wars, they would have to answer for the mess they enjoy in their own everyday lives, which would be most intolerable for most of them." Where did that come from? Now I'm listening to my own words as attentively as everyone else at the table.

The youngest man present looked at me somewhat dubiously, perhaps disinclined to admit me to their circle, and said nonchalantly, "You seem to be unaware of your own deepest convictions, Miss Amandy. Are these your words or are you repeating what others have said?"

"Yes."

Obviously annoyed, he responded with a bit more acerbity, "Which is it? Are these your words or are you repeating the wisdom of others?"

As he glared at me, warmth began to spread over my entire being. In a strange, mildly hypnotic way, almost in a trance of some sort, I felt at one with everyone there—transformed from the misfit who entered the room two hours earlier into a very old, somehow wise being.

"I meant both. What I speak is coming from me, but the wisdom is from some source far beyond me."

A murmur arose from the end of the table where four men including Jorge huddled together. I could not hear what they were saying, but Jorge seemed to smile, within more than without, as they whispered. Apparently I made a big hit with them, but why was beyond me now.

"What do you want from us?" The brevity and coolness of his question diverted my attention back to the angry young man.

What is bothering him? Why is he threatened by my presence? Oh, Oh, I bet macho man is upset because a woman is inside the old boys club.

Jorge spoke then with an almost imperceptible degree of firmness. I recognized it, yet it was unlike anything I had yet heard from him. "You will learn to recognize wisdom when and where you find it. It takes time to become wise."

The young man dropped his eyes and began examining the fringe on the table cloth.

Then the living Magus said to the bowed head, "What do you want from us? would have been a more appropriate question if Miss Amandy had been brought here at her own request, but since we have requested an audience with her, it is most inappropriate," his magnetic gaze shifted over to me as he continued, "and we apologize for the seeming lack of decorum in one of our members." As the old man spoke, the young one receded further within his skin and seemed to disappear from our energy field.

I thought, why make such a fuss over nothing? The poor guy was just trying to score points in a game I didn't even know was being played—but wait a minute! What is this about me being summoned to this meeting?

"You are our guest, and Jorge has told us you would like to hear from our storyteller. Is that not why you are here, Miss Amandy?"

As I glanced at Jorge, he smiled and nodded as though we had talked about it and I had asked to come here tonight and wanted to hear stories. Actually, I do want to hear their stories—as many as they care to tell. I may never get another chance like this again in this lifetime! This is the adventure I have been looking for all my life and it found me rather than the other way around. Wow!

"We can feel your enthusiasm and it is much appreciated, but perhaps you better wait until you hear our feeble attempts to entertain you before you get too excited." The Magus glowed from within, then beamed at me as he pointed to an even older man I had barely noticed because he blended into the mahogany colored walls. When all eyes focused on him, his eyes seem to enlarge as if gazing into a fire. In fact, I could see a campfire burning in front of him and his eyes reflected that blaze.

"Miss Amandy, I must apologize for my inability to speak English very much. I seldom visit towns and cities or meet people who do not speak Mayan. I have asked my God to speak to you through my lips so that we will not need an interpreter. If you find you do, please tell me. My feelings will not be hurt."

An amazing sensation occurred in my ears as the man spoke. I knew he could not possibly be speaking impeccable English, if he had no use for it, but what I heard was better than what is spoken on most college campuses today. I watched his lips move and a fraction of a fraction of a second later I could hear him speak in clear, yet convoluted, phrases, but his lips did not form the words I heard. It was like watching a foreign movie dubbed in English!

The lights dimmed even more, perhaps some of the candles guttered out, but this man's eyes burned like hot coals amidst ashes. Everyone and every-thing else receded from my attention as he talked seemingly to me alone.

"There are several different stories we could tell you tonight, but the ones you know are already so old we do not have to repeat them. You know about the flood and the collapse of the empires of man when faced with the rage of Godless men, and other stories of that nature, but you may never have heard about the life of the best.

"We lived on this planet for many years and never once asked why. We were satisfied with what we knew, but then one day a neighbor came to call on a very, very old man and asked him why he did not move. The old man was astonished that he would have him move."

The storyteller's voice took on the nature of another as he said, "Why? Why should I be interested in going somewhere else?"

His voice resumed the former resonance. "Why would he? The first sputtering whys became a torrent of 'whys'. No longer happy, the old man died in torment and his soul was tortured with regret, but he left Earth and never came back.

"When the neighbor heard about the death of the old man, he asked why no one had told him of it earlier, but no one knew. They all began to ask each other why. Once the whys became insistent, blame was assigned to one person after another. They ended their days in hatred, and guilt was experienced by all."

Directing his gaze toward the youngest member of the group, the storyteller added, "What the neighbor did was quite innocent, you say. But was it? You cannot know anything while you are in the midst of it, but can disagree and act accordingly. If you stop and question everything, you do nothing. You become overwhelmed with the negativity of the situation. You do not realize you are not moving, and it becomes the inert and working loss of the mind. The mind worries over why. Never ask why! You will live to be an old man if you avoid it."

Everyone laughed easily, even the youngest, and I felt such warmth flow over me. The room was not heated and I'm not menopausal, so why did I feel such waves of heat?

"You like our storyteller's gift, Miss Amandy?"

"Oh, yes, Senor. It's elegant—in the sense that it hits the target with so very few words. It's a most enlightening story. May I repeat it often?"

"Of course, our stories are meant to educate as much as entertain. They represent many generations of life—old but still new. Please feel free to take whatever we can possibly give you—that you do not already have."

Someone in the darkness said, "She needs nothing."

Another added, "She already has all she needs."

Jorge raised his hands in playful surrender. "Okay, Okay, we know she knows all she needs to know, but she is able to use the different applications which we bring to her own knowledge. Okay? Let us not get into philosophy just yet. We have time. Be patient. Mandy will be with us for a long time."

What did he mean, I would be here for a long time? I hope they don't think they can monopolize my vacation. Many old people try to do that to the young, but some of these guys aren't that old and I'm not that young—and definitely not pretty enough or rich enough to be kidnapped by anyone

"You are not being kidnapped, Mandy, but these are our elders whom you seek and they will be available to you for only a limited time—but all the time you need."

Now thoroughly confused, I thought, there he goes again. How does Jorge know what I'm thinking? Oh, oh, they all know. They are all laughing, and I can't help but laugh right back at them.

When the room quieted down, the storyteller aimed his eyes at me again. This time I felt much more relaxed—almost totally at home with these strange, alien beings. In that light not one man looked like any man I have ever known, but I already liked them better than the men at home—except for the young guy. He obviously disliked me and would not look at me.

"When the winds of winter sweep our shores, the ocean often dons a white mantilla to show us that snow is in the north, but we are not to worry. We will not be cold. We may get rain and wind, but it will not snow. We want no snow. We have no snow."

He smiled at me alone and said as an aside, "You want snow since you live where it is, but you cannot say you have something you do not want."

Interesting.

"When the winds rage at times of hurricane, we are not afraid of the children being killed. We know God is. We know that only the child will be able to decide if the time is now. We will not be too upset if the young die as children because they have the freedom to choose. We will not let the old die alone, though. The old have to die in the midst of their loved ones, if they are to be able to recognize them when they are on the other side waiting to welcome *them*.

"The world is full of old and young, but the middle is what holds it all together. If the middle is not cohesive, all falls apart and everything is lost. The middle must take care of the two ends if life is to be good. The middle span takes longer to transit, but it is not the worst time of life. The middle years are the best! They are filled with fun and action and love and death. They are good years!"

He sat silent for a few moments, then continued, "The old years are not so good for us, but for you they will be your best. You have made your middle years a long life. You have helped and done what you needed to do, but we have all suffered from the war of egos in the land. We have had our middle life taken and destroyed by the greed of the world. Our middle no longer cares about the old and the young—if not their own. They do not stay at home. They go into restaurants to eat, and drink at cafes, and work in offices, but not at home. We have suffered.

"You will know when you are old. You will feel the bones creak and the mind slow, but you will not mind because you have been good. You have not harmed your body nor taken strange drugs. Those who did will have to work with their bodies and minds and may not be able to free themselves of the effects of abuse. You will not die alone. You have been surrounded with friends all your life and will always have friends. We have friends, too. We will not die alone, but we will not be loved like you. Men are never loved as women are.

"When you leave us, you will return to a home and not remember this night, but we will have a story to remind us of your visit. We have no homes. We live as we are. We are not wanted in most homes—because we know."

The old men all nodded in agreement.

"Our wisdom is feared. We are not known. Many follow all we say, but still hate us. We know. We cannot stop the flow of wisdom, and we would not if we could, but you can act like you know nothing—your world will believe it—ours will not. Our homeland is a much wiser place than your world. We are known, and we know."

I thought he was done, but then he asked, "What questions would you ask us if you had the time to write it all down in a book?"

The suddenness of his question stopped me cold. What to say? I never thought I would ever get the chance to sit and chat with a Maya shaman—or did I? I remember meeting my old anthropology professor and telling her I was interested in pursuing a Ph.D. in anthropology, and when she asked what area I would like to concentrate in, I said without ever giving it any thought before that I would develop the Maya oral history—and here I am a few years later doing just that. Shocked beyond all words, I could not come up with a single question to ask any of the shamen present.

"We know you have wanted to study with us. That is why you are here. We have always wanted to know more about America, but the Americans who come here to study us are so arrogant and efficient. They take our ways as being unique and odd and even hilarious—in very nice ways. They nodded at each other as if to say 'I think they are cute. Don't you?' It is not meant to be degrading, but at times they talk about us to our face as though we were stupid or dead—or small children. But, it is not a problem for the wise."

"Americans can be so immature. I apologize for my entire race, and we are a race unto ourselves. We call it the rat race, but it really isn't fair to the rats. They're much more cooperative than we are."

"You smile, you jest, but there is no humor in your voice, Miss Amandy. You hate to be misunderstood, but you misunderstand your people. We do not mean to run them down, but we cannot share with them, either. We all have to be on equal standing if we are to share, and money and power is the elevator that Americans use to stand taller than us."

A jocular voice said, "We are not so tall that they actually need an elevator. We can be intimidated by simply standing close to you, and you are not so very tall, Miss Amandy. Are you?"

"Let's get back to our stories please. Mandy has a long day ahead of her, and she must leave soon." As Jorge spoke, his eyes warmed and he smiled at me alone. It was most disconcerting to realize this man had a hold on me already, and I didn't have a clue as to who he was or why he thought he knew me so well.

"Let's not dwell on the whys of this world. Let's dwell within and enjoy the wisdom of our lives in this world."

Oh, yes, Jorge. I gotcha'. You can read my mind—just look at you smile now.

The storyteller's voice cut through my thoughts. "There is one other story I want to tell you before you return to your hotel with Jorge. It is about the night."

A hush fell over the room as though everyone sat holding their breath in anticipation of shared memories.

"The night is not clear, but it is dark. It can look dark and clear at the same time if the moon is out, but if there is no moon, no one knows what is there."

Turning toward me, he said softly, "We are all very much into the moon. We love it. We think of it as a god. We want to help you understand that gods are not the same to us as they are to you.

"You have a wonderful idea of God, but it is not accurate. You believe God controls the universe. You believe you control your own life. You believe control can be taught. You think self control is what makes one man better than another. You believe in yourself. We do not.

"We do not believe in you or your ability to control life. We do not care if you can control your destiny, because you do not even know what it is. You cannot know. You are not a god. The gods of our life are very simple. They know if the weather is good or not, and they are very capable of fertilizing the crops and are able to do things we cannot do by ourselves. We know we are insignificant, but we know the gods will fill in the space and help us—or not, depending upon how patient and sincere we are.

"You think the night is an event that happens every day, but it happens every time the sun goes away. We know the sun is there behind the night. We know it is. We can sense the sun is not disturbed by the moon, but the moon is not as powerful and happy as the sun. The sun is not for us to question, but the moon is less awesome. We can ask it questions and get them answered. We like the moon, but it is not the same as our love of the sun.

"We will not let you take the sun home with you, but you will take it home on your skin anyway. You will steal some of it from us, but we will keep it safe forever. We will always have the sun. You may not see the sun for hours or days or weeks, but we see the sun every day. For us, we know the sun is a god, but you think you are a god.

"We will never question the sun's ability to be. We would never question God. We would never ask why, but you are ingrained in asking questions, yet never listen to the answers. We listen to the answers and know all our questions are in vain.

"When you die, you see the sky. You walk among the stars and know the night is not dark. You see, it is not dark at all, but the reverse side of the world—the underneath part. We see it as the belly of the day. You see it as a separate thing.

"When you see the belly of an animal, where is it? On the bottom. It lies on the bottom of the body and is large and hangs over the ground. It is not very big if the belly is empty, but can be very big if the body is full. You will never see a belly bigger than the body, but the body can be put into bad shape if the belly is too big for it.

"Only gods are able to fill their bellies to the point where they are not able to support them. The sun has a very round body and the belly is not seen, but it is there. The moon has a small belly because it is not able to eat. It never sees the crops and has nothing to give. It is light only at certain times and is never the same.

"The night has a lot of work to do. It keeps you up and does not let you sleep if your day's work is not done. It has to keep you going until you are done. If you hide in the dark, the dark will harm you. You have to shed light into the dark or you will stumble and fall. The fall to the Earth is what you need to avoid. You need light. You need the light of the sun to be all you can be, but the moon is not dark, either. It changes all the time. Mood and moon are tied together. Tides and man are not. You must live in the sun and die in the moon. It is the best of life that way.

"What you need now is a time to reflect on the light of the sun and the non-light of the moon. When you know why they are gods, you will be wise."

Uxmal

This old crate has to be the last of the last VW buses ever made. I wonder how they keep them on the road this long?

"Ah, Mandy. You can't sleep? The car is too noisy?"

"No, I'm too nosy. I don't want to miss anything."

"You got so very little sleep last night, you really should try to rest. We have a very strenuous journey ahead of us."

"I can't be any more tired than you. Can I? You had to return to your home after you left me. Anyway, where are we going? I thought we were just out for the day."

"I think you will enjoy it so much more if you relax now. We will stop at the house of a friend during the heat of the day, so you can rest. It will be a good time to eat, too. In the meantime, you can fill up on these pastries. We are going to climb quite a bit, and it will take all the stamina you have."

Climb what? Is he serious? There isn't a hill in the entire Yucatan as big as the smallest ones around Pittsburgh, but this 'not knowing where I'm going' modus operandi grows more interesting all the time. In fact, I'm getting to like it.

"You say you came to Merida to seek adventure, and your prayers were answered. No?"

"Yes. Definitely. I've enjoyed myself so far, but who were all those men last night?"

"What men?"

"Oh, come on, you know. Those old men who sat around telling stories. It was wonderful."

"Did you enjoy the stories?"

"Of course. Who wouldn't?"

"Many would not understand them. The stories get more intricate and deceptive as they weave them. But you understood?"

"No problem."

"Did you have trouble with the dialect?"

"No, that's a funny thing. I thought they might be talking in some Mayan dialect, but I heard English. What do you suppose happened?"

"You have the ear of the wise. The wise hear what the heart unfolds and ask no questions in order to prevent the mind from taking over. The mind is what blocks communication. You have to understand why you are here and accept it before you can be, but the mind wants to know why. It can't understand or accept what is given. It has to question."

"You know, Jorge, you have the nicest way of putting things. You don't seem to get upset or nervous, but I know you're on guard most of the time. Why?"

"Why?"

"I'm sorry, Jorge, but I do need some reassurance that I'm not out of my mind riding around Mexico with a man I've just met."

"I understand. This is not my world, either, and I do not fit in as well as you. I am used to going out from and coming back to the place where I belong, but lately I am seldom at home. It is not as comfortable for me, but you will feel more at home there and less comfortable where we will go. You will adapt—better than I."

"Really? You mean I'm going to be able to go back and forth from the rural life to the life of the city as easily as you do?"

He laughed too hard, then said, "Of course. You asked to be able to travel. Don't you remember?"

"Frankly, no, I don't remember asking for any of this. In fact, I'm sure I have someone else's ticket and the ride is going to be over when you find out I'm not the woman you were supposed to meet, but until then, I'm going to take advantage of everything offered and be grateful."

"That is very wise."

"You keep saying that. No one in my entire life has ever referred to me as wise, but you and your friends constantly say it. I'm not complaining, but I think you have the wrong word. You really mean something else, but can't find the right word in English."

"No, we know. We are wise. We can see through the many layers of your world's veneer and see the real You. You have a beautiful soul—one which has lived many times before and will be leaving Earth after this life. But until then, you are to play an important part in our history."

"Whhhat? I'm to be a heroine of the Maya? You really ought to rethink your game plan, Jorge. I'm not the heroic type. I'm down right silly at times. In fact, I'm prone to dizziness. I have too many friends—which shows you I try to please too much, and I drink Pepsi like water. These are not the traits of a woman destined to be great."

He laughed, but said nothing as we drove through dense foliage overhanging both sides of the paved two-lane highway stretching out in a straight line before and after us. Occasionally workers would wave and step off the side of the road as we passed and often Jorge beeped the horn and passed trucks going our way, but other than that, we chugged silently forward.

"What do you do for a living in the United States?"

"Usually, counseling. Sometimes I do financial work, but it gets boring very quickly, so then I go back to counseling which doesn't pay nearly as much but is more rewarding in other ways. I'm sort of like the author who writes one commercial novel to earn enough money to produce one literary work of art, then goes back again and writes another commercial success to finance the personal triumph."

"You are very wise."

"There you go again. I'm not wise. I'm practical or pragmatic but not particularly wise. You would do the same thing."

"Yes, I probably would, but I know what you are doing is wise and you refuse to accept it as being so. You have let it seep down into your mind that you are not worthy of being described in accurate terms. Is it because women are treated so indifferently in your country?"

"I don't know. I never thought about it, but maybe."

"Here in the land of my ancestors, women have always been honored as the bearers of life. There is no greater thing on Earth. Women are not included often in the circles of the elders today, but when a woman is, she is considered to be the wisest one present. Did you know that?"

"No, I never heard anything like that." I could not help chuckling and adding, "Is that why your young friend dislikes me so much?"

"Yes."

Wow! He doesn't pull his punches at all.

"Why was I included in the storyteller's circle last night? Was it because I was your guest?"

"No. You were the reason they gathered."

"What? I can't believe that. They all looked like they traveled there from somewhere else—pretty far away."

"They did."

"Oh, come on now, you can't expect me to believe your chieftains or shamen, or whatever they are called, would travel great distances just to meet me."

"No. They were sent."

"I don't understand. Who sent them and why?"

"They knew of your arrival and were told to be there. You were greeted as any traveling shaman would be greeted. You were honored with the recital of ancient stories, food from the best cooks in the village, and all eagerly awaited your message."

Now I feel guilty. I haven't done anything to deserve all this attention, and furthermore, I was ignorant of the honors they bestowed upon me last night and didn't do anything to repay my hosts and hostesses. I don't like the me I'm seeing right now.

"You repaid them and me for everything. Your messages were well received and very much appreciated. You were not expected to give gifts, but before you go home you may decide to give them. It will be your decision, of course."

"Of course, I will. However, I can't imagine what they would like, but I'll find the perfect things. I do have a knack for doing that well, anyway."

"Of course, you are a shaman. Every shaman knows the desires of friends— and excuses them." He laughed softly, and it made me feel funny inside, but instead of trying to say something witty, I said lamely, "What do you think of the time?"

"Time is and is not, but it does not matter."

"I'm sorry, Jorge, I meant, what time do you think we will get to wherever we're going? Are we on time?"

"Oh, yes, we are on time. I must tell you now that we are on the road to Uxmal and have only another hour to go, even if we stop for gas and rest."

"Uxmal? Great! I definitely want to see the ruins. I've done a little reading already, but had planned to go to the Museum of Anthropology and study a bit more before finding my way out there. But this is great!"

"I'm glad we are able to please you. You will recognize it immediately."

"I've never been there."

"Oh, you have. You just don't remember. Wait, you will see that I am right."

"Sounds good to me."

Happiness undiluted by any other sensation swept over me as I realized, I'm going to one of the greatest ruins in all of MesoAmerica and I have my own personal guide. What have I ever done to deserve all this?

"You have done much work, Mandy. You are very deep into our culture. You will recognize why you are here when you see the Temple of the Magician. We will climb it right away in order to avoid the heat of the day. When you are ready to return to Earth, we will go to the home of my friend to rest and eat our mid-day meal, then return to the ruins after the sun begins to decline and stay on for the sound and light shows. You will be able to understand the Spanish version which is presented first, but I know you will feel more comfortable with the English show done afterwards."

"Great! I read about the show in my guide book and hoped to be able to see it. But don't we have to stay overnight? This is pretty far out to return to Merida afterwards. Isn't it?"

"Yes, but we have made the necessary arrangements. You will be most comfortable. You may stay at the inn near the ruins where we have made reservations for you or you may stay the night in the home of my friends and sleep in a hammock. You are most welcome there, too."

"I'd love to experience life in a Mayan home, but I never stay overnight in anyone's home—especially if I don't know them."

"You deny your friends your company?"

"I hate to put people to any trouble on my account. I don't feel comfortable doing it. I want to be free to do whatever and I know they do, too; but if you have strange people in your home, you can't feel free. Sight unseen, I like your friends too much to be a burden. I have my Visa card with me, so I would prefer to just make use of that reservation."

"Oh, you are not to pay. It is being given to you. You honor the Inn by staying there. You will not be bothered and may eat all your meals there, too, if you prefer."

"Oh, no, I enjoy your food. It's really hot, hot, but I like it—which is odd since I usually avoid chocolate and spicy food—unless it's Italian."

"Ahh, you were a Roman?"

"No, actually, I'm German descent."

"No, I mean you once lived as a Roman or in Rome."

"Oh, I see what you mean. I was reincarnated."

"Something like that, but it is such a crude description. Don't you think?"

"I'm not sure what all it actually entails, so my jury is still out on that one. One of these days, though, I'll make up my mind."

"You know all there is to know now. You are wise."

Yeah, yeah, he sounds like a broken record. Can't he see I'm not impressed by this kind of flattery?

"You are being flattered only if the words are not sincere—or are untrue, but you cannot deny you are wise. Why? Because it is so. It is written."

"What is written?"

"Oh, I didn't mean it literally."

I bet! This guy means every word he says, and I'm going to figure out a way to stop him from reading my mind.

"You can protect yourself from outside interference at any time, you know. We will not be offended. You can shut down your transmitter at will. We will honor your need for privacy. I know this is a bit strange and it takes time for your mind to catch up to your soul's work."

"That is an interesting concept. In fact it almost makes sense."

"You know, and you know that you know, but the mind is still playing games. Eventually, you will disengage it, but only after you have seen enough to satisfy your mind that you are in safe hands."

"Sounds like a good deal to me, but when do you think I'll see enough?"

"Right now!"

"What?"

"You can decide right now! But, maybe it will take Uxmal."

Jorge pulled the beat-up van into the parking lot of a roadside market, managing to avoid the clothes lines hung with serapes and native dresses made in Taiwan. As he filled the gas tank, I wandered inside and found the ladies room, then bought bananas and Coke—no Pepsi in this part of Mexico. As we headed out, I smiled at the young girls behind the counter, but didn't look very closely at the man with them, yet knew he was not a Maya.

"That was some store. They had almost nothing handmade by the Maya. Why?"

"Alas, greed has entered the Yucatan. Our people are now satisfied with not designing and making things if they can get others to do it for less and sell it at a profit. It is a national disgrace. We are losing the battle against the encroachment of the world of wealth."

"I see. It's a shame. In Merida I saw a lot of things that looked like they were hand-made, but they were really expensive—for Mexico."

"If you live in the city, it is always more costly than living in the country and our handwork is very laborious and time consuming, so they are trying to get back something for their efforts. But anything made to sell is never as beautiful as what is made to give away."

"When we get to Uxmal, do you think they'll have any film for my camera? I just remembered, I left it in my room."

Jorge smiled and said softly through twisted lips, "Oh yes, the vendors are very much at home at all our sacred sites. You will be able to buy whatever you need there."

After that, very little was said. He seemed to be far away and distant in every way, so I asked no questions while trying to absorb the little there was to see of the Yucatan jungle, which consists of low growing, tightly enmeshed shrubs that cover the ground and bar entrance to it except where man has cut paths. The only real break in the jungle I could see was a short rise in the road that led up and over the highest point on the peninsula. It was at this point where I first spotted the tip of Uxmal. My native interest in all things new came fully into bloom then and I almost spoke of it to Jorge, but decided against it.

At Uxmal's entrance, we parked under a huge spreading tree in a space reserved for guides. I noticed a group of men standing nearby look up to check out who was with Jorge. They seemed surprised but too polite to say a word. Jorge left me alone outside the van and approached them casually.

Deciding to buy film now at a nearby hut adorned with a Kodak sign, I chatted with the young Maya women about the dresses they offered for sale, and all of their things were made in Taiwan, too.

UXMAL 43

"Ms. Brown!"

Jorge was smiling, but quite formal as he introduced me to the guides loitering around the ticket counter. I nodded, which seemed to be sufficient, and they all flashed toothy grins or grimaces. Most had dazzling teeth, but some had obviously drunk too much Coke.

"We will go directly to the Temple of the Magician since it will tax our strength the most. It is best to tackle it as early in the day as possible—while you are still fresh, and it is not as hot."

"Is it that difficult to climb? It doesn't look that tall."

"You will see. If you want, you can use the 'chicken chain' to hold onto while you climb. It goes up the other face of the pyramid and is for tourists who suffer from dizziness."

"I doubt I'll need any 'chicken chain'. I may look like a weenie to you, but I can take quite a bit before I get scared."

He laughed and led the way around the huge stone foundation to a spot where he directed me to stop and look straight up.

"Wow! It's magnificent! I have never seen anything like it." Shivers ran up my arms and down again as awe swept over me. To imagine these small people hacking their way through the jungle over the centuries and coming upon this huge, huge pyramid is more than I could grasp in one session. I kept saying: "It's so grand! I never imagined it to be so wonderful. No one ever told me about it. I just can't believe it."

"Yes, it is great. We worship here often. There is much power here. The stones and the air are unlike what you will find set aside elsewhere in the world to honor the gods, but the same aura is here. You will see. You will know."

"Can we climb now?'

"Sure, just follow me."

Jorge headed immediately up the monument, walking across the face of it in a zigzag manner, one foot on each step placed sideways diagonally traversing the slanting stone wall. It looked too cumbersome for me, so I started up the steps as I would climb any other steps, only these steps were not deep enough to accommodate my size 8's.

"Darn, these guys had such little feet I can't place my entire foot on the steps comfortably."

Jorge paid no attention, so I climbed about fifteen feet above the ground before realizing I had to walk on my tiptoes if I was to ever catch up with him. He was over half-way up the face of the giant temple, never looking back, and I was already nervous about the height. About midway, I abandoned all pride and shuffled over to the 'chicken chain' and grabbed it. From then on I was able to climb much faster and ignored the kids down below laughing at me as I clung to the rocks.

Jorge ascended to the top of the pyramid long before I got anywhere near it, but he never let on if he was amused by my means of ascent. He just stood in the doorway of the little house on the top and looked out over the land in silence.

The view is so awesome that words are of little use when trying to describe it. You have to experience it more than see it, and the first time is the best. I could not speak for several minutes due to strange feelings mixed with deep respect and wonder, but I let on it was due to my asthma.

"What do you think, Mandy? Isn't it powerful?"

"Oh, yes, you must tell me everything about this place. I am totally unprepared for it."

Very softly, he replied, "I am not that kind of guide. You must seek out one down below to tell you of the legends."

Embarrassment has always been difficult for me to cover, and I was even more shaken by his denial. I thought he was a tourist guide kind of guide. Who is he?

"You will learn now to hide your thoughts. This is the home of the invisible. The place where magic was born. You will be able to do all you wish, but you must make sure your wishes are what you really want."

I wish he would stop reading my mind. That is what I wish for.

"It is done."

I'm not sure if he was referring to my wish or something else, but he changed. He instantly became more distant. Maybe I had hurt his feelings?

"We can remain here on top of this mountain of man's making or we can go down below and visit the Governor's Palace, the Nunnery, the Turtle House, and other buildings. What do you wish to do now?"

"Let's just sit here. Okay? To me—this is Uxmal!"

The Earth is the Land

There were several people standing about as we walked up the steps to find seats for the sound and light show. They seemed unusually quiet for tourists—probably not Americans. We can't keep our mouths shut for ten minutes, unless we're eating or sleeping.

I saw one of the guides whom I met this afternoon, but he disappeared before I could mention it to Jorge. The cool night air, in sharp contrast to the extreme heat of the day, caused me to huddle over my lap in an attempt to conserve body heat, while Jorge seemed impervious to it. The amphitheater's huge blocks of stone retain the warmth of the sun long into the night, but the breeze chills you to the bone, and of course I didn't bring a sweater.

"I'm really going native, Jorge. Here only days and already so acclimated to the heat I think this cool evening air is frigid, and it can't be much less than 70 degrees."

He laughed softly and said, "You are a native. Don't you remember?"

Wonder what he means? Probably just his way of kidding me.

"I feel like one, but I'm American through and through. I wouldn't mind retiring here one day, but in the meantime, I have a life of my own back home that I have to work at."

"Really?"

Really? What is his problem? Can't he comprehend I have a great life at home and am just here to seek adventure?

"You may think you have a life elsewhere, but you have only the life you are now. Any other time or place is non-existent. You know that as fact."

"Oh, on a deep philosophical level I know that, but in 'reality' I have a job, a home, and a country where I pay taxes."

45

"But it is not your land. You live on Earth—that is your land. You dwell in a particular region and move about, but you are of Earth. Nothing else counts in the universe—as far as being your residence for now."

"Hmmm, I never thought about it that way. I guess you're right. We do get territorial, and in that light, Yucatan is as much my country as New York, Pittsburgh, or California. They're all part of the same land mass—North America, and I feel at home anywhere, so I guess I better start recognizing Earth as my ultimate residence. You never know who else in the universe may be present."

I could not control a giggle over the idea of my being an 'Earthling'—like some alien in a science fiction movie, but Jorge never moved a lip.

Finally he said offhandedly, "You are too short-sighted, Mandy. You have the capacity to grasp the universe in a single breath and yet you do not want to know. Why?"

"Huh?"

"You are very much aware of all that is and know why you are, but you play at being here and there. You do not like to get too serious—as you say— about the real reason we are."

Apparently I had struck a sore spot. But what is his problem? He doesn't know I am escaping from disappointments that had me by the throat and I don't want or need any more static from anyone. I just want to relax and have a good time, but I don't want him to get so sore at me that he decides to go back and find the woman he is supposed to be guiding around Uxmal. A few more days like this and I'll know all I came here to learn.

"What are you thinking about now, my lovely little 'American tourist'?"

Wow! He's turning on the charm. I have hurt his feelings. "Oh, nothing, just thinking."

"I know that, but I was wondering what had captivated your mind so completely. You look like you are thousands of years away in space or time."

"No, just at home."

"And where is that?"

I could not answer him. Nothing came to my mind. It was totally blank. I could not think of where I lived. For a second, I caught a fleeting glimpse of a room—somewhere, but not anywhere I recognized as ever having lived. Strange things are happening to me everywhere I go now!

"You look bewildered. What is wrong?"

"Oh, nothing. I was just wondering when the show begins. I'm getting cold." With a stall like that, he'll be abandoning me here and now. I better start acting like there is some sign of intelligent life in this body—even I am growing bored with my conversation.

"Notice how everyone is hushed and waiting in anticipation? It should start any moment. We are all very pleased that the fame of this humble little show has spread so far abroad that many travelers now go out of their way to see it."

"You should be proud. It's a tribute to your people. We're not very much aware of the deep ties you have to your past until we visit, but it's absolutely impressive to anyone with a brain."

Now that is a really awe-inspiring comment. I must be losing my mind or at least my ability to communicate on a deep, meaningful level. I've never sounded so inane in all my life.

"You hide your feelings behind words, Amanda."

Amanda. It's the beginning of the end. I'm about to be dumped, and I can't blame him.

"I'm sort of tired and out of sync. I need time to listen to the stones." Listen to the stones? Where did that come from?

"Yes, you are very wise. The stones tell the story of Earth and the wise can read them—but only the wisest of all can hear them."

Now I feel like a fraud again. When will we get down to just being friends—or whatever?

"I feel a unique ability to create the universe here tonight with only a stone. It's like the Earth is here and I am out there but have the means to build another world—a better one."

"Yes, Amanda, you can. You can build your own universe. The Earth is only one planet, but your plane and planet now and you are here to learn what you can do to save the Earth from the impending disaster man has precipitated upon it. You can be the instrument of creation for a whole, new world. You can manifest a world where all are created in equal goodness and able to demonstrate their worth."

What is going on now? I'm listening to me talk because I sound very interesting all of a sudden, and he thinks it's me talking—but it's not. What am I doing? What is going on here?"

"How long have you been a channel of the higher wisdom, Amanda?"

"Channel? Me? You have the wrong lady. I don't channel. Channels have these real deep voices and their faces contort into someone other than who they are in normal life. I don't know anything about channeling!"

"You protest too much. It's okay. We honor the fact that you have been chosen to speak, and you will be able to acknowledge it yourself soon. You do not recognize who you are yet, but you will."

"Really? I'm going to know who I am and why I'm here?" I could hear the excitement in my voice as though I were in a seat several feet away, but I enjoyed the feeling.

"You know already. You came to Earth with everything you need to know imprinted in your mind, but the mind does not want to cooperate. It wants to maintain control over all of this life's activities so you won't abandon it for an even more spiritual direction. It dreams its dreams and tries to keep you from meditating and doing your spiritual work. We will have to talk later. The show is starting."

The mostly Hispanic and European audience sat absorbed in all that happened, but since the entire production was conducted in Spanish, I made no attempt to translate any of it, deciding to wait for the English production later. I sat there and watched as the sky lit up with visions of hieroglyphics flashing upon the walls of the Nunnery as the story unfolded in peaceful harmonies with only occasional strident musical under-tones. The narrator's deep, expressive voice and the voices of the others who joined him in a kind of Greek chorus warmed my ears and electrified my other senses. At the end of the show, the audience clapped enthusiastically and only then could you detect a mild roar coming from somewhere behind us.

"What's that noise, Jorge?"

He laughed unexpectedly. "That is the American audience waiting for their turn. They are always very impatient—and enthusiastic. We love them best."

"You people are outstanding. You accept our rudeness and repay it with gallantries. I wish we were more like you."

"Oh, we are very much alike. The Mayan and American cultures are not so very different. We, too, enjoy life and feel its depth. We are seldom casual onlookers though. Maybe that is because we have less cash."

"There is a lot more difference between our cultures than just cash, but you have a point. Two countries aren't so very different from one another nor are any two people. It's hard to see the similarities when the customs seem to be at odds with one another, but people are people. We are all Earthlings!" I chuckled at that, but he appeared more interested than before.

"You are right. We are all the same because we live on Earth. We have no difference in our basic requirements. We all need to breathe and drink and eat and love and have people respect us in order to do what we came to Earth to do. If we lack any one of the basics elements, our health and wealth decline as does our self-esteem, but we continue to live on Earth. We cannot leave it."

"Yes, I guess we are prisoners of the planet. I never thought of it that way, but you're right. We can't get off it—except for a short time on some kind of plane or rocket."

"The planes. That is where we are. The planes of life are not obvious, but they exist and only our concentration keeps us centered within one. This plane is the one on which modern-day work is done and is the springboard for the next plane. The previous levels of this plane are in other times and places and differ somewhat from when we were on them, but they still remain the same."

"Wait a minute, Jorge. You're losing me. I followed you so far, but after that I got foggy. I'm not so sure you have it right."

"Oh, of course, you would know better."

Is he being sarcastic? I'm not sure, and why do I suddenly think I'm such an expert? I don't even understand the New York Subway System.

"Go on, Amanda, what were you going to say?"

"I was going to say that Earth is not the only planet where humans live and work, but it is the only place where WE live and work and WE have to protect it until all of us get to the next plane, which means some humans have to work up several levels on this plane first before they can be launched to the next."

"Yes, I agree, but you were saying some of my work was not thought through enough. Where am I wrong?"

"You are not wrong. You are just oriented in a different direction than what the Earth is. Your ancestral times are very close to you, but far away to me. We both lived on this peninsula in times ago, but you are still attached to it—while I live elsewhere. We are together now to save the people who have stayed here in order to hold the old ways in tact."

"Si, Si, go on."

"You're not tired, are you? We can go into this later—after the show."

"Oh, of course, you have a desire to see the English show now. I will contain my enthusiasm until it is over."

Contain his enthusiasm? What is going on here? I'm just as enthusiastic as he is and I'm the one who is supposed to be talking.

"Yes, I'd like to hear the show. I've seen it and now I want to hear it. This is absolutely the best way to experience hundreds of years of tribal history!"

"We will talk later then."

There was definitely a hint of regret in his voice, but his innate humility and consideration for other people prevented him from pressuring me to leave the amphitheater, so we sat down again and prepared to enjoy the program as the lights began their colorful progression across the sides of the quadrangle.

The End of the Week

After the show the lights came on and we all paraded out toward the parking lot, I noticed Jorge acting different—sort of fidgety. Why? He is definitely not the nervous type.

"Mandy, would you mind waiting here while I talk to a friend of mine. I see him leaving the parking area?"

"Go ahead. I'll wait over by the van."

As I approached the VW bus it did not look right, but I could not see anything wrong—at first. Upon closer inspection though I found the right front tire flat, but it was no ordinary flat—it had been slashed!

I thought, how disgusting and it's going to be pitch black as soon as they turn off all the lights. I better go and get Jorge right away.

I put my head down and ran toward Jorge, but when I got to where he was, he wasn't there. He seemed to have disappeared. I asked one of the men if he had seen Jorge, but he said nothing and looked at me somewhat puzzled. He acted like he didn't know who I was talking about. Not knowing what to do, I started to walk back to the leaning van and right then Jorge reappeared by the front door. A strong sense of relief rushed to my head. I have never felt anything quite like it. That is when I realized I had been terror filled when Jorge disappeared. Why? I don't know, but I felt something was definitely wrong—but what?

Examining the tire, Jorge said almost absent-mindedly, "It looks like we will have to walk back to your hotel. It is not far from here. I have a torch in the car."

A torch? Why would we need a torch? Oh, I see, a flashlight—what the British call a torch, but why would he use their slang? Who cares? I was becoming neurotic, but managed to say calmly, "Who do you think slashed the tire?"

"Oh, I probably drove over a rough stone or a strip of metal sticking out of the wall by the front gate. No big deal."

No big deal, my foot. I would have felt it if we had driven over anything that could slash a tire that way. What is going on? We were followed around Merida last night, and tonight our tire is slashed while we're watching the light and sound show way out in Uxmal. Something is wrong!

"You don't have to worry. I have a good spare. I will come back later to change it and still be on time tomorrow to pick you up. It does not present any real problem."

He sounds too smooth to believe, maybe that is why I don't. Up until this happened, it was such a great day—filled with so much excitement that I wanted to sit down and write about it in my journal, but now I don't want to think too much about what I may have missed or didn't really see. This is all getting a bit too adventurous for me. I don't think I want to know what is going on.

"Do you have looters in this part of the country, Jorge?"

"Wha-a-t?"

"Looters! You know! Like guys who rob the tombs of your ancestors looking for jewels and artifacts to smuggle out of the country for rich collectors in the States or in Europe."

"Or the Orient."

"Yes, or the Orient. Could there be looters around here?"

"It's possible—anything is possible, but highly unlikely. Why do you ask?"

He is still trying to put me off, but it's not going to work this time.

"I don't think you accidentally damaged the tire. I think someone is out to harm you in some way, maybe not seriously, but they are trying to make a deep impression on you."

"Now don't get upset. There is nothing sinister going on here."

"I think there is, but we better get on our way while there is still a crowd around. In fact, I see some tourists walking toward the hotel now. I think we better join them just to be on the safe side. Don't you?"

He hurried along beside me, but said nonchalantly, "You don't have to worry. There isn't anybody hiding in the bushes. This is Uxmal, sacred city of the Maya, no harm can come to you here."

"Well, I'd like to see you take one of the guides back with you to fix the tire—or stay at the Inn tonight. Can you do that?"

"Yes, I could, but I intend to drop you off and run over to my friends' place and get some help from them—so I won't have to change the tire tomorrow."

His confidence dissolved some of my tension, but I knew something was up and that he knew exactly what it was, so I played dumb.

"Do you have many occasions or reasons to come to Uxmal?"

"No, but I spend a lot of time at Chichen Itza."

I could have sworn he told me he seldom went there, but why would he lie now?

"Actually, I don't go to either site very often, because of all the tourists. We have many, many ancient burial places, cities, and temples which I enjoy prospecting and dreaming about more than those which are recognized treasures—but over-studied, simply because they can be reached easily by tourists from Cancun."

"Will you take me to some of the off-the-beaten-path sites? I would be ever so grateful if you would."

"Why, yes, I can do that, but they are not at all like Uxmal. Most are nothing more than mounds of stones covered by plants and trees deep in the jungle and require machetes to cut your way through—and boots to fend off the snakes. You have to be careful of the snakes."

He was trying to dissuade me from going along, but it wouldn't happen. I was game for going anywhere with him now. He's a good guide and he knows what he's doing.

"No problem. I used to be afraid of snakes, but I desensitized myself as part of a behavioral psych class project. Now there is no problem. I respect them."

"Great! We probably won't see any anyway, but I like to warn people."

"Who all do you take to these places?"

"We are almost at the Inn and I was wondering if you would mind if I left you here now, since there is a nice crowd milling around. You will be safe."

"So you think there is a chance of trouble?"

He tried to smile or looked like it, but said with a hint of annoyance, "Don't let your imagination run wild, Mandy. There is nothing to be afraid of around here. I will pick you up tomorrow at nine o'clock, if that is okay."

"Will you have enough rest? Last night you got almost no sleep, and how much will you get tonight after you go and get your friends and change the tire and everything?"

"Don't worry about me. I don't need sleep."

"Okay, Jorge. Do what you have to do and I'll see you tomorrow about nine."

"Great! Have a good night's sleep. We have a lot of walking ahead of us tomorrow."

As he headed back toward Uxmal, I saw him turn off his flashlight. Why? Why risk tripping over stones, unless he has eyes like a cat or something?

The crowd opened around me and pulled me with it into the center of the tidy dining room where several families were ordering dessert. Seemed a good idea, so I let myself be invited to join a table of four other Americans. We sat and chatted about nothing for almost an hour before I went off to my room.

As I approached the door, I thought I saw a light inside through the louvers, but it must have been a reflection because there was no light on inside the room and I had to fumble along the wall inside the door to find a switch. It was much lower than I expected. But after all, Maya electricians aren't as tall as their American counterparts.

The ceiling fan immediately started to whine in complaint about being turned on at that late hour, but it did not bother me. I like that kind of safe sound in a strange place. It makes you feel at home, but I heard another sound that did not. Someone was on the verandah outside my room.

Quickly I tip-toed across the room and thrust the screened door to the verandah outward, but no one was there. Must have been an animal or something. I don't think geckos run around at night—but frogs do. That must be it. No, frogs don't wear shoes. It had to be one of the staff nosing around. Who else would bother? Just the same, I locked the screened door and closed the windows' louvers, but I had to leave the louvers on the front door half open and the noisy fan going, to keep the air circulating in the damp room.

This is really a nice room. I just hope the water goes down the sink drain faster than it did before dinner. That's it! It was the plumber just now getting around to fixing the drain but found I was back. Hmmm, the sink still backs up, but maybe someone fixed it. It's hard to tell. I'm going to bed anyway and worry about what may be going on tomorrow; but just in case, I'll program my dreams and ask my Higher Self what is happening here and what I should do about it.

As the sun's first rays entered the slats on my front door, the rest of the inn was apparently up and about. The kitchen staff clanged and banged every pot, pan, and skillet at hand. Someone was actually singing! How could anyone be that cheerful so early in the morning? The sun could not have been up more than a few minutes, but my watch showed eight-thirty.

Whoa! What is going on here? You would think I was drugged or something. I never sleep that sound for that long when I'm away from home.

Rushing about, I slipped into my jeans and the hiking boots I almost didn't buy. Rubbed insect repellent everywhere bare and packed every other thing I thought I'd need to go tramping around in the jungle, but time didn't cooperate. It was after nine by the time I got to the lobby and Jorge was not there.

No need to panic! He must be outside looking for me because I know he's always on time, but the hotel manager is looking at me uncertainly. I wonder why? Oh, I forgot to tell him I want to stay another night. Jorge was going to tell him and probably forgot.

The hotel manager smiled hesitantly as I came forward, but said not a word while I rambled on about going out into the jungle for a day trip and could I keep my room for another night and about the clogged sink. He seemed confused but too polite to ask questions. He let me talk but did not respond. Finally, he sort of shrugged and motioned toward the hotel register.

"Do I have to sign in again?"

"No, Senorita, we have no room for you. We cannot extend your time with us. You must check out by eleven o'clock."

"Oh, I'm sorry. Jorge said he would make all the arrangements and I thought he did. I must apologize."

"Jorge? Who is Jorge?"

What? He doesn't know Jorge? I saw them talking together yesterday— twice. I'm sure he's a friend of Jorge.

"Jorge is the man who made my arrangements yesterday to stay overnight."

"I'm sorry Senorita, but your reservation was made weeks ago. We have no room at this time of the year otherwise. It is our busiest time."

"No, there must be a mistake. I didn't know I'd be in Mexico—let alone Uxmal, weeks ago. It was a very recent decision and I had no intention of staying overnight. I never heard of your inn before—lovely as it is—and so very comfortable, too." I started back-peddling as fast as possible in order to be able to sort through what he had said, but nothing made sense. What is going on, and where is Jorge?

"If you wish, we can arrange transportation for you back to Merida."

"I may have to take you up on that—but later. Right now I need to find Jorge and find out what is going on and where I am supposed to be. Did anyone stop by the desk this morning looking for me?"

"No, no one asked for you, but perhaps your friend is somewhere nearby?"

"Yes, he had car trouble last night and may still be working on it. Thanks for everything. I mean, mucho gracias, Senor."

He grinned, probably at my terrible accent and lack of originality, but if I talk like a native and use the few words I know they always shoot back so much, so fast I can't understand anything. Better to play dumb like the rest of the Americans.

It did not take long to walk back to the parking lot where we left the VW bus the night before, but it was not there. Where can he be? Should I wait or should I go back to Merida? I sat down on a crude bench under the huge spreading tree to the side of the ticket booth and gate in order to think over what to do next and suddenly Jorge appeared on the road in front of me, waving his panama hat back and forth like he had been waiting there for hours.

"Sorry, Amanda, but it took longer to repair the flat than I expected. I felt it would not be wise to go back into the bush without a good spare. I hope you have not waited too long."

"No, I haven't, but I can't stay at the Inn tonight. They're booked solid."

"Don't worry about it. It is all taken care of. It was just a misunderstanding. The manager didn't know it was you when he said you had to check out."

"Oh, so you talked to the manager?"

"Yes, about twenty minutes ago."

Twenty minutes ago I was talking to the manager! What is going on? I feel like a parrot—all I say is: 'What is going on?' It keeps running through my mind over and over again. I have to find out. But how?

"Jorge, when will we get back to the Inn?"

"Oh, shortly after nine. We will eat with friends. I am sure you won't miss what they are serving here tonight—a Mexican buffet and afterwards 'real' Mexicans will dance—maybe the Hat Dance from somewhere."

"Right! I don't like tourist fare, either. It's too something for me, but I'm not sure what."

"Too bland! Inauthentic! You are a native at heart. Your tastes were developed in embryo."

"Yeah, that sounds about right—in a funny sort of way. You have such a descriptive way of describing things. Listen to me! I can't even speak English anymore."

"That is because you channel so much. You cannot switch back and forth from one frequency to another rapidly when you are so far out."

"Yeah? Maybe so."

What the heck is he talking about? I need to know what is going on, but I'm so lost I have no idea where to start. Probably back at the airport, but this reservation business goes back further than that. Maybe someone used my credit cards? No, I cleaned up my Visa bill the day before I left and there were no charges for Uxmal.

"Why don't you wait in the van for me, Mandy? I'll get a few things the cook has prepared for us to eat along the way. I asked him to put in a couple of Diet Pepsis for you."

"Great! No hurry, take your time. I'll keep busy looking at the flocks of tourists arriving to visit Uxmal for the first time."

Diet Pepsi? How does he know I'm a Pepsi drinker by preference? I know he never saw me drink one and there is only Coke wherever you go here. Oh well, he knows a lot more about me than that—so what's the big deal?

The big deal is I am starting to doubt Jorge. Here I am traveling around with a guide whom I never heard of two or three days ago and trusting him to take me out into the jungle to see what? I'm even losing track of time. It seems like I've been in Mexico a week, but it's only been a few days. What day is it anyway? Friday? My gosh, I can't believe it!

I didn't tell Jorge I have to be back in Merida by Sunday because I have a date with Chip in the Zocalo and definitely want to keep it! I better mention it. Jorge is a nice guy and I like what I see, but Chip is more my style—or is he? I don't know him at all—come to think of it.

When Jorge returned, he took the road leading away from Merida to seek more adventure for me and whatever for himself but went only a mile or so when we were rudely interrupted in our personal reveries. An expensive black sedan drove right up to our rear bumper and blasted its horn. When the car passed us, a passenger rolled down a dark-tinted window and motioned at our front tire as their car accelerated and shot beyond us. No one else could be seen on the road in either direction.

Right then we heard the unmistakable 'glub, glub, glub' of a flat tire. Jorge swore almost under his breath in English and then in Spanish. Funny that he didn't start swearing in Spanish—his native tongue.

The End of Time

There were few cars at the unmarked site when we arrived, but more than Jorge wanted. He was angry. He acted betrayed or something. I couldn't see any reason to be upset, but he obviously was. When he parked the VW bus among the bushes that passed for a parking area, he swore under his breath—again in English, but said nothing else. I could hear loud voices—American tourists??

Why are we here anyway? This place doesn't look like any sacred spot to me. Something is wrong! I can feel it.

"Jorge, there is a highway patrol car coming down the road."

I pointed at the green jeep approaching us with dust playing at making clouds behind it. Jorge's eyes narrowed to slits. Maybe from the dust, but I think not.

"Hey, you two! Where are you going?" The semi-uniformed man spoke in lyrical English as he climbed from behind the wheel of the jeep. He moved faster than anyone I had seen in all of Mexico. He approached us in a sort of trot, but showed no signs of stopping to chat. Instead, he headed toward a path through the underbrush that lead toward the loud voices we heard when we pulled in and parked. We followed him closely.

There were ten or twelve people standing around in various poses depicting concern, dismay, and tragedy. One seemed to be directing the scene where mayhem and murder had been acted out recently. Laying on the ground in front of us was the 'ugly American' I had met at the Hotel Astaria's cocktail party earlier in the week. He was even uglier now with a bloody slash across his body, probably from a machete, and a gash on his forehead that looked ghastly. Whoever killed him was an animal!

I know some of these people were in the lobby on my first night in Merida, but I really didn't recognize anyone in particular—except HIM.

"Does anyone know who this man is?" asked the policeman or whoever he was.

"Yes, officer, we all know him. His name is Regis Fawley." The man volunteering the information seemed pleased to be in charge while everyone else wept or looked anywhere but at the body on the ground.

"Did you all come here together?"

A loud chorus of 'No!' answered his question, so he continued to stare at the man he now made spokesman for the group.

"Who called me?"

Of course it was the officious one, which confirmed he would be taking charge of the entire group's responses—at least for the time being. This sweaty, balding little man seemed to swell larger and larger with his own importance as the sun poured down through the tree tops and spotlighted the corpse.

The officer moved the group as far away as possible from the body, but the ground was already trampled and would yield no clues now. He motioned for everyone to be silent as he radioed for help, but one woman could not stop crying. To me, her hysteria was a bit out of place since this guy was one of the most obnoxious tourists or men alive—when he was alive and he was gone only an hour or so at most. What was he to her?

When the patrolman got off the radio, he nodded at the sobbing woman and asked with apparent concern, "Are you his wife?"

"Oh, no, officer, but he was such a wonderful man! No one deserves to die like this in such a terrible God-forsaken place."

Funny how clearly she spoke her lines for being semi-hysterical.

"What is your relationship to the deceased? Are you more than just casual acquaintances?"

A buzz arose from the group and she turned scarlet as she replied, "We were in love."

In love? In love? That is the limit! If this guy can find a woman to love him, there is no hope for American women! As though the officer could read my thoughts, he pivoted on his heel and turned to me and said, "You don't look like you liked him much. How well did you know the deceased?"

"Me? I don't know him at all! I didn't even know his name."

"Come, come, Senorita, you have the unmistakable look of someone who knows more than she cares to say. I welcome your comments now—not later. What do you know of this man? I want to know everything."

"Wha-a-t?"

"You heard me. Everything!"

"I don't know him!"

With a look of total disbelief and as much sarcasm, he said, "You mean you never saw this man before in your life?"

"Well, no, but I only saw him once. He was at the one and only cocktail party for Americans I attended at the Hotel Astaria in Merida."

"When was that?"

"Several days ago."

"Exactly when?"

Feeling stupid and suddenly tongue-tied, I couldn't say when I last saw the dead man. It seemed like months ago.

"It had to be Wednesday—or was it Thursday?"

"Which was it? Why can't you remember? How long have you been in Mexico?"

"Oh, I remember, I arrived on Wednesday and that is when I saw him. I didn't stay at the party long."

"Did you talk to him?"

"Maybe, but it couldn't have been much."

"Why?"

"I'm not in the habit of picking up with strange men the first time I meet them in a bar."

He seemed satisfied and turned back to the group now crowding around the body of Regis Fawley. He ignored Jorge who now stood several feet away from me, deeper in the shadows. Actually, Jorge blended into the bushes more and more as I watched him out of the corner of my eye.

The gang of gawkers was not well rehearsed in what to say, and it took time for the officer to question each woman in detail, yet he said very little to the men. He seemed suspicious of everyone—especially the men. There were no comic aspects in the entire scene, but when I turned to talk to Jorge, I almost laughed to discover he was gone. He had slipped into the bushes and disappeared! The shock made me want to laugh. I don't know why, but I was unhinged by his sudden disappearance again.

"Well, Senorita, you may go back to Merida and wait for the police to question you further since you arrived on the scene at the same time I did or you may wait here. It is up to you."

Definitely shaken now, I merely mumbled, "I'll just wait here. I like to take care of things right away."

Besides, how do I get back to Merida? Where is Jorge now?

I watched as the officer knelt beside the corpse and swatted flying insects away as he more closely examined the head first and then proceeded down the torso and onto the legs to look very closely at the boots—or what was left of them.

"Did any of you know why he was out here by himself?"

"No," was the unanimous answer, but he motioned for the girl friend to advance toward him.

"What did he tell you the last time you were together? Did he say he was coming out here?"

"No, we went out last night to the light and sound show at Uxmal, and this morning we all went over there and looked at the stuff we couldn't see last night, and that is when I realized he wasn't with us."

"When were you last together?"

"Last night at the show. We left in different cars, though. I had to pack up my stuff so no one at the hotel would go through it today while we were out here visiting ruins."

"I see, and when you left for Uxmal this morning, did you see him?"

She looked puzzled, then said with hesitancy, "I guess I didn't see him at all. I thought he went ahead with the guide because he left a note in my door at the hotel."

"A note? What did it say? Are you sure it was from him?"

"It just said he would see me later, but I don't know if it was from him or not."

"Why?"

"I-I don't know what his writing looks like—exactly, and he didn't sign it."

The officer barely concealed a sneer, or maybe amusement, as he turned away from the drooping, somewhat-withered blond and began examining the dead man's smashed wristwatch.

"He won't be needing that again. Will he?"

The kneeling policeman shot a look at the would-be comedian leaning over him. The silly young man's attempt at humor appeared to arouse the officer's suspicion and place him at the center of the interrogation now.

"Why do you say that, Senor?"

"Why? I just mean it's never gonna' run again and neither is he. I didn't mean anything else. I'm sorry I said that. It wasn't appropriate. I can't seem to stop myself sometimes—when I get real nervous."

"Why are you so nervous, Senor?"

Upon closer investigation he was not quite so young as he first appeared, but he looked very nervous. Nothing came out of his mouth as his lips moved.

"Speak up, Senor. What do you know of this man? How long have you known him? Why weren't you together? When did you last see him?"

These questions were fired off in close succession, if you can say that of someone speaking in Spanish and English to a dazed man who appeared to be unable to comprehend anything.

"Very well, Senor. My superiors in Merida will get the information from you later."

The now-distraught man appeared about to faint at this pronouncement, but then miraculously spilled out all his answers in one steady stream. Only then did the officer seem satisfied. He established the approximate time of death and appeared comfortable assuming that no one present was responsible for the crime. At least that is what I thought.

I waited for someone to notice Jorge's absence, but when no one did, I figured Jorge must be well known to the policeman or he would have asked about him; but it still seemed strange. Mexico has a reputation in the US of being a corrupt police state, but this was going too far—when innocent, even stupid American tourists are thoroughly interrogated while natives are totally excused from even having to remain on the scene.

As I puzzled over this, the officer turned to me and said softly, "Senorita, you may continue your journey."

I took one deep plunge into his eyes but saw nothing, so I asked nothing and cleared out as fast as I could without appearing to rush.

At the clearing, the van was gone so I ran toward the road. Why? I don't know. I just wanted to get away as fast as I could. There was something strange in the policeman's manner and attitude—not quite threatening but mysterious.

At the road I spotted the VW with Jorge sitting behind the wheel reading a newspaper as though nothing unusual had happened. Upon spotting me, he folded the paper and started up the noisy engine. How had he moved the bus from the parking area without any of us hearing it? Oh, well, I have bigger things to worry about than that.

"So, you are all clear?"

"Yes, but Jorge, how can *you* just walk away from the scene of a crime like that?"

"Aahh, this is Mexico. Remember?"

He's stalling again—but what can I say? I haven't a clue as to what is going on here.

"What did Eduardo find out? Why was this Regis Fawley out here—alone?"

"Oh, so you know the policeman? I should have known." Instant relief flowed over me, followed by a wave of confusion. What is going on exactly? Why do I feel there is something about to explode and I might get hurt? I have to get to the bottom of this now!

"When did he die? Did you find out?"

"He died at 7:15 this morning."

"Really? How can you be so sure?"

"His watch was smashed at that time."

"It might have been smashed earlier and he continued to wear it."

Stumped for a moment, I then remembered seeing the broken glass on the ground beneath his wrist. I decided not to share this evidence with Jorge. I don't know why, but I now knew Jorge was not who he pretended to be—which actually was no one. Anyway, I was not going to be his stooge. I intended to conduct my own investigation.

"You have outstanding powers of recall and observation. You are able to analyze the entire scene and reach proper conclusions. You have to concentrate. Would you do that for me?"

The tone of his voice was so soothing and comforting, I just knew he was honest and sincere, but I didn't feel like going into it then. I thought: I'm going to do my own work. Let him do his. He hasn't been forthcoming with much information when I have asked him about things—so two can play his game.

"If you are afraid I won't believe you, Mandy, don't even think it. I understand you. I am like you. We have both been through so much training and know so much that is not accepted in the world as true—because it was not arrived at by the scientific method, but it is valid. Believe me, I honor your input. Between us, we can solve any mystery."

"I'm afraid I don't know anything about Fawley. I met him once and didn't like him, but no one would kill him for being obnoxious. Americans aren't that violent yet, and you people wouldn't be that bothered by his nasty tongue. You've heard worse."

Jorge smiled faintly, seemingly concerned, but said nothing as he drove the old bus faster than it wanted to go—away from Uxmal.

"What do you suppose happened in that clearing, Mandy? Do you think he went out there to meet someone?"

"I don't know. Maybe he went with someone. That seems more probable since he'd likely not have known his way around the countryside. Would he?"

"I don't know. How did any of them know of this grove? It's not on the map or known beyond my own people as a sacred spot. Meridians are not even aware of it. It is not on any tour schedule, and no one drives out to Uxmal then continues on to see a site that hasn't been exploited. So why did all these Americans show up today?"

"I don't know, Jorge. I don't even know why I was there."

He laughed and said, "You were there at the invitation of the elders. Don't you remember?"

"Oh, yes. They did say you were to take me to some interesting spots where 'my powers would be enhanced'. Is that why we went there?"

"Yes."

This is too unbelievable. My 'powers' were going to be enhanced in that little clearing? What was he going to do to me? There wasn't anything there.

"Beyond the spot where the body lays now is a stele that depicts the grave of an ancient warrior king who gave up his life for his family. We honor him today for his devotion and see in his story a repeat of the call of family. We don't always remember our past, but many are able to recite his story. He was not able to die at home but was given a full burial and remembered long after richer men were buried in bigger tombs. He was a truly great man and gives out much wisdom."

Gives out? How, if he has been dead for centuries?

"When we return this way, perhaps we will be able to enter from another path so you may yet receive instructions from him."

"Whatever you say, Jorge. But how does he teach?"

"The same as the rest. There is little difference between those who are 'alive' and those who are 'dead'. You know that."

"Oh, of course."

You know, I actually do believe that, but to think an ancient warrior is going to impart wisdom to me just because I visit his grave in search of instruction is too far out even for me.

"Jorge, there is one thing I'm not sure about. What process is used to develop a connection between us and say—this great warrior?"

He seemed pleased to respond to my question and settled down into the cushions further and relaxed his hands on the steering wheel.

"You have to know this, but I can see you have not had the benefit of formal education in the art of seeking and sources of power as we have here in the Yucatan. We are no better for it, but it helps to know where you are and how far along the path you are before you begin to teach others. You have been teaching a long time but don't realize it yet. You think you are still a student. Right?"

"Absolutely! I'm no teacher. I don't know enough about anything to teach. Anyway, I prefer to listen."

"That is the wisdom within you. All who are wise listen and fools seldom do, but not all who speak are fools. You cannot learn as much from fools as you learn from the lips of wise men because nothing much memorable flows from wide open mouths; but from the open minds of wide intellects flows much wisdom. If you are open, you will overflow with wisdom, but if you deny your ability to leave the role of student and refuse to accept the responsibilities of the teachers, you will be unable to ascend to the highest level of this life. We know we are there, but you are not convinced you are."

"What? I really don't know what you mean. I've never done anything unusual with my life. I've never done anything really odd with my psychic abilities, either. I do practice, but very little happens, and I never studied with anyone, either."

He laughed merrily, would be my best description of how he reacted to my confession. Up until now, he had never relaxed so completely in my presence, but he did not speak.

"I know I'm *psychic.* Everyone is. But I don't see things like some do and seldom do things that the New Age crowd likes to do. In fact, I dislike *so many* things being taught in that area, and I dislike listening to people who stand up at such meetings and brag about their out-of-whatever experiences. I feel nothing and can't connect to them."

"As I said, the fools who would teach have little wisdom to impart, but it is there for those who look deep and go beyond the obvious. However, it takes a wise one to be able to do that."

"Hmmm, but who teaches me?"

"Your teachers are the same as mine, but I have others here in flesh to help me absorb the process and understand why we are different. Now I can see this is a help. In the past, I often wished I did not have to spend so much time with the elders. I wanted to spend more time at the university or working alone with my spiritual teachers."

"Oh, you have teachers in Spirit who tell you what to do, then the elders reinforce their lessons?"

"Yes, of course! I am sorry. You have not had elders to teach you since the one who raised you died. That is indeed sorrowful. I never before realized my luck. When I chose to be born again in the Mayan way, I obviously chose the easier route, while you chose the much more difficult course of being born into the American world. Here I have prided myself for being able to understand and accept more than you, but I am totally humbled by this revelation and accept the lesson for my ego which is long overdue."

"Your ego has been chastised. You will not suffer. I am here to learn from the elders and you, and now I am ready." I looked around to see who was talking, then realized it was me.

The End of the Road
Rises Higher
Than the Beginning

The best way to see around anything is to look straight through it. Fortunately, most people are quite transparent, but not Jorge. He has so much light and energy around him you cannot see into him. Your eyes begin to blur the lines and you see nothing after awhile.

For me, the tone of the day was set when we left the clearing with a dead body laying on the ground, but not for Jorge. He did not refer to it again and ignored me when I did. He was quite content to quietly drive and drive and drive. We stopped only to refuel. Fortunately, I'm gifted with a major league bladder and can last all day if I must.

The sun was high above us and bore down on the car relentlessly since the trees along the roadway provided no shade. We had not seen any villages or pedestrians for miles and miles, only an occasional vehicle going the other way. I had no clue as to where we were or what direction we were traveling, but I felt quite comfortable in my ignorance.

"See that tree on the horizon?"

For Jorge to say anything, we must be wherever we are going.

"Yes, it looks to be quite tall. But how can that be?"

"There is a big spring beneath it and an outcropping of rock upon which it stands. It is a guardian."

"Did you say, garden?"

"No, guardian. It protects the water from intruders."

"Interesting. How can a tree do that?"

"You will see. Right now, pull your arms inside your jacket. They are getting red. I forget you have white skin now."

He's always making weird comments like that. I wonder why?

"Ow! You're right. My right arm is burnt. I'll have to buy some after-sun stuff and put it on."

"Don't worry about it. Mexico is the home of aloe. Remember?"

"Oh, yes, but I have stuff that takes the sting out without fading your tan, instead of all your skin sloughing off like the 'creeping crud'."

"The 'creeping crud'? What is that?"

"When Caucasians get too much sun, a few days later the dead skin comes off and clings to the side of the tub and shower. It's not a pretty sight. So, when I was a teenager we called it the 'creeping crud'. Believe me, it's an apt description."

"Oh, I believe you. You cannot lie, and you are *very* descriptive in your word usage."

"You're right about the lying, anyway. I've never been able to do it. It shows all over my face and I feel like such a heel—I always have to confess."

"It shines from your being that you are one of us, so you cannot lie when truth is necessary. You cannot be untrue to the light. If you are, the time factor will erase your lie and tell it as it is."

"What time factor?"

"When you talk, you think time is going by, but it isn't. You are merely inputting information into the data bank of another and the time is of no importance—only the content. If the content is of no use to anyone, the facts are distorted and dropped immediately from the field. But if you speak of knowledge not known by that soul, it is retraced to its root and you are given a new light to carry."

"Sounds interesting, but I'm confused."

"No, you are never confused. The mind is, but not You. You have the capacity to be all you ever thought in this life. You are here now and you are the one who made all the choices this past week to enhance our meeting today so there would be no way it could be delayed or avoided. You are here to learn why you are—and no dead bodies, police, or anything on Earth will stop it from happening. Do you understand?"

"No."

"Nonsense, you know. We will not waste time now discussing it, because you need to know a few things in advance about the procedures to be followed when we enter the cave. There is a definite protocol to be followed."

"A cave? I hate caves."

"Don't we all! But they are used for the matters of Earth and you are not to be left behind. You will enter directly upon hearing your name called. You will not hesitate or ask questions, but step forward quickly. You will remain quiet of mind and never question anything you see or hear while in the cave. You will let them explain the manner of ceremony we are to witness and why it is necessary. You will say NOTHING. Do you understand?"

"Yes, yes, but why can't I at least know now—from you, what is going to go on?"

He looked irked, but I knew he would tell me—probably against his better judgment. I could tell by the way he kept clearing his throat and looking away to his left.

"You know everything already! You came to Earth totally prepared. You do not need to be 'prepped' as you say. You have it. Just think! Just listen and don't say anything. Let the event unfold. You can do that. Can't you?"

"Yes, but"

"Yes, but, but, but. Why always a but? You can wait."

I know he will tell me now. I just have to whine a little bit more. "Why do you act like I was born and raised the same as you? I am not Maya—at least not in this life and cannot possibly know everything you take for granted. You should help me. I need to know why I am expected at this cave today."

Jorge's shoulders sagged, then he shrugged and said, "You are here for the same reason I am here and everyone else is here. You have been called!"

"Called? To do what?"

"Wait! Don't question anything—just listen and enjoy, then take your knowledge back with you and study it at your leisure. Today is a day of religious significance to all Maya—this life or any other. It is the time of the end and we all know what that means."

"Whoa! I don't. I need to refresh my memory."

"You are getting to be annoying, but why I don't know. I have never really been annoyed by anyone before. We Maya are not used to the ways of your people and your wheedling and begging for what you do not need or want. I am not prepared for this."

"You are doing just fine. Now tell me why I'm here, why I flew down here, and why we are out here in the wilderness together, then I promise I will just watch and wait."

He stared at me long enough to make me blush, then seemed to relent. He said hesitantly, "I can see you are genuinely puzzled and don't know why you came to the Yucatan at this time—even though you should know."

"Finally, the man sees the light!"

"Not me. You have not seen the light! You are glowing and afire, but still do not realize the time has arrived for you to fulfill your life's work. Don't you know yet? You are here to help the Maya in their last days."

"Wha-a-t?"

"You heard me. You are here to help us ascend. We are not here to be leaders of a new religion or carry the torch for others to follow. We have completed our annual and biennial and triennial, etc., etc., celebrations and rites for the last time. We are nearing 'our end of time'. We do not intend to stay until the bitter end. We will deliver the world from its own disharmony—if we can, but we are not responsible for it and will not carry the guilt with us. We will not be here."

"Be here when?"

"When the Earth is destroyed by the hands of man. Your people have been the plague of the universe. You started out with the energy and goodwill of all, but now you have been so contorted by ego and greed that there's nothing left to hold Earth together. The Earth moans in agony. The Earth is dying and none of you care. You are all rapists and murderers."

"I think I agree, but why am I here then? I'm an American."

"Not really. Many Americans are not of that society. You are not. You don't even vote."

"How do you know that?"

"It is in your head. You record all events. You have not voted in any election of real worth in twelve years and feel no need to because you do not care what they do. Apathy is written in your heart. You do not enjoy life there anymore. You are not as into the life of others who are much involved in politics and merchandise. You think nothing of them or their wares. You are tired of the marketplace mentality—as you put it, and you are still an American?"

"Yes, and proud of it. I have always been pleased to pay my taxes."

"Taxes? Oh, yes, I see what you mean."

"No, you don't, but never mind. Just tell me what I asked and I promise that I will be good."

"You have such curious phrases. You are good—basically, innately. How can you be otherwise?"

"Never mind, you are too literal—and obviously stalling for time, and I can see we're going to be there very soon."

"All right, and I can see you need to feed your mind something to get it to stop interrupting the flow."

He settled back in his seat a little further, smiled, then began, "Before you arrived, the word was out that an American woman of your description would arrive at the airport on Wednesday. I was to greet and help you in any way possible—after all, I am a Guide, so we met and I found you were not aware of your mission. I have been showing you ever since what it is, but you keep denying any knowledge of it. You really have to let up on this pretense."

"Oh, my gosh! Now, I see! You really do have the wrong woman! The woman you want was with me on the plane coming down here. I saw her. She is the same height and build as me, has dark hair and brilliant eyes and was covered with crystals and celestial symbols and stuff to let you know she is here on far-out business—psychic or something."

"She is a phony! She is no more evolved than the fashion model in the seat beside her."

"What do you mean? How did you know she was with a model?"

"They are friends. Birds of a color or whatever you say."

"How do you do that?"

"You do it! But let us not get off the track now or later you will say I did not help you enough."

"You got that right. I'm planning on reporting you to the highest authorities, if you don't tell me now."

He looked startled until he saw I was laughing. Wonder why?

"You take few things as seriously as I do, but perhaps that is why you are so high. God loves a merry spirit."

"So high? Never mind, just go on."

"When your mind gets going, you are in high gear and can roll for hours and hours, but if you get off the track, you cannot move an inch. Before you get off the track again, let's seek the middle of the road so you can use the berm for balance if we should digress a bit. We need to keep centered, otherwise it is too hard to live."

I don't mind his opening up and saying what he thinks of me or preaching to me, but it seems to make him uncomfortable to be so forthright. Now he is gritting his teeth, but he'll talk.

"First, you have this need to know everything. You don't. You can be happy knowing nothing about anything. You do not need to know why anyone does anything, but the humanness you love and admire is so addicted to nosing into the business of others, it can't do its own work—at least do it well enough to ascend."

"Oh, I see, Jorge. You're talking about spiritual work."

"What other work counts?"

For some reason I felt very foolish and wanted to blush, but could not.

"You will now sense the inner being—which is the real You—acting differently. You will fear nothing. You will be free of all restrictions of voice and mind soon. You will be able to communicate using only the eyes and inner ears."

I could feel he was right because when I tried to voice my agreement, nothing came out yet he knew what I was trying to say.

"We will be there momentarily. Try not to talk, if you can. Listen and know that you know. If you clutter up your mind with nonsense, it can't move. Let it alone. We will be moving in spirit and you will be able to see and feel the difference. Don't be afraid. You are just coming home, that's all."

Now, he's trying to soothe me! I have been scared out of my wits by dead bodies and people following us, and he never said a word, but now that I am here to meet some old people, he thinks I'm scared.

"Your mind is shutting down now. Just let your body transfer its energy and light your way, Don't worry about walking. We will all be in spirit soon."

What is he talking about now?

"There is a rise in the road up ahead and after that you will see the guardian. Watch how the roots of the tree lead you to it, but there are pits between the roots that can lead the unsuspecting to their death. You will fear nothing. The guardian is expecting you."

How can a tree expect anything? This is beginning to sound too weird— even for me, but I'm sticking to the end. I have no intention of going back empty-handed now.

"When you meet the elders, just nod your head. No need to speak."

"What would I say anyway? I can't speak Mayan."

"There will be no need for any interpreters since we will all communicate in spirit. You will see. Now be silent within."

A Trail Leads to the Top

The trail of the elders was easy to follow. However, they moved so rapidly I could not keep up. When they got to the bottom of the cave, I was at least two minutes behind them. Jorge did not act impatient with me, but I knew he was.

With my entrance into the 'room', they all stopped their seemingly casual conversations to take time to introduce me to those whom I had not met in Merida. They all looked pretty much the same to me in the semi-darkness, but I recognized the storyteller and Fernandez, the angry young shaman, as well as a few others. After exchanging a smile or a word with those whom I remembered and nodding at the rest, I sensed they were embarrassed by something but didn't know what. Maybe me? I felt sort of strange and didn't know what to do. They seemed to be expecting me to do something. What?

"WELCOME!" Hearing my own voice boom out into the cave startled me more than any of them. I had definitely caught their attention and all stared expectantly at me.

Now, I'm stuck. I don't know why I'm here. Nevertheless, I loudly proclaimed, "We are here today to celebrate the end of the old world and initiate into the new one the youngest shaman to ever be admitted to this holy spot."

Whoa! This is too much! I'm acting like I'm the emcee and they're all letting me do it. What the heck is going on here?

"Today is a great day for the Maya. Fernandez Cueverras is not going to be the name they will remember after today, but Jose the Honest. The oldest mission in America is here to honor those who have placed his name in the work and asked to have him initiated this day, and I am pleased to be here to do the initiation."

Fernandez, now Honest Joe, looked totally shaken. Apparently, he never expected me to be here let alone initiate him; but he could not have been more surprised than me.

"Jose, you are chosen by the elders of the tribes to take charge of the latter days. You will continue to study and learn all there is of the old ways until you are told to work with the new ways. You will never deviate from the path. You will maintain the work of God and do it always. You will remain true to the work of God. You are to be honored for the work you do now and in the future, but your new work will not begin until the latter days when you are old."

Wow! I really know how to give a speech. Everyone is smiling now and bobbing their heads—even Jose looks happy. But, why me?

The oldest elder present spoke then, very strongly for someone who looked so frail, but his hands shook as he handed a beribboned staff to Jose.

"We wish to thank our esteemed emissary from the New World who has been here for only a short time and made such a deep and lasting impression upon us all. We will host a celebration today in her honor as well as to celebrate the occasion of Jose the Honest entering into the realm of shaman of the Maya."

Things got a little jumbled after that with everyone talking and congratulating each other on the initiation of one of their own, but no one seemed at all concerned that I was a woman—the only woman in the group. I wondered why.

"All shamanic work is best done by women, but you are the only woman of our tribe left. We are sorry for the delay in your work of the world, but the time is here now. Our women show no interest in shamanic work until too late in life to learn all the disciplines, but perhaps your appearance here among us has awakened them and they will want to be like you."

"Thank you, Jorge, but I don't think of myself as a role model. I am more like a patient or maybe an intern or someone who looks on at operations. This has all been very interesting, but I feel I need time to digest everything before I can rationalize my behavior here today."

Jorge smiled and patted my hand as he said quietly, "You are most powerful. You know so much that the conscious mind refuses to accept it. Now you will be able to understand why you are here and when you can leave, but let us celebrate first."

I followed the parade of feet ascending the stairs above, leading me back to the light of day. Strangely, I never felt the darkness down there. I was in a cave with no light and yet we didn't need candles. Why?

"The glow of your being outshines all the rest here today, Amanda. You are most admired. You have long been waiting to shine. We will have you back often. We wish to share in your energy and help you in your work, but you must tell us about it so we will know how to help." The elder's behavior as he spoke was cordial and refined, but his eyes glistened with hidden meaning—or something different from what I am accustomed to seeing in a man's eyes.

"Thank you. I have a problem that needs a lot of work before I can even phrase it, but your help will be most welcome. We will talk later."

"Most certainly. I have all my life waited for this day, I can wait another."

What does he mean? Is he referring to me or the celebration honoring Jose? I'm still getting lost, but not as much as when I first got here. Maybe I do belong? What other explanation is there?

"As we enter the light, let us give thanks to God for all that is!" I can't believe I keep saying these things, and they keep listening. "You have all been to the bowels of the Earth and back with no harm, but you will not return there without light. It is not the time to be brave or foolish. We will wait until the moon of the world is shy and we are not heard before we all return to this meeting ground again."

Hushed words seemed to agree with my pronouncement. But why? What is the big deal about this cave? Listen to me. Three hours ago I was scared of caves, now I'm wondering why we shouldn't go there again *soon.*

"Take care of the work you do, Amanda. You will honor all of us when you return to America, but you will be in our constant attention here. We will keep you present in a form not abstract enough to hinder you there, but strong enough to be able to witness your work. We will help you. We know why you have to spend this time in America, but you will return to us. We will take care and do what you have asked. You are the wise and witty one. We will have many days to think back and remember all you have said, while you are gone and onto the next assignment."

The storyteller spoke so calmly I had to believe him. After all, he isn't the storyteller for nothing. He knows how to spin a tale and keep it going.

"You are very humble, Miss Amandy, but you will remember this: We have honored you and your work and will never let you suffer. We will take you into the work of the gods of the past in order to promote the work of God, but you must not let anyone else ever enter this work. We will not permit anyone to decipher this work. You will be the only American."

I could only nod. After all, if I'm doing so much here that I can't figure it all out, how am I going to pass it on? Furthermore, I don't have the stomach for telling people what they should do with their lives and initiate anyone—even if they drag out *ten* chickens!

"You say you did not know they would sacrifice chickens?" Jorge looked at me indulgently while patting my wrist. "Of course! *You* don't use chickens. You live in a city and can't. We live in the country and the blood is all we need to sanctify the blessing of the gods of the underworld and above who are not happy that the end of time is here."

"You know, Jorge, you really get to me. I can't figure out who you are and how you know me so well."

"I am your Guide. I keep telling you that."

"What kind of Guide?"

"The kind that keeps a shaman on track and lets her know if she is needed elsewhere. You are never off the path because of your Guides, but you do not realize it. We all have them, and you have been one yourself, but you don't remember it now. You will."

Great! Just when I start to think I know what is going on, another mystery appears. What is it that I know but don't know I know?

"When you get back to your home, you will know all. You have had many 'strangers' approach you and tell you much, but you told us far more. We need you here, but you still want the life there. When you decide to leave it forever, we will be here." The oldest of the elders almost bowed over my hand as he spoke and his shortness of height was almost as noticeable as his shortness of breath. I instantly felt a surging—almost electrical connection to him when he added, "You are the only one who keeps me on Earth, Miss Amandy."

"What? I am keeping you here? Why?"

"You are my replacement. You are the one to take my place in the circle of elders, but you need not hurry. I will outlast several others here. I know the secret of long life. I am already much over the age of the oldest and will be here. You will come one day, then I will leave—happy."

Tears welled up in my eyes, but what is it all about? I can't get my mind together. Everything is strange and weird and different, but nobody else sees anything wrong. What is going on with me?

Jorge asked softly, "Would you like to stay the night or must you keep that engagement in Merida?"

"What engagement?"

"You made a date with a handsome American to meet him in the Zocalo. We would not intentionally keep you from meeting anyone once you have promised."

Oh, yes, I totally forgot about Chip. Now, what to do? I'm starting to really dig this stuff, yet I want to see Chip.

"Perhaps it would be better to go back to the inn right after the meal and pick up your clothes so you will be able to meet your friend. We will have many occasions later when we can talk—after you rejoin us."

Oh, sure, they initiate shamen on a regular basis. I don't know, yet there is something irresistible about Chip. What can it be—besides sex?

"You are tired after so many busy times among us. We cannot keep you from doing what you are sent to do by your own people. You have to do that work now, so we will help you get back."

"We must be eight hours from Merida. We have been traveling forever to get here."

A tiny twist of his lips that almost revealed his upper teeth was Jorge's only response as he led me by the elbow into the crowd at the feast to honor Jose the Honest. We ate quietly together and then went toward the area where he had parked the old Volkswagen, only it wasn't there now.

"Where is the van?"

"It could never travel as fast as we need to go, so I borrowed another car."

Smiling more than I thought he could, Jorge pointed at a red convertible obviously built to travel at the speed of sound. There is no way I'm going to ride with the top down over these dusty back roads.

"You will enjoy yourself more if I put up the roof. No?"

"Yes, please do."

Within minutes we were 'flying'. It was as though we had never ventured into the ancient one's territory. It was weird. Everything has been weird since I arrived in Mexico, but tomorrow life will return to normal.

"You are most anxious to see this man. Aren't you?"

"Not that much, but I did make a date and I don't stand people up. You have to be nice to everybody, they may be your boss one day."

"You really talk funny, Mandy."

After that we drove in silence over seemingly impassable back roads until we hit a main highway where he *really* tramped on the accelerator.

The End of the Road

We no sooner spotted Merida then we were there, but Jorge reacted strangely. He practically melted into the frame of the car, almost disappearing under the steering wheel. I could have asked why he was slouching down like that, but why bother? He wouldn't tell me, but he had to be hiding.

"We will soon be at your hotel, and I will have to say good-bye."

His words sound so final, but he can't mean it.

"Good-bye?"

"Yes, I'm sorry, but my work takes me far from here by tomorrow and I won't be back before you leave, but you know my warm feelings and best wishes travel with you wherever you are."

He is serious. I can't believe it! We meet in a flash and then he's gone—just like that. What will I do without him? He can't just abandon me like this.

"You now have time to assimilate all we have talked about and the people you have met, as well as the many things discussed over the past hundred hours. Never fear, you will be back again and then we will spend a long time together."

"Really?"

He acts so sure. Why? What does he know? How can he be so certain I will be back—and that we will spend time together then?

"Yes, you will be back. You have to return. You have no other destination more important in this life. You have been programmed. You are imprinted, as it were."

"Imprinted? That is a curious word to use. As though I inherited some predilection to return to Merida, like a turtle to the land of its birth or something."

He looked at me oddly as he said, "You don't get it. Do you? What did they do to you, or what do you know that lets you erase it?"

What is he talking about? He is always spouting mumbo-jumbo, and some of the stuff I say in return isn't any better. Something has to happen soon to let me know what is going on here. But if he leaves now, how will I ever find out?

"Mandy, it is amazing! You sit there and look at me like you don't recognize me or know anything about what is going on, but you do. You know everything. Why do you act like this? Have you truly lost your identity? Have you really forgotten what your connection is to the Maya—and your mission?"

"I don't know what to tell you. I don't know much of anything about anything on a rational, logical basis. I'm just a middle class, middle-aged woman from mid-America who's down here on a vacation that turned into the adventure of a lifetime. I don't know what has been happening or why, but I'm sure having a great time anyway!"

Shaking his head, Jorge forced a smile as though to indicate satisfaction with my response, apparently too polite to push me any further. Not another word was spoken between us until we pulled up at the side entrance to the Hotel Astaria. The same idlers stood in the lounge where I last saw them several days ago, but I could not be sure of it in the twilight. We sat still for only a moment of emotion-filled silence—like lovers parting. Really strange!

Jorge looked more deeply into my eyes and said softly, "You will have more adventures before you leave Merida, Mandy, but you will know what to do. You are up for anything. You are wise—you know."

For some reason I felt terribly irritated and snapped back, "I wish you would stop saying that, Jorge. I don't know. I never know. Anymore, I don't even know what I'm going to say next, let alone know what I'm going to do tomorrow."

He reached over and held my hand for only a split-second and smiled as he said, "Adios, Miss Amandy. We will meet again and have many adventures and more time to share them then. Take care. You are wading through a more dangerous jungle here in Merida than in all of the Yucatan. Watch out for the snakes. They can be killers."

A shiver went through me as he released my hand, but I took the hint immediately and grabbed my stuff and got out of the car. Standing on the sidewalk, I watched him round the corner still slouched down in his seat as if sneaking out of town.

Only the desk clerk looked up at me when I entered the hotel lobby. Everyone else had obviously drunk more than enough margaritas or whatever and cared nothing for the intrusion of a disheveled woman, so I grabbed my key and took the backstairs up to my room.

Once inside the room, I felt hot and sticky. The width and breadth of the room seemed to have shrunk while I was gone and been disturbed by someone with a purpose other than robbery. The cell-like space intruded ominously upon my consciousness as though someone was watching me from within the walls.

Someone planted a 'bug' in here. I know it! It may be beyond all logic, but I have to check it out anyway.

Working diligently, as though a trained master spy, I found hidden in the scrollwork of the mirror above the dresser a small metallic disc—like a hearing aid battery. I looked at it, but did not remove it. In the event it was a camera or something other than a microphone, I hung my bag over it.

I could not find anything else out of place in the walls or furnishings, but someone definitely had gone through my luggage. Some people may not have noticed it, but I pack my things while traveling in such a way as to reveal if someone does something they are not hired to do—like poke around in my stuff. However, this was the first time I ever found anything amiss. So why do I always set such traps? Maybe I was practicing for today?

Little sun shone through the window, but I hesitated to turn on the overhead light bulb due to its glaring ugliness. I found a candle in the dresser drawer and lit it. I could tell something else was going on in the hotel, but why and how it could affect me did not come to me.

Maybe it's those clowns in the CIA? Yeah, I bet that's what it is.

There was little to detain me in my room and I was hungry, so I went downstairs the same way I came up and left the hotel by the side door. No one was around, but I had the feeling someone was just around the corner. Hotel Astaria was beginning to bug me and whatever was going on inside the hotel was outside, too. I felt the same tension. The hair on the nape of my neck stood erect then lay down constantly as though in a rhythmic flow of air. It was getting on my nerves. I felt electrified. I walked rapidly toward the center of town and when I saw a group of noisy Americans standing outside a cafe reading the menu, I approached them as though a part of their group—just in case anyone was watching or following me.

"Hey! How y'all doin'? Amanda's your name, isn't it?"

A tall blond, washed-out-denim kind of guy with no upper lip waved me into the inner circle, but I know I never saw him before. What is going on now?

"Yeah, that's me. How's everybody doing?"

A sort of happy chorus of 'fine' and 'great' and other stuff that means nothing returned my greeting as my would-be host pulled me into the core group. I let myself slide forward. Why not? After all I've seen since I've arrived in Mexico, what more could happen?

"You really shouldn't run around the countryside all by yourself, Amanda. It's not safe down here for American girls. These Mexicans think they're God's gift to women and will take what isn't given to 'em."

Although extremely annoyed by his rudeness, I managed to purr, "Oh, really? My misfortune. I haven't met any of those kind yet."

The oldest woman in the gang rolled her eyes upward and clasped her hands to her breast and said, "Well, you're lucky!"

Imagine any man bothering her! She really has a high opinion of what she has to offer. It was all I could do to keep from sneering at her. Why am I so testy with these people? I don't even know them yet, but I detest them already. Why?

"We're Americans, so all these natives think we're loaded. They think they can screw us out of all our money, but we're on to 'em!"

This guy is so inebriated I really can't cut him down for what he is saying, but I'm going to try anyway—just wait.

"Those cute little white smocks with all the embroidery the women wear when they get all dressed up are so precious. You would think they'd be glad to sell them, but I asked this woman at the concert hall on Thursday night where she got her dress and how much it cost. You should have seen her! She got all high and mighty and said it was made by loving hands and was therefore priceless! Get that. Priceless! It's just white cotton with stitching all around the neck and on the skirt. I bet they run them off in sweat shops on the back streets for less than five bucks."

"Now, Virginia, her dress was beautiful. It could never be run off on a machine to look that good. She probably made it herself, and you insulted her."

"Girls! Girls! Girls! She's the wife of the biggest banker in Merida. You don't go up to a woman like that and ask her what she paid for her dress. She thought she was all dressed up!"

Now I'm mad! I'm really mad! But I'm going to avoid looking into them.

"Come on everybody. We got the biggest table in the house and the Mad Mex is finally ready to serve us. Come on, Amanda, you can't skip out now. You're in for it just like the rest of us."

A less than cheerful woman's voice said, "Let's hope we don't get Montezuma's revenge."

Heartily agreeing, the small crowd plus me followed the courteous, if somewhat disdainful maitre d' to a table far from the front entrance of the restaurant. If we had gone any further back, we would have been able to watch the cook and dishwasher work, but no one complained. Most were too drunk to notice.

Why do I suddenly loathe my countrymen so much? What is happening? They don't know any better. But why don't they? Americans are not stupid and ignorant. Are they?

I could not stand to listen to their loud, nasty remarks about the servers as though the waiters did not understand English, when in fact they probably spoke five or six languages fluently. It was degrading to be with a group of people who were so obviously fond of being obnoxious. Why would anyone want to get so drunk they couldn't see what was going on around them—especially in a foreign country?

"These Mexicans are so-o-o-o slow you can see them sweat."

"Really?" I have to cut down on the amount of acid if I want them to take the bitter pill. "That means they are at least working. I haven't seen many Americans sweat lately—only at the spa or playing games."

I can't help it. I have to siphon off some of this negativity or burst like an over-ripe pod of seeds, no one is listening anyway.

"Why don't you ask the waiter for water, Amanda? You seem to have a way with them."

My host's snide behavior was beginning to flow over me—not hanging up anywhere, but I had to free myself of him before we ate.

"Thanks for the compliment. I'm sure he has served thousands of drunken Americans in his time, but he still seems to like us. Doesn't he?"

"Why, yes, he does. Doesn't he? We'll have to leave him a super big tip. Won't we gang?"

Everyone seemed to be in agreement until Virginia said, "That is just an act they put on to get big tips. I think he secretly hates all of us and would slit our throats if he had the chance."

Believe it or not, someone did agree with her and that ended my participation in the whole fiasco they called a fiesta.

* * * * * * * *

The evening air coming through the slits at the bottom of the window in my room cooled my body and calmed my mind, but I could not stop comparing the ignorance, conceit, and downright nastiness of my dining companions tonight with the gracious and wise Maya whom I had dined with earlier in the day.

What to do about it? Nothing. You cannot change anyone, let alone a whole generation, or two, or three, who have the self-conceit to believe they are the inheritors of the Earth—every last acre of it!

I could not sleep for wondering about Jorge. Why did he come into my life only to leave so abruptly? I had gotten attached to him. Hmmm, that is probably why we were separated.

It is hard to solve mysteries without a clue. I got on a plane, met a handsome stranger, made a date—which I never do, then ran around the countryside of a strange and wondrously foreign land with yet another handsome stranger, and on top of that, I'm gone for days without a care in the world and meet Maya wise men who tell me fascinating stories they claim I created and they merely repeated to me out of respect. What next?

I must have dropped off to sleep, but heard something outside that caused me to bolt upright in bed—shivering all over. I could make out a scratching noise of some kind. What was it? As I crept across the room to the slightly open window, the sound grew louder. It was impossible to see anything by peeping through the crack, but I knew something was out there.

Oh, my God!!

My heart stopped for sure. Just as I looked out the window, a big wild cat of some sort stared back at me. I must have scared it as much as it scared me because it jumped to the ground and tore away into the darkness, but I wasn't sure.

"How can a wild cat live in Merida?" The sound of my own voice calmed me down a bit.

Jorge said there were wild things in Merida, but I hadn't believed him. How could such an animal survive in the city? Wouldn't everyone know about it and trap it or whatever?

My hands shook as I lay back down in bed, so I did what I have done to chase away the night frights since I was a little girl, I sang: "Happy trails to you, until we meet again....."

There is No Tomorrow

The only thing I can remember about that time in the restaurant was when the bill was paid. The guy who asked me to join them, asked me to pay my own way. It struck me as funny at the time, but now I don't see it quite that way. I don't know why, but I think I turned out to be someone other than whom he wanted to join the 'party'. Which makes me think.

The other day at the elders' feast I was busy pondering all the ways I could help them and now see they are all better off than I am. Why did I think I could help them, and why did they say I would?

There is so much to do now that I'm back in Merida, but I don't remember why I'm so busy and why I want to do so much. It's strange, and yet not at all, but I think nothing I ever did before this time was important. I don't even remember much. When the other Americans asked me about myself, I told them I was an intern writer and was visiting sites of Mayan culture where there were reported sightings of UFO's. I can't believe I said it, and I can't believe they bought it, but they did. Now I have a pack of characters on my back demanding I show them what I've seen and tell them what I know.

What to do until I meet Chip? I could just sit here on a bench and watch the little kids play and the teenagers making out, or I could shop at the little booths, maybe even buy a potion from that 'medicine woman' over there who seems to scare everyone. Funny, but her booth is the only one that appeals to me, maybe because it looks like a gypsy's wagon. Could she be one?

The sun's heat quickly took the damp and chill off the whitewashed seats scattered around the Zocalo, and the square continued to fill with noisy families all having laughing times, but still no Chip. When it got to half past twelve, I sought shade with no inclination to leave this wonderful atmosphere and the joyous people who strolled and chatted as their children played nearby.

It was fun to watch the young women parade around proudly displaying their babies and usually, but not always, a smiling papa by their side. To me, the younger women look envious as they watch the slightly older matrons strut their stuff. In fact, I'm sure they were. What a difference compared to the women at home!

Why isn't Chip here? I'm sure he said he would meet me at noon in the Zocalo, but then I'm always early—while most people are late. No need to panic or get impatient. After all, nobody at home ever arrives at the stated hour on any invitation, so why expect it here? If he is not here by one o'clock, I'll get a table at a nearby cafe and sit and watch what happens here. That way if he shows up late, I'll be able to flag him down or catch up with him.

There is No Place Like Now

After a few hours of wandering around in all the smaller plazas near the Zocalo, I felt things were slightly off center, but not me. Did you ever feel slightly disoriented—like maybe after a bout with the flu or if you stayed in bed too long and got up too fast? That is how I feel now.

The trees seem okay but a few are shaking, yet there is no wind and the sidewalk lines quiver then align again. I have this feeling I'm not quite all here now. It is disconcerting to be all alone, feeling well and enjoying yourself, and then the world starts fading in and out on you. What is wrong? Maybe the heat and humidity are playing tricks on my imagination—like seeing a mirage in the desert? No, it can't be that. It's not that hot—in another month maybe, but not now.

What could cause the world to shrivel, then expand? Time, that is the key! But why would I know that? Why am I so sure? And I am. Time is standing still and I am the one who moves. What would happen if I refused to move? A twig snapped somewhere right behind me.

"Who is there? Owwwllll."

* * * * * * * *

Where am I? It all seems strange, but I know I am in Merida. I can tell by the smell. Every city has its own smell—or perfume, if you prefer, and Merida's scent cannot be duplicated. I am definitely in Merida. But where?

"So our sleeping princess is awake?"

Oh, no, deliver me from another ugly American. No, it's not another one, it's the same one from the restaurant. What was his name? I can't remember, but I know he is obnoxious—drunk or sober.

87

"Oh, my head hurts. What happened? Where am I?"

"You're here at my place."

Obviously, but where is your place, dummy?

"Don't you remember what happened to you?"

How would I? This character gets on my nerves every time I see him, but I guess I have to thank him for something.

"No, I don't remember a thing. Where did you find me? What do you know?"

His laughter cut through me like a jagged piece of glass might as he said, "You were sprawled out like a drunk in the middle of the park over by the little church. You looked like you'd had a *really* good time. Know what I mean?"

"No, but I'm sure I didn't have a good time. What else did you notice? Was there anyone else around?"

"Yeah, a small group of peons was standing around trying to figure out what to do with you. Someone had gone for a cop, but I told them not to worry you were a *really* good friend of mine and I would take care of everything, so I just picked you up and carried you over to my car and brought you here."

He doesn't look like he could pick up a dead cat. How could he manage to carry me?

As though reading my mind, he said, "I won a few 'power lifting' contests back home, and the training sure came in handy today. You know, you could take off a few pounds and not do yourself any harm."

That laugh of his is going to get him killed someday, but I have to figure out now what his game is. He is stronger than he looks and I just know he knows more than he is saying. But what?

"Well thanks for rescuing me from an angry mob of Maya." I tried to laugh, but it did not come out that way.

"You can laugh, but these people aren't to be trusted. They have it out for Americans—especially women. You better watch where you walk. In fact, you better not go around alone anymore."

"Yeah? Why? I've been here almost a week and nothing happened to me until I sat down in the middle of the day in the middle of town."

"That is my point! You are not safe anywhere. You better stick with me or my friends. We tried to tell you that but 'Oh No', Miss High-and-Mighty, defender of all Mexico. You know it all. See where it landed you? If I hadn't been driving along the street right then and seen the crowd, you would be sitting in some stinking jail cell right now."

"Oh, come on, why would I be put in jail?"

"You could pass for the town drunk right now—let alone when you were sprawled out in the middle of the square."

This room being almost identical to my own, I peered into the mirror above the shabby dresser standing opposite the bed I had been laying on. Though I could barely make out my face due to the darkness in the room, I could see he was right—I was a fright. What is going on? I don't know what this character is up to, but I'm about to write out his part in my play.

"What time is it?"

"What time? Is that all you're worried about?"

Why did he jump? He's too nervous. What is wrong with asking for the time?

"It's about nine."

"Nine?? Are you serious? Nine at night?"

"Yes. What time did you go to the plaza?"

What is going on? There is something weird about this room and he is not who he was yesterday, either. I know I don't know him, but I observed him enough last night to know this is not the persona he normally projects. In fact, he looks menacing right now, and then he was just a run-of-the-mill jerk.

"I don't remember."

"What do you mean? Of course you remember. When did you go to the plaza and why?" The urgency in his voice betrayed an interest over and beyond that of a good Samaritan.

What is he up to? Something is up, so I'll just play it cool.

"I don't know. I guess I'm in shock. Maybe it will take a couple of days for me to remember—you know, amnesia or something that comes with a concussion. I'm just lucky to be alive after a fall like that."

"A fall? Is that what you had? I don't think so. You wouldn't look like you—"

"Like what?"

"Like you had just been dumped there."

Really? Why would I look like that, and where could I have been for so many hours? I arrived at the Zocalo about eleven—maybe twelve, but no later, then waited around for an hour before I visited the nearby plazas. I have to get out of here and find out what is going on, but first I have to ditch this guy.

"Gee! I'm really grateful that you came to my rescue. I must have tripped and struck my head on the concrete, came to, and then moved around trying to get help. I'm really lucky you rescued me. You're quite a guy—a true friend." I almost gagged as I said it, but the look on his face was one of total satisfaction.

He thinks I'm a fool, and that is disgusting!

"Now don't get up and start running off in all directions. You can stay here tonight. I won't bite. In fact, I'll just run out and get you a bite to eat while you clean up a bit. The bathroom is over there."

I nodded in the general vicinity of where he was pointing to suggest I was accepting his offer—no chance of that ever happening though. I may not feel like myself, but I still have some sense left.

"You stay quiet. I'll be back soon. However, that is soon in Mexican time."

His nasal snicker irritated me even more, but I smiled back at him as he left the room, then walked into the bathroom where a quick check in the mirror established that I have looked a lot better. Unfortunately, I have also looked worse, so no worry about running around town at night looking like this.

Where are my shoes? What has he done with them? The oldest trick in the book to keep a houseguest. If I can't find them, I'll borrow his. His feet can't be that much bigger than mine. Having thought that, my toes touched a familiar pair of huaraches under the bed. I quickly slipped my feet into them and rushed to get free of the room. I tried the door and thought it was stuck but it was locked.

Why? He didn't seem the type to try force, but then he is the classic weasel! Good thing he has as little respect for women as he has for Mexicans because he will be shocked to find out I can pick any lock in Mexico—maybe in America. It was definitely the best thing I ever learned in Girl Scouts.

Once outside the room I saw no one in the hallway and knew it was not the Hotel Astaria; but the layout was about the same. I sneaked down the back stairs to the first floor and crept out the back door to enter a dimly lit alley that looked much brighter at the far end of it—maybe downtown Merida?

It did not take long to join the usual evening strollers out looking for a place to have dinner somewhere along the main drag. I saw no other Americans, which posed a slight problem, at five feet six-and-a-half I stood out above most of the crowd; but having slouched and crunched down inside my spine since junior high, I felt I could cut me down enough to get by in a crunch.

Within a few blocks I recognized the area adjacent to the Zocalo. Once across the center of the plaza, it was easy to find my way back to Hotel Astaria. Only when I was outside my room did I realize it was not a great idea to have taken such a direct route there. If something weird was going on, they were certainly smart enough to watch for me here.

I decided to stay put, but weariness won out. I had to sleep. I could not go any further. I may have been in a coma all day, but I felt like I had walked miles and miles and been awake for hours and hours, and as I lay down on the lumpy mattress on the iron trimmed bed, I felt coldness creep over me. It was too late to do anything. I fell asleep.

When I awoke, the sun was streaming in the window since I had not lowered the shades. I saw an alley cat perched on the window ledge peering in at me. How could a cat climb up and sit on such a narrow sill? I will never know because as soon as I got up, it appeared to fly away. I rushed over to see where it landed, but by the time I got to the window there was no sign of life anywhere within the courtyard below.

I wanted to go back to the little square I had visited the day before to see if I could reconstruct what happened, but decided to eat a big breakfast first.

Obviously, I could not wander around in that heat with an empty stomach and not have the devil to pay for it. I would not risk fainting again.

After a hearty Mexican rendition of what they believe Americans eat every day before they go out to plow the back forty, I waddled away feeling at least ten pounds heavier and very grounded, which is what I had to be if I was to reconstruct what had happened.

Once at the park, I easily found the bench where I had rested the day before, but now two elderly men sat there kibitzing about something funny. No problem, I sat down on a bench opposite the two old friends and noticed that bushes overgrew the bench. It would be easy to sneak up on anyone sitting there.

As I watched, a figure moved in the shrub right behind the laughing men. A pain struck me in the gut. It subsided as a child—a beautiful, impish boy parted the branches and tried to surprise the men. They made a pretense of being caught off-guard, but were not. Apparently the boy pulled this prank often. Wow! Maybe I took their favorite seat yesterday and interrupted their little game and they will remember seeing me?

As I approached the trio, the boy stared up at me through luminous large black, virtually pupil-less eyes fringed with thick black lashes. He hung precariously over the back of the bench midway between the two old gentlemen and waited. The men stopped chattering to look at me more closely. The boy seemed to recognize me, yet appeared ready to dart away. I haltingly spoke a few words in Spanish hoping they spoke English and would pity me and speak slowly. It usually works. It did this time, too.

Perhaps the boy recognized my ploy or understood English, because the two men softly returned my greeting then said nothing, while he looked ready to talk. The men may not have wished to address an American woman traveling alone since we had not been formally introduced. The Maya are quite formal—as are most Mexicans.

"You are an American?" The inflection in the boy's voice indicated he was not sure.

"Yes, I am, but if you are not sure I am an American, where do you think I come from?"

His fidgety movements were ambivalent as though he felt torn between lingering and fleeing, as though scared, but not of me. What is he afraid of? I have to find out before he runs away.

"I do not know. I did not think you were American. You look sort of Mexican. Maybe Mexican-American?"

Wow! This is the first time I ever passed for a Mexican. I have been welcomed by Jews, Arabs, Italians, and a few others—never the Greeks, as being one of their own, but this is the first time a street-smart Mexican ever saw any resemblance. Don't tell me I look like a Maya now? It's bad enough talking like one, but looking like one is too much!

"You look at home here, Senorita. Did you used to live here and go to the university or something?"

"No, a couple of years ago I visited for half a day and vowed to return. I was on my way to Chichen Itza then and didn't get to see much of Merida, so I came back—on vacation."

He seemed relieved, and mumbled, "Oh."

With my biggest smile, I asked the boy, "I was wondering, do you come to this plaza every day?"

As I spoke, I could see the wizened men turn their sharp, hawk-like noses and questioning eyes to better see the child. I could tell they disapproved my furthering our acquaintance, but they said nothing. Perhaps sensing their disapproval, the boy turned and rapidly spoke to them in Mayan, and strangely enough, I knew what he said.

This is too much! I can't speak enough Spanish to buy dinner in a grocery store, but I think I understand Mayan! This place is really getting to me.

He told them I was having trouble getting around town and had asked him to accompany me for a fee. Then he turned to me and said in English, "Senorita, these are my uncle's friends and they are wondering why you are all alone. I told them you have friends here but are just strolling around taking in the scenery. Right?"

This kid is a scream. He is running some kind of scam. But so what? I'll go along with him. Normally, ten-year-olds are my favorite males because they are honest and straight-forward—usually, but this guy may be different. Time will tell.

"What is your name? Mine is Amanda."

"My name is Freddie and I will call you Mandy. Okay?"

His familiar tone caught me off guard and raised the hair on the back of my neck—But why? Mandy is an obvious way to reduce my foreignness to a size that doesn't frighten him, but Freddie doesn't look like he is frightened of me—maybe somebody else, but not me.

"I was wondering, Freddie, would you like to escort me around Merida today—for a fee?"

Now *he* looked scared! His eyes darted back and forth between me and the two men, then it dawned on me, I was speaking Mayan. They had to be more shocked than I was!

Freddie appeared taller as he stepped out from behind the bench and asked with bravado, "Who are you, Senorita? We saw you yesterday, but you disappeared mysteriously and then reappeared last night—as if by magic."

Wow! What is going on? I can't let Freddie get away from me until I find out everything he knows and/or suspects about what happened to me yesterday. I feel these men sense something, too. I wonder if they will open up and talk?

Simultaneously, both men folded their arms over their chests and crossed their legs in the universal symbology of an intention not to reveal anything to me, but Freddie came closer and offered his hand as though he really were a helpful, hopeful child expecting a treat. I knew it could not be for real, but what is a poor girl to do?

As we walked away from the seated men, I felt my legs tremble slightly at first and then more obviously. We barely made it back to the bench where I had been sitting when they collapsed under me. Freddie did not seem to notice. Why?

"You will be fine here, Mandy. I will help you. I will make sure nothing bad happens. You sit here and I will go in the woods and see what is there, then you can follow. Okay?"

The woods? What is he talking about? This is a poor, old denuded park where tiny feet constantly walk out the grass, and the trees are ancient. Where is he going?

"Mandy, do you hear me?" He would not leave until I nodded.

Everything seems okay. I feel warm and cozy and safe, like I am sitting inside our old house on a snowy day watching the fire glow in the hearth. Freddie is moving further away from me. I don't mind.

"Okay, Mandy, you can come now. Everything is okay. You are expected. They want you to come alone, but I think I can sneak in. Do not worry. I will be there. I will bring you back."

Hurtling through space, I felt incapable of doing anything but submissively following the bright lights until I fell asleep. It took a flash of lightening and a bolt of thunder to wake me, but I knew I was not in Merida anymore. A wise looking man, like the Magus, approached and shook my hand. He seemed somewhat concerned about my appearance but too polite to comment. He pointed toward a chair of satin and velvet and told me to sit down and wait, then he left.

I could sit here forever. It's so peaceful and the music is so 'heavenly'— sounds of strings and flutes and guitars and things—nothing brassy or discordant—no words.

As I waited for whatever to happen, some sort of beings floated by me and looked at me curiously. They were not ugly or weird or evil looking—sort of angelic, for want of a better description. Waves of these beings, bands of light and vibration more than flesh or solid material, flowed over me and I felt comforted by their presence, like one of them—only on a different plane.

Eventually the old wise man came back toward me but stopped when he spotted Freddie. He took Freddie by the ear and pushed him in my direction. I had just enough energy to indicate that the boy was with me and I wanted him to stay. With obvious disapproval, the seer released Freddie into my custody.

When we entered a room-like structure not far from where I had waited, there were several discussions going on at the same time between a small group of 'beings'. None of the participants looked up or seemed aware we had entered the area, although we looked outrageous compared to their brilliant splendor.

"Why don't you and your ward sit here?" A wispish being, perhaps female, flowed by and motioned for us to follow, but something strange happened, I wasn't there. I just disappeared. Freddie continued to sit still and watch, but I disappeared. I felt weightless and wonderful, but my body disappeared!

After a long time, Freddie approached and motioned for me to come back with him. I followed reluctantly since I did not want to leave this wonderful place where time does not exist and no one notices you, where you are totally free to be You! You are all you are and ever will be. It had to be heaven.

With a jolt, and then a sliding sensation, I was back sitting sedately beside Freddie on the park bench. He still retained an alien look, but appeared to know nothing.

"Well, Mandy, we have seen everything in Merida and I have to go home now, but I think we should meet again. Can I work for you tomorrow?"

I was not about to question him about his idea of a tour of Merida, but I did wonder how long it took?

"What time is it, Freddie?"

"The church clock just chimed four. Didn't you hear it?"

"Oh, yes, how absentminded of me." No, I can't believe it. "Time escapes me here in Merida; and yes, I would like to go with you tomorrow, but I need to make arrangements to visit Chichen Itza. Would you like to go there with me?"

"Yes! We have not been there at all this year and it is time. I will find out from my brothers what bus to take and where you should stay. We can hire a taxi there—to go to the cave."

"We? Are your brothers going to go, too?"

If it was a lie, he was able to smoothly change into his wistful appearance again as he said, "Oh, no. They will not go with us. I sort of use 'we' a lot when I am talking about myself. I am sort of loco, I guess."

"Aren't we all?"

I decided to let his little subterfuge pass rather than part us, but I intended to find out what my boy was up to. Why would he have no problems leaving his home for days at a time? More and more mysteries arrive daily, and I didn't even know the hour.

"Freddie, before you go home, what day is today?"

"That is easy, Amanda. Today is now. Now is the only time we exist. We may never know why we talk about tomorrow, but we do, yet it will never be. Tomorrow is only today repeated until we change today, and if we never change, it will be as it is forever."

"Wel-l-l-l, that is some answer! You have given me a lot to think about and I'm grateful. By the way, how old are you?"

"Me? I'm 21."

"21? You're kidding. I thought you were just a kid."

"I am. 21 in our world is young, but we are expected to take on the responsibilities of being old and young now, and I keep slipping back into childhood because I never got my fill of it. I moved to the city too soon. I still like to act the child. Are you disappointed in me?"

"No, you are perfect the way you are, but why would you sneak up on your elders in the park like a small child would?"

"I don't know what you mean."

"When we met this morning, you played a game with the old men in the park. That's when I first saw you."

"I'm sorry, Amanda, I don't know what you mean. I was at the university this morning, and we met shortly after noon here at this bench. Don't you remember?"

"Oh, yes! How could I forget?"

"Now you remember. Now you are here and all that is past is gone, but all that is to come is not here, either. You can live only now."

"Right you are, Freddie. Your name is Freddie, isn't it?"

"Of course. You say the strangest things, Amanda, but then again, most Americans do."

"Yeah, well I'll see you here tomorrow morning. Okay, Freddie?"

"See you then, Mandy. Take care to be free."

What an unusual thing to say—and very beautiful. I wonder what is really going on now? Someone is going to great lengths to drive me mad, but I'm not going to let it happen—at least not while I can still have fun!

There is Nothing

I knew I alone had to have all the answers when I realized no one else was going to tell me why so many strange things were happening to me. Why would they happen? You cannot imagine what has never been and you cannot see what the mind has never discerned, so how can so much happen and yet seem foreign and weird?

I decided to go to dinner early and see what would happen, if anything. I sat alone, like others in the cafe, but not alone in disliking the meal. It was in such negative contrast to the food I had eaten while dining with my guides that I felt extremely disappointed to be reminded of just how unsavory American fried food can be.

I knew when I sat down that ordering 'home-style' food would cost more than Mexican fare, but hoped it would be worth it. I should have known better, so when the bill came in under $20 I didn't feel quite so defrauded as I might have. You have to wonder why we crave American fast food while traveling, yet never touch it at home. Are we weird or what?

Speaking of weird, nothing has happened. It is a boring night, just like millions of other people are living right now, so I might as well sit and act like I'm enjoying myself. It is not likely the strolling musicians will come over here. They *know* I'm not a big tipper. Waiters have a way of telegraphing that kind of stuff. Furthermore, I am not the type to jump in bed with a musician after hearing a few romantic melodies, so they are better off playing the rest of the room.

What about that guy over there? He sort of looks like me—in a way. Medium height, medium build, medium complexion, your 'average American man'. Mmmm, he is good with the knife and fork and smiles at the waiters,

98 An Adventure in Time

but he doesn't look around like me. Wonder why he is here? He must come often or he would watch more. Could be he is just tired.

From here I can see the street filling up with diners unable to decide between this restaurant and the one next door. I should signal them to go there. But why? Why would I know what's best for them when I can't even figure out what's happening in my own life? Ego—the good old, all-American version: I know what's good for everyone else—even if I don't do it myself. It's too bad if the first batch of late diners suffer the consequences of my small tip, but it's not my problem.

What an evening for rambling about Merida! I can smell poinciana blossoms mingled with other heady fragrances I could try to figure out; but why bother? Names mean nothing. Look at me. I have two names now. One, Amanda Me, and the other, Mandy Brown, but I'm still the same person. Aren't I? Probably not, now that I think of it.

Back home as Amanda Sheridan, I'm not subject to flights of fancy and weird goings on and I'm hardly ever followed by men anymore, but here I have been chased all over town by men and watched by cats—wild and tame, and had my room bugged! Things definitely happen to Mandy or Amandy, as the elders say, that never happen to Amanda. Wonder why? What *is* in a name that makes things change?

Why I would dare go down a dark street into the dark side of town is a mystery to me, but my feet took me there. What if I run into trouble? Who will rescue me? I guess my feet will.

What you need to do is face fear and cut it up into little pieces in order to handle it better. That is why I am facing mine now. I want to know what is in the shadows, and I want to know why women are afraid of men. At my age, we don't need them—that much and don't really want to marry, but we still think about them too much. I wonder if it is because we want to be men? Probably not. Men in America have more respect instilled in them than women do. Women don't really respect anyone anymore and it is hurting us and taking away from our lives, but the men brought it on.

What a joy to walk and sense that you are able to take care of yourself! What a relief to know that should someone suddenly appear, you will know if they intend good or evil before they speak or do anything. I could never tell before, but now *I know.* I really do!

I know, that is what Jorge always said about me. Yeah, he was great. I wonder why he thinks I will be with him someday? He sounded very confident of it and his assurance is here with me now. I can almost see us together. Yes, I can see it now. We are together!

What a great vision! If I could see like that all the time, I wonder if I would change my life?

"You can."

Oh, my god! I never saw this guy coming at me. Where did he come from? Don't tell me I'm about to have another adventure?

"You startled me, Senor. Do you read minds for fun or fortune?"

"Yes, I do. I love to read and am seldom wrong—or so they tell me. But many times I know I planted the seed and they made it grow. Why else consult a shaman?"

A shaman? Just walking around Merida at night like he's going to work? Oh, well, I asked for adventure.

"You're a shaman? I thought shamen lived out in the country and didn't consult with people on frivolous matters?"

"What is frivolous? Nothing. Nothing is real but all is real to the tortured mind. I help the people of Merida, but generally live outside of town. It is too crowded here to be yourself. You have to know peace to know why you are here, and in a busy city you lose yourself in the details."

"Yes, you are right, and the bigger the city, the more likely you are to get lost—and stay that way."

"Not necessarily. I have 'students' who come here for *courses* in shamanship. Really! That is what they call our visits, and they tell me of the changes in vast cities like New York, London, Chicago. They say many there are remembering the old ways because they want to return to a simpler time and place, but stay in the cities to help others. Why are you in Merida? You are not from here, but you speak our dialect perfectly."

Oh! There I go again, talking Mayan when I think I'm speaking English.

"Actually, I came to Merida to practice. I was getting rusty and this is no time to be inept and without words. It has become necessary to prepare people for the end times, even though they are aware of them. You have to wonder why they would know about them, but still not have a clue as to what to do or how to live?"

"We were negligent. The Wise are responsible! We have not taught them enough. We have assumed they would not want to know, that they are better off ignorant, that we are powerful enough to delay the end; but we are not."

His words lost energy as he looked at me through narrowed eyelids, and said, "You have not answered my question. Why are you here?"

"I guess I am here to learn more about the end, too."

"Nonsense! You know. You have always known. You will not be here in Yucatan, but you want to help. That is why you returned now. We will help you remember, but you must be honest—always. You cannot say you do not know when you do. You cannot ignore the evidence of your senses, either. For instance, you are in danger and yet do not act prudently. We have intercepted several different emissaries who are not of you and wish to be. We cannot do it all. You have to be on guard. You have to acknowledge that you are being followed and pursued by the hounds of hell."

"Wh-a-a-a-t? The hounds of hell? I don't believe in hell. How can I be pursued by it?"

"You know of the end. They do not. They want to be in positions of power and take over when all collapses. They are of the world. They are not of God, but they pray and speak of God. You will hear them. You will know of their false work, too, but you will not disturb it."

"What is the point? If someone is trying to harm the whole human race, why wouldn't you try to stop them?"

"You can only stop a few. If you let them all think they are superior and know more than you, you can control them. That is what we are doing. We let them act superior and talk nonsense. Sometimes, we even agree—just to get rid of them. We will not let you go, though. We need you. You are of the elite."

This guy is crazy. He is really trying to oil my motor now. He says I am a great shaman, even though he just met me, and he thinks I am one of the elite—whoever they are, yet he never heard me speak before. He acts like we are partners in crime. What is going on now?

"You are nervous. It is understandable. We stand here in the shadows and you cannot see my face—except maybe my eyes, but we are known to each other. We met the first night. You were at the celebration. I was in the back of the room when the storyteller amused you with the retelling of your most famous tales."

Whoa! My tales? This is confusing, guys. What is happening? Where is all this leading me? I need to know now! I don't have time to meditate and travel to some mountain top to think this over. I need help now!

"You will find more ancient ones returning now, but you are different from them, you have returned before and reconnected with us many times over the centuries. We remember you well. You always come as a woman. You may not be one, but you always appear to us as one. We like your stories because they are timeless and to the point. You are always very practical, and we appreciate that even in this life you are a big business success."

"Well, yes, you might think so, but in New York and Chicago, anyone making less than a million isn't regarded as much, so it just depends upon whom you are talking to about money. That is the only success I have achieved."

"You are humble. You always are. We know of the work you have done—regardless of the hindrances of being a 'Yuppie'. You have had difficulties absorbing the value systems and your people's responses to the life that evolved since your last visit, but you will find here in the Yucatan we are still the same—definitely hard-headed, soft-hearted, and not very bright when it comes to understanding the outside world, but we are prospering once again in the cities."

"Now it is you being humble. You are all doing great! In fact, I am amazed at the changes. You have all known so much pain, but have never called it to the attention of the authorities world-wide. Why? All the others do. Our families in

Tibet are moaning more than mourning in order to bring salvation to the Chinese; but you do not care if the Americans and Mexicans are not saved or so it would appear."

"Ah-h-h, we are hard on them. We do not like to go into the past, but Americans love us only for it. We want to move ahead, but they will pay only to dig up old and forgotten temples—and then they try to rob us for fun. It is degrading and disgusting, but the young here are able to adapt and use the money for their own purposes. We cannot condemn the money, but the greed—that is where the evil lies.

"First the English, now the Asians, and there have always been Americans carrying on like children in Mexico, but not so much here—even they seem to sense this is hallowed space, that there is something different here that must be preserved. They think it is the old stonework, and we do not try to dissuade them."

"Why? Why not get them to cough up money for the children? The kids could use art materials and clothing that is their own. But, forgive me, I can see you think they are fine. It is just my 'yuppieness' overflowing again."

"The children must learn that they already *know*. They are so recent from God that they know why they are here. They chose this life and will be content until they are half-way to being adults. That is when they must choose their path—the world or God, but they do not know it then. They think they are just being young, but they are choosing sides for life. Today, you hear many do not honor God, but there are more who do than do not. We know. We will help, but the children are safe—only the adolescents are in trouble."

"You can say that again."

"Only the adolescents are in trouble."

Funny. This guy is a real comedian, but he seems to be in trance. I better watch myself.

"You seem to waver between two worlds now, Mandy, but you are growing more centered here. We will help you learn to be in both, but you have to strengthen your ties here first. You cannot help if you are not here. You have to know how to enter and end a session, but it is not as important as being able to know, and you know now, but you question. The questions must stop. You cannot question if you are to move forward. Questions are diversions placed by the mind to stop progress. You will have to stop worrying, too. The mind is in control less and less now, but you are totally in control of all that is. You know it and you are better now. We will walk."

The street brightened as we walked further away from the Zocalo. Why? Oh, yes, I am not going to ask questions. But can I survive without asking questions? Yes, I can. I know I can. Asking questions is just a bad habit. I know, yet I continue to ask. I have to learn to listen, to be, to know, and let go.

"Why are you so uncertain, Mandy?"

"I live in a time and place where money is the god of all and time is the handmaiden of that god. Time is so important to people that entire cities would collapse if the schedules were to change all at once. I can't believe I am so messed up by time, too. I feel like I need to check the time, but I am not wearing a watch anymore. It is something I started to do before then stopped, but I vowed on my way down here I would stop now."

"Yes, time is evil."

"Evil? Isn't that a strange thing to say—I mean, a strange way to look at it?"

"No, time is a device of the mind. It is the mind's way of controlling the Earth. It has always been so, but in the ancient times man learned by it and affected changes to the life cycle. You do not see time helping anyone today. It never tells people to plant crops or resist doing much, it just is. It serves no purpose other than to confuse people already stressed beyond common sense."

"What about common sense? Why not use it? Why have time and space and other concepts? Why not just sense what is right and do it?"

"Why not? You tell me. We live that way. Why can't you?"

He got me there. Caught in my own sophistry. I deserve it, but I still want to know why. How can I learn what I need to know if I can't ask questions that direct conversation to my point?

"You continue to question when you should listen and think. The thought energy form will enter the mind of those whom you need to learn from and will help you, but you cannot expect to think of things and learn at the same time. You have to think out what you need to know first, then the teacher or teachers will present themselves and provide all you need to know, but be prepared for additional work. Teachers are prone to do that. Once they have you, they pour on the challenges."

"Wow! I just thought it and you answered it. I like this kind of conversation. It is such a relief from New York, Chicago, LA, and the rest of the places where everyone jumbles their mumbles so you won't know them. They are so afraid of life they can't face you. They sort of smile and say stupid things as though they were wise, then drift on to another and another until the whole room is filled with utter rot. It really smells in some of the offices and clubs!"

"Yes, rotting flesh, material, ideas, energy. It is all the same. You have to use it to generate more energy. Happiness is the illusion some seek. You know peace. That is greater than all the rest, but how many know that?"

"Only a few, I'm sorry to say. I better get on the stick when I get back or all of Manhattan will sink in the mire of self-hatred."

"No, you do not have to do anything. It is okay. They will find themselves. Do your own life. You can do things for others, but you have to finish your work first. It only makes sense that if you do what you came to do, they will get the message and work on what they are supposed to do, too. Life is that way. Mimics follow a leader."

"What leader? Who is in charge? Nobody wants to assume the role of leader now. Everyone points their finger at the top of whatever organization and says it is their fault that everything is slowing down. I haven't heard one person comment on it, either, because I think everyone thinks it has always been like this."

Not hesitating a moment, he rejoined, "They know better, but the time to adopt new laws is rapidly coming—so why bother with what they have now? They want them to fail. They want the old ways of business to collapse and have good reason to celebrate when they do. They want to be miserable enough that they can seek God in peace. Is not that what you did?"

He knows! How? When will I ever learn? Oh, dear, I just can't remove questions from my life.

"There is nothing you need to know you do not already have all the answers to now. You came to Earth preprinted. You have only to light up the interior files and read. You can enter the files anywhere, any time and know whatever you need to know. Remember that."

There is No Secret

What we have here is a situation where I am unable to go home now because my round-trip ticket forbids it, yet I am not sure why I am here or if I should be. Odd ideas, ideals, sensations, isms, and schisms keep going round and round in my mind, and nothing is coming out straight.

Why am I being squired around Mexico by all these Mayan guys? Will I wake up and be able to go home or am I at home having a dream? I couldn't be more disoriented if I were drugged.

"That's it!! I'm being drugged!"

Why didn't I think of it before? I am being slowly and insidiously drugged into some sort of mind state where I believe I am on an adventure that will lead me to the secret of life. If I can't leave the country yet, at least I will get out of Merida. I will run over to the corner pharmacia and buy a Coke and sit in the Zocalo and think this out. I'm not going to eat anything that doesn't come straight out of a can or bag and drink only Coke. Within 24–48 hours max, I'll be free of anything that could possibly be in my system. I'm not going to die of junk food poisoning if I eat it for a few days. Anyway, it can't produce moods worse than what I already have.

"Senorita, do you wish me to put the Coke in a bag?"

"Sure."

Why is he opening the bottle? What is going on? Don't tell me he is one of them, too?

"Stop! What are you doing?"

The man behind the counter looked up with a smile, and spoke softly as though I were a child or very, very stupid, "I am opening your bottle of Coke. You asked me to put it in a bag."

"You don't have to open the bottle to put it in a bag."

Now he is looking at me as though I just grew a beard. What gives?

"I must open it if I am to put it in a bag for you." As he said this, he waved a zip-lock plastic bag in front of me.

"I don't understand. I thought you were asking if you should put the bottle of Coke into a paper bag. How can a bottle fit into that bag? He is still looking at me funny, and the kids by the old pop case are all laughing. What am I doing that is so weird?

Patiently he showed me how the bottle was to be poured into the plastic bag and he would keep the bottle.

"Oh, I see!! That way you save me from paying the deposit on the bottle?"

"Si, si, Senorita. We never let the bottles go out of the store. We save you money."

"Oh, I'm sorry, but I never bought a Coke in a bag before."

What could I do but laugh and take the saggy, sloshy bag of Coke and accept the straw he held out for me. This is not very promising, is it? I can't even buy Coke in a can or a bottle. Thank goodness the pretzels are in a sealed bag.

Upon leaving the pharmacia, a woman jostled me, but I said nothing. She was too pointedly aggressive for me to believe it was unintentional. Several blocks later it dawned on me that this is Merida—not New York, and women here don't push people. Quickly I checked my bag, in the event she was a pickpocket, but everything was there.

As I turned the corner to walk toward the plaza, I almost collided with the back of a tall blond man standing in the middle of the sidewalk. He was ranting and raving in Spanish at a tall Castilian-type guy whose mouth moved even when he wasn't talking. Neither man was happy with the other, and both voices grew shrill in an odd sort of male way. The heated argument snagged the stream of humanity trying to flow around it, and though no one appeared annoyed, everyone was.

After crossing the street to the opposite corner, I casually glanced over at the two men as I pretended to be hunting for a bench to sit on while I drank my Coke.

Oh, no! It's Chip what's his name. After he stood me up, I completely forgot about him. What is he doing here? He didn't seem the type to haggle on street corners anywhere—let alone in downtown Merida. Wonder what is wrong?

As I sat and watched them wind up what had to be a totally unsatisfactory piece of business, the woman who jostled me earlier came up to them and gave the Castilian a slip of paper.

The plot is thickening! What is she up to? The guy looks happy about whatever is written on the note, but Chip is still raging. His voice rose almost loud enough to be heard by me—clear across the street. The other man thrust the piece of paper in front of his nose, which silenced him instantly. Chip stared at the note as though it were some secret formula or a winning lottery ticket. Suddenly, he draped his arm over the shoulders of the Castilian, and they stooped to talk quietly to the woman.

I see her smiling. She looks like she is feeling very good. They must be telling her she has done a great job. Wonder what she did?

As they continued to talk—you know how long it takes to say something in Spanish—the woman's eyes began to rove over the crowd around them, then she spotted me. I know she did, but for some reason she didn't examine me as closely as she did everyone else.

It struck me as odd, but when Chip eased his body around them to face me, I felt my hair standing up again. He couldn't help but see me, but apparently did not remember me or recognize me in this get-up—or chooses not to. The Castilian and the woman abruptly left Chip standing on the corner. He appeared not to have a care in the world, but I kind of doubt it after all their crazy antics.

What is he up to? Who are the other two? They don't look like the kind of people Chip or any American tourist would be talking to, let alone arguing with, on a downtown street corner.

What am I saying? Why do I assume Chip is a tourist? He never said a word to make me believe he was. In fact, I think he said he was here on business. But who can remember? The flight was ages ago. It seems like I have been in Mexico for years. Lost in thought, sipping on my little bag of Coke, I forgot to watch Chip. At some point, he had disappeared.

"Amanda! Amanda Sheridan! How the hell are you? I never expected to see you again after you stood me up last Sunday. What happened? Why didn't you show? I waited right *here*—for hours!"

I almost jumped out of my skin. His voice boomed at me from out of my blind spot on the left side. He must have sneaked up on me on purpose, so I will act like I never saw him yelling on the corner. After all, a girl can't be too careful.

Trying to act mildly surprised, yet sophisticated, I purred, "Why Chip, how are you? I'm sorry. I wanted to let you know, but I got caught up in so many other things I simply forgot what day it was. Really! I totally forgot! Will you ever forgive me?" How can he? I was here, but he wasn't. I can't wait to hear what he says to that.

He looked perplexed and fumbled for words before he said, "You forgot— oh, I see. Time has a way of slipping by when you are on vacation. Are you having a good time? Been to see any ruins? Can you recommend any restaurants?"

All he asks are questions. He wants me to be on the run or defensive, but I can't be bothered. I'm too tired of foreign intrigue to take on any new domestic conflict, so I'll say nothing.

"I see you bought a Coke in a bag. Isn't that charming? They won't let you take out a glass bottle that is biodegradable, but give you a plastic bag that can only foul up the planet. They make no sense. Do they?"

"I don't know. The kids are the primary targets, and they can't very well cut themselves badly on a broken plastic bag if they trip on the street while drinking it."

"That's you! Always looking on the bright side."

What's me? He talks like he knows me. Wait a minute. This has to be for the benefit of anyone listening. I know it. Something is happening and I don't intend to be taken for another ride—or be taped.

"You don't know me at all. I never see things as totally one way or the other. I seek balance, but I don't look down on others if they don't."

Where did that come from?

"Oh, I'm sorry, Amanda. I guess I'm tired. I've been out all day scouting the territory to see if there is any sign of intelligent life hereabouts—and found none. These people want to stay in the stone age forever."

Why did I ever think this guy was attractive? He is as ugly as any of the other Americans down here. No wonder I don't have any luck with men. I can spot a loser only after I get my nose rubbed in it first.

"I think you are a tad too tough on these people. After all, they still let us in the country—even though we constantly abuse their hospitality."

"What do you mean?"

"I mean the way we come down here and run them down verbally, physically, and whatever other way we can. If we are not stomping over their work, we are stealing their sacred art and whatever else isn't nailed down."

Chip's eyes flashed. Now he is the one assuming a defensive posture. Wonder exactly what hit home?

"I'm sorry, Chip. I know you are not like that, but some of these people get to me. I have been riding too many tour buses, I guess."

With his face partially hidden in the deepening shadows, he seemed to relax a bit, as he said, "Yeah, those buses get to you every time. Have you been on many?"

"In my life?"

Sounding slightly exasperated, he said, "No! Of course, not. I mean here in Mexico—this trip."

"Oh, I get around, but one town is pretty much the same as the next. Don't you think?"

He did not seem to be interested in continuing the conversation any longer, but was not budging from the bench. What could I do to make him drop me completely? Then I knew.

"What are you doing tomorrow? I'm going to go to Uxmal and see the ruins with a couple of women at the hotel. You would have a great time. Why don't you come along?"

Straightening his shoulders, he said, "Oh, no. Thanks a lot, but I have business that takes me out of town tomorrow. In fact, I will be going in the opposite direction. I plan on going to Chichen Itza."

Oh, no!! How will that work out? That is where I'm going, and I sure don't want to run into him. Something is definitely up! I don't know what, but I'll know by this time tomorrow.

"Why go to Chichen Itza if you are here on business? Isn't that out in the boondocks?"

"Wel-l-l-l, yes it is, but even businessmen have to have some time off. I have been here as long as you, but I haven't seen a thing. I want to be able to compare notes with you later and see who and what we know and did in common, but right now I have to run and do a few errands in preparation for my trip."

"Are you staying there for a few days?"

"Oh, no, just a straight shot there and back. You know, photo opportunities at the main stops and then back to the hotel for a long soak. I can imagine what they have out there to entertain the traveler, and what I see isn't for me."

"Too bad! Well, I'll see you when I see you. Have a great day tomorrow. Maybe you can join me and the girls another time."

"Oh sure, sounds great. See you around."

It works every time. When you tell a Romeo you want him to meet your girlfriends, he knows he is dead meat. At least Chip did not run!

I sat there until the dampness drove me out of the park. Before returning to my hotel room, I stopped in another little store and bought two cans of Coke and a fresh bakery roll from the middle of the stack and placed it in my own bag. They had little I could buy to flesh out my evening meal, but then I have plenty of flesh stored up behind me already.

After crossing several streets, I sensed someone walking behind me, but could not see anyone reflected in the windows, so I stopped dead in front of a shop window and turned around and leaned up against it. That is when I spotted the 'aggressive woman' again. She was not fast enough for me. She popped into a little storefront, so I hurried around the corner and took off. When I got to the end of that street, I turned and saw nothing out of place. Not one person on the street, yet it was not late.

What is going on? I'm getting tired of all these mysteries.

As I turned around, the door of a car opened just in front of me and out jumped my newest Mayan friend, Freddie. How was that for perfect timing? As casually as anyone can after abruptly accosting you on the street, Freddie said, "Oh, Mandy, how nice to see you. Can we give you a ride to your hotel? We are headed that way—and it may rain."

Who cares now? I'll figure out later what is going on.

"Sure. Don't want to ruin my beautiful hair."

Freddie joined me in laughing at my little joke, but the other two men in the car said nothing and made no move to introduce themselves or look at me.

In fact, I could never pick them out of a police line-up because they carefully kept their faces averted from me. Within two minutes the car pulled up at the rear of my hotel and Freddie barely had time to renew his instructions about the morrow's trip to Chichen Itza before they dumped me out. That was how I was beginning to feel—like some kind of garbage being passed around because nobody knew what to do with it. Toxic waste—that's me!!

As they drove off, I checked to make sure nobody saw me enter the hotel. I'm getting the hang of this stuff and act more like Jamie Bond every day. I should be able to solve all these mysteries pretty soon, even though I have yet to meet Dr. No or whoever the villain is. Wonder where he is hiding?

Slipping the key into the lock, I quietly opened the door, then closed it firmly behind me. As I put down my bag and reached for the light switch, I *knew* someone was in the room. What to do? I did the only thing I could. I threw the switch and there sat Chip!

"Welcome home, Amanda. Sorry for the intrusion, but I just couldn't leave you like that, so I came over here to see you before you went out for the evening. Since my Spanish is meager, the desk clerk thought I wanted to wait for you here, so he gave me your desk key. Here it is."

I have never seen an eerier look on any man's face as he dangled the key from his little finger, but I managed to be my own irrepressible self and snipped at him.

"Sorry I can't say I'm glad to see you, Chip."

Managing to look somewhat puzzled at my response, he said, "What do you mean?"

"I don't take kindly to strange men entering my home or my hotel room when I am not there—and even if I am. You have no right to be here, and you will leave immediately. The only way you got that key was by insinuating we were more than friends—or a bribe. That is not the way to impress me, so get out!"

"Whoa! Whoa there little lady. I just stopped by to take you out to dinner and make up for not being more attentive, but you are making me look like some kind of pervert or something."

"Or something is more like it. I want you out now or I yell and keep on yelling until every American, Mexican, and whomever else is anywhere within a mile of this place knows you are in here and I don't like it. Do you catch my drift?"

As I raved, he jumped up and flew to the door where he now stood with his hand on the knob making a sickening attempt to look boyish and innocent as he said, "Oh, Amanda, I'm so sorry. Please forgive me. I never meant to upset you. I thought we were friends. I'm so sorry if I came on too strong, but you are such a beautiful woman."

"Now I'm really getting mad, cowboy. Get out of here NOW!"

Who is he playing to? Ever since we talked earlier, he has been acting a part—and very badly. He seems to be talking for the benefit of an unseen audience. Oh, no, don't tell me there is another bug in the room!

It took less time than before to locate the bug, but this time I put two fingers in my mouth, curled my tongue and whistled into it as loud as I could. If someone has nothing better to do than listen to me, they will pay the price. That is how I see it. I am really mad now and won't stop until I find out what is going on here.

The secret to success is to be aware of what everyone else is doing, but act like you are doing nothing. It always worked before and I bet these small-time jerks would take the bait, too. I decided to keep on acting like I did not know whatever it was was important, which would not be hard to do since I did not know what it was everybody thought I knew, maybe that would make some people mad enough to come out in the open.

My secret weapon is that I haven't got a secret.

There is Space Between Us

After my run-in with Chip, I did not feel like myself until Freddie picked me up the next morning and we were almost half-way to Chichen Itza. Chip definitely had done a number on me. What was he trying to prove?

A little Mayan village straddled both sides of the road and created a minor traffic snarl at its one stop sign. As I sat there looking at the little kids looking at me, I felt at peace—finally. The permanency of the town and the people reassured me that things are just as they have always been here and everywhere. Little kids looking at big kids thinking they are having all the fun going places and doing exciting things.

The wistfulness of their expressions made me laugh. If they only knew what was in store for them in the years ahead, they would sit down and start playing and having fun right now. No one can rob you of your youth the way you do it to you. I know it, you know it, but they don't.

What about this guy Chip? Where did he come from? What is he doing down here? He is obviously no businessman, but I *was* entirely taken in by him at the airport and later on the plane and I am usually not that gullible. What would I be up to if I were Chip?

"Look, Amanda, there is a turkey. Someone is going to miss their fiesta main course unless they catch him."

"Turkey? Where? Oh, yes, I see him. But look over there! That woman is on to him. He is not going to be free much longer. She looks like a woman with a mission."

"That is a funny expression. I like it. You look like a woman with a mission, too. But then, of course, you are."

Wonder what Freddie knows? He is so deferential and courteous—too much so for his age, but it is nice to be respected—at any age. At home, you never are—no matter what you do.

"What do you know about my mission, Freddie?"

Watching him squirm slightly, I made my voice as smooth and calming as possible as I pushed him to respond, but at least a minute passed before he settled down and stretched back into his seat.

Apparently feeling more secure, he said, "I do not know much of anything, but I have never been asked to show anyone really important around Chichen Itza before. They always told me to study hard because someday I would, but I was never told when or why. So, when they showed up at the University yesterday and said: 'The time has come,' I came. I do not know why and I do not know anything about you except that you come from America and will be here for only a short time now and will come back later to stay."

Oh, my god! What is going on now? Where are they getting all this stuff? I can't keep it all straight, and now with Chip and friends and all the other stuff—not to forget good, old Regis Fawley's dead body in the jungle, I am beginning to feel like I am so far over my head that this has got to be my last trip anywhere. Why would they say I am coming back? I like adventure, but this is getting to be ridiculous.

"You're a very good student then?"

I could tell he was flattered, but his only response was a brief nod.

"You can fill in all the blanks for me now, Freddie, and I will let you know if there are any gaps."

"I am not sure I understand."

"You will. Just start talking about every little thing you know about these times we live in and how they are changing and what you think we are supposed to do—stuff like that. If you get off the track, I'll just fill in what is missing so you can figure it out. Okay?"

The movements of Freddie's face betrayed puzzlement, but he manfully started talking about his background and philosophy of life. He didn't seem to question my authority or right to know, but obviously felt inept and not prepared for the assignment. As he rambled along from phase to phase of his earlier education and his selection by the elders of his village to be advanced to the university, he seemed to find a rhythm and feel the impact of his story—he overlooked nothing. In fact, the drive to Chichen Itza was over before he reached today, but I had enough background on the Elders' methods to see what may or may not be on the agenda for me.

It seems they all feel I am an emissary of the ancient ones and I am an ancient one myself—reincarnated or something. I'm not sure, but they are comfortable with that concept and contacted me intuitively to come down here to check out what is going on and why so many foreigners are trying to make contact with the higher beings now.

They believe my assignment in America is almost over, and I know as much as I need to know or will ever figure out about Americans—that it is time for me to come home and do what I have been sent back to Earth to do. Whatever that is. Anyway, they seem satisfied with me as I am, even though I cannot figure out what is going on most of the time.

When we got out of the van, I spotted a few idlers standing under one of the huge spreading trees near the low wall that leads to the main entrance, but by the time we approached the spot, no one was there. Strange. I figured they were guides, but guides would not disappear, at least I do not think they would.

"Freddie, what do we have to pay to get in here? I have some change in the bottom of my bag. I can dig it out."

"For *you??* There is no charge! You are our honored guest. You will be able to stay as long as you wish and take whatever pictures you care to take, but you will not speak. We do not want anyone to notice that you speak Mayan."

"What? Oh, yes, I understand." Good grief, I'm talking Mayan again and don't even know it. It's absurd! I don't know Mayan, and if I did, how could I talk so many different dialects? I guess it's what is known as the gift of tongues. Oh, well, better continue to play dumb. I am getting good at it.

"What do you want?"

"What do you mean, Freddie?"

"Do you want water or anything to take with you? It is hot and the climb to the top of the pyramid and the other temples can be very hard if you are dry."

"I don't see you and the others carrying water bottles—only the tourists. Actually, only the Americans."

"That is because Americans are only now aware of the need for water and figure that if they use their intellect and take care of their own bodies the Earth will last long enough for them; whereas we know the Earth is running out of water but the body has enough for such a trek if properly paced. We fill up and then refill at convenient times—not when the mind says it is time."

"That's an interesting concept. You say you fill up the body and let it tell you when you need water, and we let the mind tell us. I think I see the difference, and I bet you are right. The body should know what it needs, but the mind loves to mind every *body's* business."

I chuckled at my miserable pun, but Freddie apparently did not get it or was too polite to groan. We moved toward the water sales counter, but I decided to go native. After all, I should be able to pace myself when I am with a guide. As I turned around to speak to Freddie, he was gone.

"Freddie! Freddie!" Oh, oh, I'm not supposed to speak, and obviously, I don't sound like an American, because only the Maya are looking my way.

Panic strikes more and more often lately. Before I came down here I had gotten to the point where even hearing footsteps running up from behind me while walking down a dark street in Manhattan barely raised the hair on my arms. I credited my belief in God with my lack of fear. But down here I feel out-of-joint or out-of-sync or something and worry about being lost. I don't know why.

"Amanda? Do you want to follow me now?"

Where did he come from? I *know* he wasn't here a minute ago.

"Oh, yes. Let's go."

"This is the finest example of European cultural rape we have in all of Mexico. You will see it is not at all like what we would do ourselves if we were restoring a site, but then we are ignorant savages. Are we not?"

He did not sound bitter or even snotty, just calm and matter-of-fact. I feel more and more like that myself. I definitely resent the intrusive behavior of my own fellow countrymen in such a beautiful culture and country. Why do we think we are so great?

"You will find the greatest pyramid is the worst of the conversions. It was destroyed in order to protect the rest of the city, but the city is now destroyed to make it look good. The only side in good shape as far as visitors are concerned is not at all what it is supposed to be. They robbed the site and put in whatever fit. There was no reverence for design. They simply painted pictures and said, 'This is how it was.' We were not consulted. We knew, but we did not bother to tell them since they were so arrogant—and ignorant. We regret it now, but *then* we were poor and thought they would all go away sooner and leave us alone if we just let them go. Obviously, we were wrong."

"Obviously."

Freddie shot me a warning look. There were a few tourists approaching us and within earshot.

"You will find the Arabs and other diligent keepers of the fragile ecologies of the Earth are all considered to be ignorant, but it is the terrible ignorance of your past that has destroyed the Earth—not the poor and nomadic." Freddie turned to the group of eavesdroppers beside us, and asked, "What do you think it will take to end the destruction?"

The hangers-on dropped back immediately when faced with the dilemma of answering his question or continuing to get a 'free guided tour'. They all decided to act like they were not intruding upon our conversation.

Freddie is a born guide. He won't be taken advantage of easily.

"Whenever anyone comes too close, I get nervous. I want to keep them away, but I did not mean to insult them and certainly did not mean to sound like I thought you were a destructive people, but I could not stop myself."

Yeah, I know what you're saying. It happens to me everyday, but it is sort of fun.

"I can hear you, Amanda. You just said it is fun to be able to, what do you call it, channel." His smile was one of triumph.

So, we are well matched after all, and now it is my turn.

"Mandy, you transmit. I will talk and you just think. Okay?"

Okay.

"Good. We are going to have lots of fun. Let's go over to the pyramid before all the tour buses get here. I want you to go up inside the stairway between the inner and outer pyramids and see the jade jaguar—without any interference. We better hurry."

As we rounded the corner of the pyramid, I saw Chip. My alarm was immediately transmitted to Freddie. He stopped and looked at me as if asking for directions or instructions. All I could say was, let's get out of here fast. We ran.

In the bushes nearby, Freddie found a flat stone left over from the 'restoration' of the pyramid which apparently had been discarded as unusable. We sat down on it and he asked me why I sounded the alarm. I told him about my recent adventures with Chip and he looked scared. Just as I finished, I saw Chip enter the path leading directly to where we sat.

What else to do? I pulled Freddie's arm around me and started to nuzzle his neck in an imitation of grand passion. Freddie giggled at first because it must have tickled, but he really got into it as Chip and another man came closer and closer, slower and slower. I could hear their heavy breathing. Before they reached our rock, Chip stopped and said something in Spanish to his companion, whom I assumed to be the Castilian, but could not sneak a peek to make sure. Chip and the guy left abruptly, but I suspected they were on to me.

Maybe Freddie knows what to do?

"No, I do not know what to do. Perhaps we should not go to see the jade jaguar now."

Now I felt driven to visit it. I shook my head and stood up. Freddie followed me slowly out of the copse and watched to see if anyone followed. I found a seat on the bottom tier of the pyramid and sat down while 'telling' Freddie to check around to see if he could spot Chip and friend.

When he came back alone we carefully advanced toward the central stairway where the entrance to the interior pyramid is located. There were three Maya standing by it, but they looked more like guards than guides. In fact, I have never seen such menacing looking Maya in my life. As we walked up to the entrance, one of the guards/guides opened the door to the little shed protecting the inner stairway and ushered me in. No one else was inside and everyone waiting was forbidden to enter the stairway until 11 o'clock.

Wow! I have plenty of time to explore whatever it is I am here to see. I wonder why Freddie isn't allowed in with me? It's really cramped and humid, but another person isn't going to hurt—especially if he is Maya.

Just then a feeling of overwhelming grief descended upon me. I could sense blood and tears and hear the weeping and wailing of a woman close by and somewhere above me. I peered into the gloom and could barely make out her shape standing on the upper steps. She beckoned me to climb. I followed the essence of her being. She was young, but not very strong. She was barefoot and a little feather or flower was stuck in the back of her hair. I could see it floating above me. I followed it. She wailed as though distraught with some terrible grief. As she cried, she climbed the slippery steps ahead of me.

Finally I saw the sculpted cat looking down at me from the top of the stairway. It stood in stately splendor daring me to come closer. I could see why they fear it. Its majesty is not in the stone. It has its own life and a soul. It is not of Earth.

What did they do here? I can feel it wasn't evil, but it was so scary people could be compelled to do anything. Why would they do that?

Now there are only a few things in the small room where the jaguar keeps guard, but I know there should be more. The walls reveal nothing. They once told a story, but it is all gone. Nothing could withstand the humidity. However, I can tell her story easier now because I feel her sorrow like dampness in my bones.

There were only three things a Maya maiden had to do, but she had to do them well—and she had to do them all. Her life was not a life of hope or love, but one of obedience to the work of the Lord. She had to do what she was told. If she thought she had nothing, she had nothing. If she thought she was beautiful, she became the greatest beauty of her village, but she had to have a child. She could not escape destiny.

Once there was a lovely maiden in a very small village who thought she was very beautiful, and when she was told to have a child, she wanted no one to touch her. She went every day to the temple of her father and asked for a blessing and a release from the stain. She wanted no blood to issue from her. She asked to be relieved of the menstrual cycle so as to be unable to bear a child. This prayer at the stele of her father's family was heard. However, she went as required to Cozumel to pray to the goddess of fertility and enjoyed the trip to the sacred caves to swim in the grotto with other maidens—even though she would not bear children like they would.

When told she had to obey all the rules like any other young woman and seek a husband, she balked and announced she did not want a husband. She wanted no one. She felt she had all she needed in her family— especially her father and her lovely body which men wanted but could not have. She enjoyed her power. She wanted to keep it.

Her rejection of marriage meant she had to be sold or bartered, but before it could be arranged, she was asked if she wanted to work in the place of the elders. Aware this was a rare honor, she accepted it readily. The only possession she could take with her was a little feather from the eagle her father gave her at puberty.

She could not wait to arrive at the elder's town, but her discoveries there shocked her maidenly delicacy. She was to be shared. She was to be a woman who served and serviced the men who came and went from the village. She was not to be married and would not be allowed to bring forth a child. She had her wish. Her prayer was answered.

Her life there was not at all what she wanted, but she could not leave. Her own ways were so delicate she could not walk long or do much work. She was not lazy, but she had little strength. In time the stopping of the blood sapped beauty from her body and her weight dropped even lower. Many men thought of her as a child and some were thus attracted more to her than to other women.

The lonely woman had nothing and got nothing, but she hoped one day to be queen. She continued to pray, but had no altar or temple at which to worship, so she went about the countryside looking for steles and found one buried in a remote section of the wooded area beyond the north end of town. It was not easy to find, but she determined it to be powerful and useful for her purposes. She prayed there for three nights and then in the moonlight, she felt a presence beginning to emerge.

When she returned the fourth night, her face was bathed in moonlight and she felt the hand of God. It was a power-filled vision and she knew ecstasy. She knew her life would be totally transformed. She would no longer be loved by men. She would be a goddess of the night. She would be a jaguar!

Her life was over only to the elders. She lived on in the jungle and at night prowled over the remains of the village years after all the people moved to another area. She entered the temple of the most high and slept there until one night she was cat napping when she heard a woman crying aloud to the moon. The woman did not want a child. She wanted to be free of the blood. She wanted to be able to be beautiful all her life. She wanted to be a queen.

The jaguar descended from the temple and devoured her and became the new goddess of the time. She became the jaguar within the pyramid. She is still here. She is still on guard. She wants only women who have no children.

"What do you think she wants from you, Amanda?"

The shock of hearing Freddie's voice right behind me on the narrow stairs caused my throat and shoulders to constrict and slightly convulse. I could move only with difficulty, but I could see in the dim light his large and luminous eyes.

"Don't be afraid, Freddie. I am safe. I am not going to be devoured. I have come to the temple where time and space unite to keep out the old or the young who would not appreciate the time and space preserved here. The space is not much, but the time to reach it is gone. You have to understand the maiden is here, but she is not here. She has her own hell. She created it herself. She wanted youth and beauty and no responsibility and she has it, but life is not for those who want to do no work. You have to work. I have. I continue to work. I am not here to be devoured. I am here to end her misery."

"H-h-how? How can you end her misery, Mandy, if she is not alive or able to be seen?"

"I see her. Don't you?"

"No! I am not a shaman—yet."

"I keep forgetting. You won't ever be able to see her. She will be gone. I am going to release her into the wild. She has been entombed for centuries and unable to escape. I will take her into me and release her. She has not eaten for a long time but will not hurt you or me, but she will eat whatever comes across her path after that."

"Oh, Amanda, do you really believe that?"

"Better take that back, Freddie."

Now it was Freddie who looked frightened and 'spooked', if you know what I mean. I made him leave before I entered the mood I had been in earlier. I felt he was unable to help, but I didn't know what to do either.

As I lifted my head, she was there again as before. I let her descend and enter into my auric field and smother herself in my hair. She seemed to be enjoying the intimacy. I felt somewhat used, but not abused. She ended her caress by holding my nose. Was she thinking of entering me by way of my naris? What would she do?

As I waited, a strange feeling of non-resistance or subsidence of all energy came over me. I thought I saw her, but she blended into my aura until I felt only a tingle in my right eye. She seemed to be there. I awoke from this hypnotic trance or whatever it was and felt I could do anything. I was very hungry. I felt totally alive and indifferent to all fear. I wanted to get out of there!

I dashed down the steps and flew out the door almost trampling the three startled guards as I headed for the bushes where Freddie and I had hidden from Chip. I decided to sit on that same rock and watch the paths beneath me, but this time I perched on the rock—both feet under my hips, in a crouch like I was going to pounce on someone.

Wait a minute! I am no jaguar and I am not going to be one. Just get out and bother me no more. I can do anything! You are just my imagination. I am not a jaguar and never was! You are! You will run and roam and live forever, but I will not. I am human. I am a shaman. I will set you free. You will live. You will not devour me—ever.

Whatever I said, it worked. Energy catapulted me off the rock and I felt like I had jumped out of a tree. I rolled on the ground and suddenly felt a wrenching from beneath my rib cage that stopped my heart and breath. My abdomen erupted and there stood a jaguar! Really! A jaguar! A real, honest-to-goodness jaguar.

There is Nothing Wrong

The cat sprung out and away into the jungle, but soon I heard her back panting close by me. Surprisingly, I was not afraid of her—not at all. I felt sort of like Androcles and the lion, if that is possible, and knew she would never harm me because I rescued her. She was part me.

I wondered: Should I leave her here like this? Maybe I should say something to her? Better not. Freddie said not to talk out loud *at all.* But it can't hurt, can it?

"Go gently into the forest my little friend. You will not be harmed by me. I will not tell anyone about you."

You better believe I won't. They would think I had really lost my mind this time. The sound of loud, low purring emanated from the bush directly behind me. It almost made me drop my drawers, but I'm okay now. She's just a big pussy cat—really.

I must have become mesmerized by the rhythmic breathing, because it startled me to discover someone was creeping toward me in the underbrush from the opposite direction. I should have listened to Freddie about talking out loud. Now I was in trouble again.

"Well, what have we here? Our little lady of distress. I thought you were supposed to be in Uxmal? What are you doing here?"

Oh, my god! It's Chip. I couldn't speak, so I just shrugged my shoulders and cocked my ear in the direction of the jaguar.

"What is the matter? Cat got your tongue."

His sneer did not scare me and his attempt to sound menacing was too melodramatic for belief until I saw the gun partially concealed behind his back. My heart slowed as he pointed the pistol at me with chilling ease. He did look menacing and cruel. My heart could no longer stand the strain of trying to beat slowly. I had to let it race. Panic was the only thing I could not use, yet it was all I had.

Chip waved the gun at me and said, "Come on, you and I have a few people to see."

He no sooner finished the sentence than the jaguar sprang from the undergrowth straight for his throat. It was terrible to watch. He never had a chance. The pistol dropped to the ground, and I hurried to pick it up while he and the cat rolled around in a death grip that only one could survive, and I already knew who that would be. It was over quickly and I made no move to shoot the bloody cat standing over this vicious stranger's body. She just looked at me, and I knew I had to leave.

I ran out of the woods, down the path to the pyramid and almost collided with Freddie and two of the guards. They were apparently coming to find me, and their eyes never left my hand which clasped the revolver.

Freddie was the only one to speak, "What happened, Amanda? Where did you get that gun?"

"It's a long story, and you would never believe it. We better get out of here fast. There is going to be all hell to pay for this."

"Why? What went on? You flew out of the pyramid and into the trees no more than ten minutes ago. What could happen in such a short time?" Freddie looked panic stricken, as he if he already knew what had happened.

"I'm telling you, Freddie, you won't believe it."

The other men looked immovable, so I decided to show them rather then tell them about the attack. I led the way back to where I last saw Chip and the jaguar. At first I thought they had disappeared—been a figment of my enlarged imagination, but upon closer inspection we found what remained of Chip.

Freddie whispered, "What went on here? Who is this? It is a man, obviously, but what happened to him?" He gagged and retched while one guard poked the toe of his boot through the torn clothes and what remained of a human being. The jaguar had devoured Chip almost entirely.

"You are so calm, Amanda. How can you stand there and look at this disgusting sight and not feel sick?"

"He was going to kill me, Freddie. I know it."

The older guard grabbed my arm and asked, "Do you know who this is? Why was he trying to kill you?"

"Yes, I know who he was—I think. But I don't really know who he was. His name was Charles something or other, but he went by Chip, and he crept up on me a few minutes ago while I was resting here and threatened me with this gun."

"How did you get the gun from him?"

"Was anyone with him?"

"Do you know why he was threatening you?"

The trio talked so rapidly I did not bother to answer. I waited until their shock subsided. The two guards no longer looked so tough. In fact, they looked scared.

"He sneaked up on me, like I said, and pulled out a gun and talked like he wanted me out of here, but he didn't get very far when a jaguar attacked and killed him—right in front of me, so I picked up his gun and ran out and straight into you."

"A jaguar? There are no jaguars around here. They have been gone for years. Besides, they cannot kill a man with a gun. That is too incredible!!"

"But look, Freddie, there is evidence all over that he was devoured by a wild animal. Look at the tracks! They are those of a large cat."

"But how could a jaguar eat so much? There is hardly anything left." Freddie suddenly sprang into action as though awakening from a deep trance and told the two men, "Do not disturb anything. Get the police. Tell them you found the body on a routine check and don't mention that Amanda and I were here. Okay?"

Both guards nodded, then the younger one ran down the path toward the pyramid while the other said quietly, "You both better go down the path to the sacred cenote and leave by way of the old road. I will get someone to take your car over to the hotel for you. Go and register like you just arrived. Okay?"

"Good idea, but will you be all right?"

"Of course, but you and Amanda better be careful. They are starting to play rough now. We must be close to something big."

Who are they talking about? What is going on now? My worries or thoughts were interrupted by Freddie wrenching my arm almost out of my shoulder socket trying to take the gun from me.

"Don't ever try to take a gun away from me again, Freddie. The next time you might get shot."

He looked shocked, then started to laugh.

"Oh, Amanda. If you could just see yourself. You look like a woman playing John Wayne—if John Wayne spoke Mayan."

Don't tell me I'm still talking Mayan! What goes on here? Will I ever be myself again?

"Yes, Amanda, this will all be over soon. I know it. It cannot continue at this pace without coming to a climax soon. But why not give me the gun?"

"I don't know. I really don't know. I never had anything to do with guns before, but it sure feels right now—'and I sure know how to use it, Pilgrim'." My John Wayne impersonation brought some comic relief to the situation, but not much.

Freddie shook his head and said, "Okay, you look like it, too, but isn't it a bit of over-kill? What if someone sees you twirling it around? They might connect it to this dead guy, and then where will you be?"

"Right. I'll put it in my bag—right next to my tortilla chips, because I know I'm going to need it. I can just tell."

Poor Freddie! He looks ten years older than when we met this morning. Now he is afraid of *me* and apparently doesn't know any more than I do, but he is Maya and I'm not.

"Why do you think this guy wanted to kill you, Amanda? Did you know him?"

"I met him on my way down here, then accidentally sat next to him on the plane out of Houston where we made a date to get together last Sunday in the Zocalo in Merida, but he never showed. Then yesterday 'I ran into him and some heavy after some woman fingered me'—that's movie mob talk not John Wayne—but I gave him the brush-off. Then he showed up *inside* my hotel room last night and I threw him out."

"What?"

"I am not going to repeat it. Just remember it."

Poor Freddie. He is aging now. I want to laugh for some reason, but I better not. He will think I'm some kind of fiend if I do.

"You are very strange, Amanda. Things that would upset most people— especially women, do not bother you. Do they?"

"Normally, yes, but down here—nothing is normal. I don't even know if I'm here. How can anything be wrong if there is nothing to judge it against? Right, wrong, what is the difference? When you start trying to figure things out, you get upset. It's best to just keep bouncing back and looking up and knowing there is more to this than you will ever know—or want to know."

"Right. I mean, I guess you are right. I don't know. It just seems wrong that a man was killed and we are running away. But then, what is he doing here in my country? What were he and his friends after?"

"You know, Freddie, I think we are about to find out. Why not just wait and see?"

"Of course. You are wise, Amanda. You are obviously of the highest level. I will never be able to do what you do. I will still be trying to figure this out when you are back in America and have no memory of it."

"It's true, I remember almost nothing. I am ageless. I fear nothing, and I am not going to learn to fear at this late stage in my development. You have to understand that death is nothing but an illusion and you are an illusion—then it all makes sense."

"Yes, I guess so." His look of bewilderment belied his words.

"When we get to the car, let's jump in and drive up to the lobby entrance like we just arrived, like your friends suggested."

"I guess it is better than having no plan at all, but do you really think no one saw us arrive at the main entrance earlier?"

"Don't worry, Freddie. No one was around then who can swear we went in or not. We will act like anyone else who stops to check out where the entrance is and then decides to check into the hotel—only we never intended to check in. Did we?"

With a mischievous grin, Freddie admitted, "I did. I wanted to stay here as long as the elders permitted. I have never had a chance to visit the Mayaland Hotel, and the elders feel you can stay no where else now."

"Great! It must be something."

"It is. It has the most beautiful gardens in all the Yucatan and the food is very good—for a hotel, and their maids are the most beautiful. They make very good tips, so they get the best of the best. If I had not gone to the University, I might have aspired to work there."

"Oh, really. What a waste that would have been. You're too bright to be expended on menial work."

"No one is too good to work, and I am not that bright. I am nothing compared to one who lives in my village, but he was never offered the University."

"Why?"

"He is a mighty shaman like you. In fact, he was recently named the youngest shaman in Yucatan. He is very proud of it, and so are all we who come from the same village."

"Oh, I know him! I was there when he was crowned."

"Crowned? Oh, you always make jokes. But, of course, you were there. They waited for your arrival before he could be solemnly established before all the elders."

Wow! I really did miss what was going on!

"You are a mystery to me, Amanda. You are so much like my father, who is also a shaman, but so very different. I guess it is because your ways are so ancient."

"What do you mean?"

"About what?"

"That my ways are ancient. How could they be? I live in New York. They couldn't be that old."

"Well, for one thing, you speak a dialect most of the time that is very, very old, then you use phrases and stories that are more recent than the old stories of our old books, but older than the meaning of the stories now being preserved. You speak in a tongue that is different. You look old/young, serious/sober like a very elderly elder, but you never change."

"I'm just a bit mystified by your account, but it sounds okay. You have made some good points. Maybe I am an ancient one—come back to make sure everything is done in accordance with the ways of God when the last days arrive here in Mayaland." I felt strange and strained saying this, but Freddie went for it and smiled more than I ever hoped to see today. Whatever I am here to do, I seem to know what it is at some base level, and now on a conscious level I am not afraid of doing it, either.

"Watch, Amanda! I see the car coming. Flag them down and get them to pull up here."

The fellows parked the van under a low-spreading tree that obscured the front seat as they crawled out and disappeared into the underbrush. We slipped in the same way, backed up, turned around, and headed back to the hotel entrance. As we walked in the lobby, I felt that same strange sensation that someone was watching me—but this time I had a gun! I don't care who it is, but I won't be happy until *I* find out what is going on around here.

Freddie made arrangements for our accommodations, telling them I was here to photograph flowers and needed space on the second floor overlooking the gardens, and he needed a small room beside mine. It took only a short time before the bellman showed us to our rooms, but the feeling of being watched intensified. I sensed several pairs of eyes on me and one of them was crossed.

Not knowing what might come out of my mouth, I continued to say nothing. When we got to my room and Freddie whispered it would be okay to talk, I started to jabber. The bellhop had some trouble understanding me, but it was because he spoke very little English and I talked too fast. Never stopping, I followed him out onto the verandah where Freddie was waiting to be shown to his room. Freddie looked surprised, then shocked, as I said very loudly, "See you in the lobby in an hour, Freddie. I want to go to the cave. You know the one I mean."

He appeared about to say something, but apparently thought better of it or was too stunned to act normal. His voice never rose above a whisper.

Freddie was scared. He was sure we were going to get into big trouble; but after all, I had a gun, and a shaman with a gun is more frightening than John Wayne could ever be—now or in his lifetime. I had to laugh, but Freddie refused to join me. Maybe he could not read my thoughts anymore?

* * * * * * *

It turned out that there was nothing in the cave to keep me busy there, but when I later entered the hotel's garden presumably to photograph the foliage. I found a large flowering plant with a huge white blossom that was open and aromatic but covered with ants. While meditating upon it I discovered I was the flower and the flower was in me, but the ants were Maya and I had to return. I would not be able to shirk my work. I would have to return and see what was going on and why the world was not ready for the work.

The work is not open yet, but you will see that we have to be open if it is to work. I will depart and return to New York, but I have to see what happened first.

The hotel had a few guests who were not my kind. I felt them. I knew what they were going to do, but they did not know if I was onto them or their intentions, so I had the upper hand. I caused no shame to come to the Maya, but I put them all on guard. I made them all see that we would fully digest everyone of the foe if they got into our work.

The end of my time in Mayaland was not over when we checked out of the hotel, but it might as well have been since I was unwilling to do whatever it was I was supposed to do to ignite. I went inside and never arrived. I refused to do whatever, but it came back to this: I was afraid of being myself and had to wait until another day.

What to do now? I don't know, but the time is not right. What is to be done when you cannot act as you are and you are part of a single one who is unable to go any further than you are? You retreat and let the night begin again. So I left the Mayaland Hotel and went home? No, I went on to do whatever I had to do, but it has left my mind. I don't care to remember and it was never part of my plan.

Somehow I came through it all smiling and left alone. How? You have to admit you experienced it with me and you don't care to go into it either, so let's split.

Time Out!

There is no time now to explain, but if you have ever been in a whirlpool or done yourself in with shopping, you may understand the feeling that swept over me when I saw Chip, the jaguar, and every other thing that happened during my weeks in Mexico. I could no longer cope, so I bombed out and gave in.

Work cannot make up for lost time, and there is nothing left in me. My mind absorbed too much while my body ran too fast, so Spirit took over. Maybe it is shock and maybe it is time, but I cannot continue as before.

WITHIN

THE

VEIL

The Evil of Men
is in Their Egos

The weird thing I remember about the Chichen Itza affair was that when I returned home and looked at my snapshots, I found the same people pictured in them over and over again, but I did not know any of them well or talk to any one of them for any length of time during my stay. So, why so many pictures of them?

Looking back, I often think of Freddie and how much he knew but did not know about why I was in Chichen Itza. He was not aware I was there merely for the adventure or had a life here. He believed I was part of his society and had a role to play—but when?

Now I think the two dead men were produced by my imagination. I never heard anything about them. There were no reports of two Americans mysteriously killed while traveling in Mexico or any of the other things you would expect to hear if it had really happened. The only problem with that theory is that they both appear in my snapshots.

Funny, I never recognized Chip until I saw him on the corner across from the Zocalo—after he stood me up, yet he is in the background of several pictures taken earlier. I wonder who he *really* is or was? Why would he be on the same plane with me and then never return, yet no one cares? Maybe no one expects him back? Maybe he was a gun runner or drug dealer?

What sticks in my head most is that I conversed in archaic forms of Mayan dialects with numerous people at numerous times and was never doubted. I was totally accepted. I have never been so honored or well received by my own people!

Where would I be now if I had never gone to Mexico? Why did I go any-way? I was content and happy and all of a sudden, wham! I'm off on an adven-ture that includes murder, mayhem, and mystery, and now I am back at work doing what I do—just like nothing ever happened. It's enough to blow a poor girl's mind away.

When I got back to the office, no one acted like I was different. They all said I looked good—tan and sort of rosy, nothing unusual, and they all want to go to Cancun, but Merida does not appeal to anyone. 'They're not into indians.'

Guess, I'll just wait and see if everything stays as is or if I feel compelled to do something different again. I can't imagine why no one wants to question me about Chip, but then maybe the authorities don't know of any connection between us or still haven't got a clue as to who he is—or don't care.

I am planning to do several different things, but first I have to talk out loud about all this. If I go over all the details aloud, I can usually figure out anything. Besides, it will clear up my confusion and any fears I may still have buried in me somewhere—possibly bring me some answers from above.

Yes, folks, I believe in prayer! I find a good, old-fashioned talk with God clears the air—of anything, but I haven't done it lately. I'm going to drive to Connecticut, get off the Merritt Parkway somewhere and talk to the trees. They are great listeners, and God is obviously close by there.

The only difference between the woods in Central Park and Connecticut is that in Connecticut the trees aren't as cautious. The trees are just as manicured and just as frail and feeble from all the pollution and over-building, but they still trust man a bit. Once there, you pick out a park or a lake and amble about until you find a spot that looks perfect for meditation—or just keep walking. It doesn't matter. My style is to sort of keep walking and if I find a bench I might sit for a few minutes but not very long because people check you out too much if you become stationary.

There is a saying in my family that if you want a straight answer you don't ask a liar, and few of my friends can be accused of always being straight with me. In fact, do you know anyone who *really* tells the truth? All the time? I doubt it. Egos are so fragile today you have to fib constantly or lose every friend.

* * * * * * * * *

What about the air here is so clear? I can taste it. It feels different from air anywhere else, but it isn't. Is it? I think air has to be the same everywhere, but why doesn't it look and taste the same?

Oh, I see, you think air in the tall hills and mountains is fresher because it is not shared with millions who have taken all the oxygen from it. That is inter-esting. What else? You think the air is cleaner up here because the particulates are less dense. Now that sounds like God talking to me, too, because I never use words like particulates. I wonder who else is here talking to God? Is anyone else talking now? I bet some are, but won't admit it.

There is a tree that needs a hug! Got to hurry and do it before someone comes along the trail looking for his dog or whatever. Better hug and run or they might try to put me away.

This tree looked young at a distance, but the bark is so old and dank up close. I can't reach my arms around it, so I guess it's about 150 years old. No, just 98? Okay. You know best. I think of things like that when I'm out and about, but I am never sure if it's God or me. What the hay, why not believe it is God?

There is something I wanted to ask you. Do you know why Chip was in Merida?

Nothing. You are not going to tell me? Being rooted here in Connecticut, I guess you weren't there. You probably don't like gallivanting all over the world like I do, but I bet if you think about it, you can come up with something new to say about the case.

Yes, I think I know now. Chip was there for a special conference on the environment, but he wasn't there to represent the interests of humanity in general—only himself. He wasn't there to help teach the Maya about new farming methods to end the centuries-old way of slash and burn, either. He was there for something else—mostly money. Why? Why go to Merida for money?

You would go to Merida if you wanted to sneak around the Yucatan, but it is eight hours from Cancun. You would want to do a few things while you sneak around, too, like look at ruins and act like an anthropologist who is trying to study the ancient ones, stuff like that, but he didn't run that scam. He acted like a legitimate businessman from the beginning. He never acted like a tourist.

"What was his real business?"

Not going to tell me? Okay, I can take a hint. I am being too nosy now, and I have plenty of time to find out about all this once I return to Merida.

"Did I say that? I'm going back to Merida?"

"Hello! Are you in trouble?"

Now I've done it. I had to practically yell—instead of mumble, and now I have been discovered by the local matrons and their broods.

"No, I'm okay. Just slipped and let out a few choice words. Nothing wrong."

A determinedly assertive matron eyed me suspiciously, but said in a syrupy voice, "You look so casual, but we thought you were hurt. You sounded surprised or in pain or something, but we're glad that you're okay."

The other women continued to gape as their kids crashed through the underbrush and trampled or broke off every branch or plant standing in their way. None too soon, another woman spoke cheerfully, "Come along kids, we have to get home by half past five or your father will be wondering where we are."

"Oh, Mom, can't we just walk? I'm tired of hurrying. I wanna' play."

"No, children, this is good for you. You have to learn to keep up. You can't just sit and stare at things if you want to get ahead. The world will pass you by if you sit and look at fish or whatever. Come on, we have to hurry."

They are so busy, they don't even know I exist. Great! That's what I love about this country. Everybody is so busy doing something, but nothing gets done. The whole place is a shambles because nobody has time to do anything and that is because everybody is too busy. Doing what?

Whoa! I'm running in high gear again. Just one brief encounter with the suburban set and I am all wound up. I'm better in the city. There I can blank out my feelings, except acute attention to anything odd or unfamiliar that might produce pain. Here I haven't a clue as to who is okay or who is a latent homicidal maniac. They could all have guns or machetes, but act like they are on a family outing. Down in Merida, I never feel like this. I wonder why?

There is only one thing to do once the spirit is gone. Go home. But where is that? I want to be at peace, but more and more I can't find it. I am always sort of anxious to be somewhere else, but I don't know where. I want to be with others, but I am not sure I care for anyone. I want to see my friends until I do, then I rapidly tire of them. I want to be alone, and then I get sort of lonesome, not lonely—never lonely, but sort of lonesome. If I were to cash in all my chips here, what would it take to move to Mexico?

"Is that all?"

No, that is not realistic. I can't sell all my 'stuff' and move out of the country—maybe forever. That's what weirdoes do who can't make it here, but I am a success. I can make great money and I have a great life here. I don't need anything. I have everything. I don't even need my BMW, but I have one. I don't need a thing, so why would I sell it all and move?

You're right! I'm not very happy. I think I am, but I know that where I work and where I live no one will remember me beyond a few years or maybe even a few months once I'm gone. But in Mexico! There I am remembered for centuries. I have to live where I am of use, and I don't count here. I am just another stockbroker, excuse me, Investment Counselor—just another Yuppie—just another mid-management female who cracked the glass ceiling and has a glamorous, empty life of work and faked passion.

Yeah, I might as well go. Why not? I can always come back and go to Chicago and get in the commodities market. I would fit right in there. I would find Chicago less sophisticated and well mannered than Merida, but otherwise about the same.

Yes, the air is good, and hugging a tree does make everything look more reasonable, but to leave Manhattan and go to Mexico to live is a bit bizarre—if I do say so myself—which is all I'm doing—talking to myself. I don't have to sell out and move away. I can support the Maya from here. But who are they, and what would I be supporting?

There is another thing I don't quite understand. What about Mexico intrigues me so much? Why would I want to live there? I love Paris and all of France. I love the South—especially the Great Smokies. Why not live there? No, I don't belong. I may have lived there before, too, but I am not as attached as I am to Mayaland.

What about the Maya is so convincing? Maybe it is their sincerity and lack of notions about being important. They are not egotistical—much. They don't appear to be very humble until you ask them about themselves, then you find out. They carry themselves very erect and walk carefully as a proud people must, but when you talk to them, they drop their eyes and reflect upon your words and think before they answer you. That's it! The Maya are honest. That is what I miss. That is what I crave.

I am an honest person lost on an island of dishonesty and fraud. The fact I can succeed in a lying profession has always bothered me. I know I don't lie, but everyone else does, or so they say. I wonder how I made it then? I never really thought about it before—and that is scary.

Maybe I was appointed? Maybe I was just lucky? Or, maybe God wanted me there to help the poor old investors who needed help in doubling their income for the upcoming depression? I don't know, but it was fun. I have to admit it. I really enjoyed amassing money, but it doesn't do anything for You. It really doesn't. Once you have all you need, what do you do with the rest? You let it accumulate in accounts presided over by would-be weasels who can't wait to raid your nest and suck your eggs dry.

You have to be so careful when you have a lot of anything. You have to worry about others taking it or not being able to use it properly and letting it go to waste. In fact the happiest people I know have just enough and never worry about money. Can I trust God that much?

If I go to Mexico now, I will end the most fruitful time of my career and can never hope to reenter it again—anywhere, not even in Chicago. If I stay on this job, I will spend my most productive years earning money for what? This is hard.

Wow! I just thought of the two dead men in Mexico and suddenly saw them!! I can see them walking and talking like nothing happened, but it did. I know they were killed. But who did it? A jaguar and a lone gunman? Really, Amanda, you have to get your act together before you start running all over the city selling out.

"Selling out. Who said anything about selling out?"

I guess I did. I wonder why I am so sure I will? What if I just sort of keep a small place here? No, that wouldn't work. I would never want to come back to no job and renting a dump in NYC that would cost more than a huge home in the Yucatan.

It is scary, sort of, but my mind is letting me go. It really is! The Spirit of All is trying to move me, and my mind is now accepting that I can live well else-where—even in Mexico, so now I only have to decide when.

There is nothing like the mind to keep you on the job, but it can be such a pain when you decide to leave. I think it is the mind or ego that produces all trouble. If you had only the spirit to contend with and the body to care for, you would have no time for all the stuff you fill in the rest of your life with. I think I will let my mind idle and shift gears real slow so it doesn't know I am chang-ing and try to stop me.

Why do I think men are evil?

Because they are!

Who said that?

Yes, they are—not always intentionally; but they can get that way inten-tionally.

Hummm, what is going to be the outcome of my moving to Merida?

Nothing. Nothing ever comes to me when I ask a question about the future, but if I ask philosophical questions or ponder things other than the future, I get quick answers. I guess we are not supposed to know what is coming to us.

You have to make your own decision, then we of the upper regions can help you. It is a universal law that no one can interfere in the life of another entity unless asked to do so by that entity. You will have to tell us if you intend to go to Merida or not, then we can all help you.

Wow! Now I am hearing in stereo. What about the times when I asked about coming to New York? You told me to come here.

No, you told the universe you were going to New York when you finished graduate school, so we saw to it that you got your way, but you decided.

Oh, yeah, that's right. It's a bummer when you have to accept responsibility for all your own actions. Isn't it? But life wouldn't be much fun if someone else called the tune or told you what to do. Almost no one I know really believes they own their own life. Wonder why?

Ego. Ego is what keeps you here on Earth and binds you all together. You will never use the ego framework once you leave Earth. It is like the body—an instrument to be manipulated and used for a short time while the spirit evolves and grows beyond the need to con-flict within itself. You will find that the negativity of Earth is what attracts you—a positive being of light—to this planet. You will find out

later why you chose it to begin a new life, then lost your way. Now you are trying to knit the frayed pieces of several lives into one. We will watch. We will help if you ask. We will not be far away.

Okay guys, I can feel you. It is comforting. I like to feel like this. I remember when I was in high school and would sit and stare in the mirror and say how ugly I was. You would yell back: Stop that! You are of God. You are not ugly. You are here for a purpose—stuff like that. It got me through the terrible teens But what to do now? I guess I better meditate. Maybe if I look up stocks and money markets that infiltrate the Mexican market I can help them? No, that is never a help to the common man or woman. I better do it myself.

"Do it myself? What? What can I do? I'm no big shot! I can't move bureaucracies—and I don't want to." Wow! I'm getting warm. It happens every time they are around me. I wonder why?

You feel the Spirit of God and it is all around and flows within you. It is not that your body cares one way or the other, but your spirit is welcoming the light. Your Guides are here and will always help you, but first you must tell them what you must do—where you are headed.

Welcome Guides! Welcome, welcome, welcome. I really need guides. In fact, maybe I can become a guide in Mexico?

Yeah, that is a terrific idea! I know my people and get around in Mexico pretty good. Funny thing though, who are my people? Americans or Maya?

There is No Time to Wait

There is never enough time to say good-bye, but I found it, and found I did not have much to say—so it took longer, but I finally broke away from everybody. It isn't likely to be a total break, but one never knows, and you never know who your friends are until you go.

My return trip to Merida took half as long as the first time because I didn't have any layovers. I flew directly to Cancun and hopped immediately on the local commuter plane to Merida. I shipped everything by boat, believe it or not, and probably won't see it for months, but by that time I should have a place and be able to move it all in nice and easy. The boat will dock in Merida's refuge from summer, Progresso, and from there it will take a couple of hours to move it anywhere in Yucatan. Who knows how my eclectic collection of contemporary and oriental furniture will look in the tropics but it should be a hot topic of conversation.

When I decided to sell out and move to Merida or thereabouts, I never realized how much time I would lose. I walked out on an entire life and can barely remember it now. Strange, but what was so important in Manhattan counts for nothing here—or almost nothing.

Nobody is rushing me or shoving me or asking me for money. I walk around like a native and talk like one and generally feel accepted as one. Something that never happened in Manhattan. Now I go shopping and enjoy it. Actually, I buy only a couple of things each day in order to pass my business around to the local merchants and get a feel for what is going on now. My way of being the local Welcome Wagon—in reverse.

You think a lot when you are by yourself, yet somehow the time glides by. It seems strange, but I have not been contacted by anyone I met during my previous trip. Maybe I'm not expected yet. Anyway, who knows what to expect? I have run into a few Americans who say they met me before, apparently at the Hotel Astaria's 'cocktail hour', but I don't remember them at all. When I finally get around to calling on Freddie, I think I will ask him if he knows Jorge. He has to, but he never mentioned it, so I'll play it cool.

When the time comes to do whatever it is I am to do, I want to look good. I hate to look like I'm studying to be a Maya, but I bought a few books and magazines at the local used-book store. There is not much in them, but I found some of the rituals I participated in during the last trip were not that old—certainly not ancient. I previously thought everyone in Yucatan kept the ancient ways and only adapted them in part or not at all, but it's okay. I feel like I know where they went off the path—but who am I to say? I also feel like I know more than the men who wrote the books and articles—but again, who am I to say?

There is nothing going on now. I'm just waiting—not sure for whom or what. Maybe no one will come. Maybe I will be left alone? Maybe this is real and my first trip was only an illusion, and nothing is going to happen now? But it can't be. I speak Mayan. There is no denying that!

A corny sense of humor is about all that remains of my old Yuppie self, but maybe I am imagining the transformation. No, the Americans are aware I have changed, too. They now think I am some sort of anthropologist who is able to bridge cultures and learned Mayan to get my Ph.D.. I let them think it, too. It's easier to just agree, otherwise you end up in an argument—and for what? I would like to drop my American identity, but with them around, I can't. Anyway, the hotel staff knows I am different now. They say I speak Mayan like an old lady. I have to laugh. I feel like an old lady!

When I eventually see Jorge, I am going to ask for help, but until then I don't need anyone to guide me around. I will bide my time and do whatever comes to hand. I know it won't be long before something happens.

When you see yourself in a new town, wearing different clothes, and acting like a native, you have to wonder why, but there is really no point guessing. I have the time to be myself and I am, but there is no reference point to the past. I just feel like I am me. I bear little resemblance now to the old me who worked for days on a single, narrow-minded project in the search for hidden assets or more dividends. Now I can't imagine doing such stupid work. It scares me that I could have lost my soul and nobody would have cared, but here I fit in already—after only a few weeks.

When you get down to business you have to have an office, but here I don't. I am in the business of dispensing medicine and don't even know what I am talking about. I just point at some plants and herbs and sort of motion to chop or crush or boil, show about how much, and the women take the stuff home. In the last two days, three of them returned to thank me for helping to heal them or their family. It is most gratifying, if mysterious.

When you think about it, what is healing? It's not you. It's probably not even the medicine. It is the person. You have to convince the person who is ill that they can heal themselves, and if they believe you, they will. If they don't have any faith in you, you can't help them much, and since I am odd or strange or whatever to these people, they think I have more knowledge or power than they do, so they believe me.

I know it sounds weird to be practicing medicine within a week of moving to a new city, even for an AMA-approved doctor, but nothing is strange here in Merida. I feel like I have always lived here and helped out the medicos and midwives—and the younger women act like it, too.

Do you ever think about when you get old and aren't able to work? I never did, but now I wonder what I would have done if I had stayed in New York? Within days, weeks, months of turning 50—you can expect that little rap on your office door and someone saying, 'Happy Birthday, you're retired'. Down here, nobody retires. It's great. Old men and women work, little kids do, too, but not as hard.

Which reminds me, I think the schools are what I really want to work on down here. They are not very good. The kids are intelligent and very talented, but there is no art material and good story books available for the poor. I am going to check it out before I do anything, but I think I can endow one of these schools for the cost of what I paid monthly on my old BMW—could probably build a school for the cost of a new one.

When you run over a bird, you think: Why did I hit that poor innocent bird? But if the bird crash-dives into your car, you wonder why it hit you. That is how I feel. I wonder why they all ran over me the first trip and now I'm not running into anybody.

I know, I know, the analogy stinks, but you get the message.

When you have time to think, you start to worry, so I started this journal to keep my mind busy and organize my time—since I have so much of it. I want to sit and develop a way to meditate wherein I can live in meditation and never actually come out of it, but I guess that is impossible. Anyway, I'm meditating a lot now. It makes the time go away fast.

Funny, but time is either for you or against you. Sometimes you feel like you can't catch up and then you feel like you haven't got enough to do to fill your time. Seldom a happy medium, but that is my goal. I am taking the middle path. No more fooling around on the edge.

When you feel yourself grow, you know you are, but sometimes you can't tell until you meet someone you talked with in the past and enjoyed their prattle but now they drive you up the wall with their inanities, yet the person has not changed at all. You have. That's sort of how I feel with my 'old' American friends. Truly, I can't stand them, but some of them are beginning to sound more sincere. Maybe there is hope, but I doubt it.

What do you do when everyone you know is no longer like you? You have to go. You have to do your own work in your own way. I'm enjoying myself now. At first it was confusing, but now it's okay.

I was going to say that sometimes I feel like I could stay here in Merida forever, then think that as soon as Jorge and the guys arrive I'll leave and go somewhere less congested. But where?

The first week I took the bus out to Progresso to check out why everyone here always talks about it, but found it depressing. Maybe because it was dark and rainy. I found nothing of beauty there, and the prices for an out-of-season resort in Mexico were a lot higher than I expected. I guess beauty is in the eye of the believer or is that deceiver? I kind of forget.

When you think back on your childhood, do you ever wonder why you picked your parents? I know why I did. I wanted them to be old and wise and have it all together, but not so old that I could not grow up with both of them. I think it was important that they were there during my teen years, but it was okay to go soon afterwards. I miss them, but I know they are okay. I know it. I can tell when they are around, too. I get real misty eyed and feel sort of warm. Everybody can tell if their deceased parents are around, just ask them. I'm not the only one who is crazy.

When you go to bed here you have to check to make sure your bed isn't full of bugs, but you don't have to check that much unless your room is over a hotel kitchen. I have a room over the hotel kitchen.

When you read what I write down in this journal, you have to wonder where my mind is, but I know. I can tell I'm bored, but not so much that I don't like what I'm doing. If you know what I mean.

If you are reading my journal surreptitiously and get to a page where I say I am having a hard time differentiating between today and tomorrow, you will know I am about out of here, but right now I am fine. I am not tired and I am not ill at ease or upset by anyone, which is more than I could say for any given day back on the job.

There I said it. The Job! I don't really miss it, but I wish I had something 'real' to do here. I figure after this length of time I should be able to see people and find spots where I can do something, but I never run into any shamen. I look, but I don't see anyone. Maybe if I go over to a restaurant by the University every day around lunch time I'll see someone who knows Freddie or Jorge—or somebody?

This town is not very big when you live here, but it has lots of little streets and little buses. You can ride around all day long and not be sure you saw the same people or the same shops. It's a little village within a big village, but you repeat it over and over again and it begins to blur. I still prefer the main boulevard for my evening stroll, but I don't linger around the Holiday Inn anymore.

It's too full of Americans. See! I am already anti-American, and I haven't been out of the country a month. What gives?

When you own property in Mexico, you have to have a co-signer or sponsor who is Mexican, but they don't seem to notice I am an American when I go and look at what is available. They rattle away like I am a Maya who has come into a fortune and they can't wait to take it away from me, the same as Realtors everywhere—except with a softer accent.

When I set up housekeeping, I intend to keep a kitchen closet full of paper products even if I can't use most of them. The toilets are so old and antiquated the soiled paper has to be placed in buckets which have to be cleaned constantly or they smell. It's the one thing I really dislike, but you always have to put up with something. It could be worse. I could be living out in a Maya village with no running water at all.

When this place goes to the dogs, it really does. Every night about seven o'clock, or just before dark, the dogs roam the streets—so happy to see one another. You can tell they are old friends, but they really leave a mess behind. But what's new about that? In New York, we had the same old stuff, and the dogs weren't nearly as happy.

When I find out what is happening, I'm going to fight for the new ways. I'm going to introduce women to the ways of equality, but not right now. They seem happier than the women back home—much happier, in fact. Maybe we missed something?

What is printed in the newspaper here is nothing compared to what you get back home, but you aren't depressed reading it, either. When you think of it, what are newspapers for today? They can't give you the scoop on anything because television reporters have swarmed all over every living survivor of anything and radio stations broadcast news all day and all night, seven days a week; so what do newspapers have to do but give you all the itty-bitty, nasty details you may have missed in the big glossy presentations? No wonder they don't sell. Down here the papers get straight to the point. They tell you where, when, and to whom something is happening—that's it. You can find out anything you need to know. That is important today, but the big picture is quite blurry.

When I go home, or rather, if I go home, I intend to find out what they are doing with my taxes. Down here you can see where every single dollar goes—good or bad. It's like a dry garden. You can easily see where the water runs. You watch droopy leaves perk up and can see where there is too much—big mud puddles form. Like I said, you know where your taxes go down here.

When I see all the citizens line up to pay their taxes, I sort of enjoy listening to them talk and carry on with each other. It takes hours for each person to matriculate through the lines waiting to get to the cashier. Before and after the cashier there is a slew of clerks who do nothing but stamp papers. But everyone seems to enjoy the process—even the guards who stand around trying to look very official. In New York there would be a murder if people had to wait half as long. Down here, when time hangs heavy on people's hands, like waiting in the tax collector's line, they resign themselves to it and enjoy each other. I think that is the civilized way to handle your civic duties. Don't you?

What about when you have to go to the country? Do you hire a cab or rent a car or take a bus? You wouldn't be caught dead on a bus, you say, well down here everybody rides the bus. They're fun. You get to see a lot and hear so much that you could write a book after each fare. No wonder they don't need to watch soap operas as much as they do at home.

Whatever you do, don't sit down without looking. The seats in the buses are usually a mess, and the birds drop doo-doo all over the benches in the plazas and the seats that escape that fate are usually covered with kids' handiwork, so you have to watch. The kids here are cute, even cuter than at home, if you must know, but you have to watch them, too. Whenever you look at them, they start playing peek-a-boo and other games like that and you don't know how to end it—and another thing, whatever you do, don't eat out. It is addictive.

I can't imagine cooking now, and I have been here how long? You think you will just eat a meal or two a day, but now I am eating five meals a day—well, almost five. I eat breakfast, mid-morning snack, lunch around one-thirty or two, snack at four-thirty or five, and dinner later. I have no way to cook in my room and I doubt if I would because it is so cheap to eat out, and they need the money. See, I'm not only lazy, but charitable, too.

What I need now is a full schedule, and I am going to have one. I know what to do. I don't know why I am here and if I am supposed to be somewhere else instead of Merida. I like to know what is happening, and right now I feel like everything is breaking out all around me and no one is telling me about it. Oh, well, time will tell. I have nothing better to do than wait.

The Time to Die
is Never The Time

What about all this seems weird?

Sometimes I think it is because I am here and everyone else is there, at other times I feel like it's just not quite right—but what is? Why can't I be like all the others who run around saying they don't understand or can't figure it out and let it go at that? Why do I try?

Maybe the rest of the world does know what is going on, but acts the way it does in order to confuse the uninitiated? Maybe *they do* know where they are going and just say they don't in order to keep you off the pace—to make you seek deeper? I wonder who does know?

Anyway, now I want to be more like other people, not so much like them as to be miserable or afraid—but not quite so odd. The fear people exhibit today demolishes the character of the land and can't be helping anyone. It has to harm the mass of our work and behavior. Do I really want to remain a part of them?

What if I just say I know what I am doing? What would happen? Would everyone run out and say, 'She knows it all?' I wonder. Maybe they would shun me or put me out to graze? Maybe I am supposed to know what is going on, but nobody else in my dimension is supposed to know that I know?

I get crazy wondering why nobody else cares; but if I am the only one who does, then why can't I do anything? There isn't any time for people to say they don't care, but everyone says it automatically. If you say the Earth is going to shatter, they say, 'I don't care'. If you say they need to improve or do something for the sake of humanity, they say, 'I don't care'. What is to become of us? When are we going to wake up—to care?

When you first see yourself in the mirror, do you automatically say, "I look great!" Not if you are sane. But if you aren't, then why wouldn't you say you look okay? Probable insanity.

I don't usually like to question myself, but lately that is about all I do. I can't find anyone to talk to about why I am here or why it was necessary to return to Merida, but I know I did what I was supposed to do. It gets a bit jumbled, but you know what I mean. Maybe if we just go and do a few things together, we can find out what the devil is going on.

My spiritual self and I are quite a pair! We hang out a lot and get to see a lot more than I ever saw by myself. I think of myself now as 'we' instead of 'I' and it slips out all the time. People ask me who I'm traveling with or who I am going to see or where are my friends, and I just smile and go on like I have a partner. Maybe I am cracking up, but if I am, I feel really good about it and I don't think you're supposed to—if you are cracking up.

Maybe this latest thing about the dead bodies being washed up on the shore after the last storm was a hoax. I never saw anything about it in the paper, but then I never heard about Fawley's death in the jungle near Uxmal, either, and they certainly never reported anyone devoured by a jaguar at Chichen Itza—maybe it has to do with promoting tourism.

When I met this fellow who told me about the massacre, or whatever it was, not far from Progresso, he said I was not to repeat it or he would be in big trouble. He acted scared, but told me and seven or eight other Americans about it. They all believed him, too. I wonder where he went? Nobody has seen him since.

Whatever they are doing, I wish I could handle the implication that I have something to do with it. It feels strange to walk around and know so much, but not know where they are or who is behind them. I want to know why Chip came to Merida—and arrived on the same plane as me. I want to know who killed Fawley and why, and why no one is talking about it—not even his 'friends'. I want to know if these latest victims were killed in the jungle, too, then put out to sea on a boat to rot. What about all this sounds fantastic? Every bit of it! Nothing makes any sense anymore and neither am I. I better go outside and walk around. Maybe I will run into somebody who knows something.

I gathered my bag and left the room with the intention of walking a mile or two. As I rounded the corner of the nearest square, I saw a few people backing away from a Mayan man staggering about waving his arms and shouting—probably obscenities at some unseen person or persons.

Oh, my god! He has a gun. Not here in Merida, too! This is why I left New York. I can't stand it. What is wrong with people? Don't they know they can kill somebody or don't they care?

The crowd scattered in every direction leaving the lone gunman to wave his weapon over his head and yell in slurred Spanish that he was going to kill the governor. In Mexico you are sure to get the death sentence when you talk that way, even if you are drunk; but maybe they will take his age into consideration.

Who can say why, but I kept on walking toward him with my hand outstretched and open, motioning for him to give me the gun, but he didn't see me at first. When his blinking, bleary eyes focused first upon my hand then my eyes, he wilted. All the belligerence slipped out of him and he wobbled toward me with tears running down his cheeks. He started mumbling a prayer—part rosary, part Mayan something. When he gave me the gun, he made the sign of the cross and tried to back off in a sort of crouched position which caused him to totter. I lunged at him in an attempt to keep him from falling, but succeeded only in terrifying him. He ran after the crowd.

With nothing to do but wait for the police, I decided to sit down and keep the gun until they got there, then thought better of it. The police will take *me* to jail, saying I was the one in the plaza threatening the Governor, so I left the gun on the bench. Most of the crowd regrouped around me, but no one tried to touch it. I decided to take off and ask questions later.

Whatever happened to good, old quiet Merida, capital of Yucatan? Maybe I am responsible for all this mayhem? I never heard there was much trouble in these parts after the uprisings years and years ago, but all of a sudden we have murder every other day.

The thing about death is it is not permanent at all but most of the population is convinced it is. I try to tell people all the time that death is just a phase of evolution, but you can't get it through to them. They want to believe this is what is and all there is, even though they hate this life and don't do well. Why wouldn't you do your very best if you really believed this was all there was and that it counted for everything?

I think I will go and sit in the park across the way, feign sleep and watch what happens. Maybe they will figure it out. Maybe the police will react with initiative and directness. Nahhhh!

Why don't people look you in the eye? As I sit here with my eyes closed and sort of stretched out full length, but still quite erect with my feet crossed at the ankles, they all look at me. Some even check me out super close. I wonder what they would do if I sort of opened one eye when they poke their nose in my face? No, better not scare them.

Everybody is shocked with all this stuff going on, but nothing is happening according to the police and the newspapers. Wonder what these people think? I doubt if they have a clue, but I do think I'm some sort of witch or sorcerer to them because so many cross themselves after they pass me on the street. I probably look different.

That's it! I never looked in the mirror today. I just stuck on a Panama hat and ran out the door—going more native than the natives. I didn't even put on lipstick. What would it take to find out if I look strange? I mean, why would I look strange? Maybe because I talk to myself. This whole thing is way out of control. I better get myself together or they will be sending me back to New York to Bellevue in a box—a padded one with a big lock.

When the police arrived, the crowd backed away from the gun and no one volunteered a word about what happened. One little boy looked in my direction, but if he was going to say anything, he could not speak. His mother yanked him by the arm and hustled him away. Otherwise, no one ventured to tell the police anything of value. Some said an unknown man, others said a drunk, had waved the gun around and a man or woman came and disarmed him. Finally the police put the gun in a plastic bag and waved their batons to disperse the crowd. No one seemed too miffed.

Whatever happened, I don't want to deal with it, but I better check out how I look, just in case I am now Maya in appearance, too, not just linguistically. It is fun to be so mutable, but one of these days one of the Americans is going to catch me being a Maya—then what will happen?

Wherever I go now, I feel Mayan. I don't know if I am or not or if I look the part, but I am treated with respect anyway. Whatever else goes on, I really don't care as long as I am not treated badly or lose my ability to be me. I couldn't care less if I have too dark a tan or not, but I like to look decent. I don't want to look like some hobo or worse.

"Senora! Senora! I saw you at the plaza. You took the gun away from that man. You were very brave."

The small boy who had been dragged out of the park by his mother now stood at my side tugging on my belt. He could not be older than seven or eight—just my size.

"Not brave—not really. I knew he was not going to hurt anyone, but he might have gotten thrown in jail and that would have hurt him. I did not want him to get in trouble. Where is your mother?"

"She went in the house. She is making soup for supper. She does not know I am here."

"You better run back in, then. I will see you around. Okay?"

"Oh, yes, Senora. I will watch for you."

"Okay. See you later."

Now that is my kind of man! Doesn't waste my time or his. Delivers the message and then goes. I wonder what he wants to be when he grows up?

I know! He is going to be a priest. Isn't that weird? I just look at a little kid, fantasize about him, then see pictures. He was dressed in black and had a crowd of kids around him, so I figured he was a priest—not a teacher. Wonder why? Oh, I see, he would not look that formal—teachers dress casually.

At the rate I'm picking up visions lately, I will never have to go to the movies again. I merely look intensely at someone, and depending on who they are and where I focus, I can pick up all kinds of information. I wonder if it is accurate, though? I should start asking people—as a sort of confirmation to see if I am clairvoyant. Stranger things than that are happening, so why not be clairvoyant, too?

Wonder what the people in the plaza think? I bet they are all talking about what I did. Why else would the little boy be so impressed? He looked at me like I was Wonder Woman or whoever the kids equate powerful women with today. Wonder who kids do equate powerful women with today? Whatever happened to the kind of woman who could be depended upon to wait out the war and keep the homefires burning while the man of the house butchered a whole nation of whomever? I wonder if women will ever want to be like that again. No, that is why there aren't any really big wars anymore. No one wants to raise a big family and have them marched off to war. I am sure Today's women won't tolerate wars.

Whenever you talk about death, it always gets to war sooner or later—why it is and what causes it and why not end all war, but when you go to war, you never think *you* are going to die. You always think *they* are going to die—or lose, or whatever, but the reality is that you both lose and you both die.

When you think back to how much you knew as a little kid, did you ever think you would be so dumb now? I didn't. I figured I would have everything memorized and know everybody and everything by the time I was an adult—certainly by the time I was fortysomething, but here I am and I know less than then.

Whatever became of innocence? I feel so guilty about everything. If someone says the world is a mess, I feel I made it that way or at least contributed my share. If someone says the planet is dying, I feel like I am killing it, too. I wonder why?

You are responsible!

This new me keeps me on my toes. I merely think about something, then loud and clear I hear this voice respond and tell it the way it is—no holds barred. I wonder why I never heard it before?

You were too busy. You had too much to do. You could not find time to meditate. You had a very 'important' job, and you gave it your life. You had a million excuses for staying out of reach, but now we are all in this together.

"Yep."

Better watch. I talk out loud so much anymore that pretty soon I will be carrying on whole conversations with me alone, and they will be carting me away to wherever they take crazy ladies in Mexico. I wonder where they do put the delusional and insane here?

Immediately I caught a flash of me hovering above and looking down at my body. I was wearing a white outfit and a big brimmed hat. A serape covered my top and part of my flowing pants. Not exactly the traditional Mayan dress nor the traditional Panama hat, but someone dressed to play a Maya in the movies. Yeah, that's it and that is what I asked for. Didn't I?

Whatever the day, this week is beginning to be a bore, but I can't complain. It is nice to be lazy and let your mind play games, but I have to get used to it. I never had this kind of time at home. I ran here, there, and everywhere and let every pest I knew take up hours of my time if I was home alone. I was often annoyed, but I always thought I was helping them out—meanwhile they were eating up my life.

Regardless of what I do down here, it has to be easier than what I did before, and now that I know I am going to be here for a while, I might as well get used to sitting longer and longer and talking less and less. It is the wisest thing to do. It is the Maya way.

The End of This World

There is nothing I enjoy more than sitting and watching others work, but it is not allowed. You have to work or you will end up a bum. That is the message I heard all my life, and now I know it is true. You have to work in order to understand why others do. You can sit and stare into space all your life and someone will take care of you; but why merely exist?

When you look at all the things you can do in one lifetime, you figure you would need several to do it all, and you do, so you have more than one 'life' running at the same time—if you are ambitious. I just got through the hardest part of one life and now I am wading around in the shallow end of my next life here on Earth waiting for an invitation to dive into the depths, but *I know* it is all one life.

If you ever found yourself wondering and wandering around and around, unable to figure out what you were doing, you were just sitting in several sessions of one life while another one took off. You can't take off on several levels at the same time, but you can end several at once. I know I did.

I sat in New York and ended several episodes of the 'past' as I watched that life on Earth disappear. I let them all go and now am sitting here in Merida letting go of the life I once knew in New York. It's easy. Start flying and let it all drop! But to pick up the next life takes practice and I have never been good at picking up threads, but I drop them very well. I have done that many times, but now it is time to start to weave.

When we were in New York, I thought I was in control of my life and had it made but truly had no clue about how many lives I was living and that all I had to do was what I came to do—but now I do. How did I gain so much knowledge? I didn't. It was in me all the time.

The time you have now is not very much different from time in the real-est essence of the word, but we all see it differently. You are not able to do things without finally realizing you do what YOU want to do and not what others say you should do. In fact, you get mad if you have to do what another says you have to do and You do not want to do it. Then why do we act like we are living our lives for someone else? I never thought much about it then. I would blame others when I didn't do what I wanted to do, but now I know I hated to admit I was different from others and did not want to do what they did, instead, like so many others, I took the coward's way out and blamed Mom, Dad, or some other boss.

When you act the role of the coward, you begin to hate yourself so much you have to be very brave in order to reverse the flow. I never was much of a coward, so I did not have to be courageous, but sometimes I think I was brave.

For instance, I never wanted a career in business, but I went after it anyway. Why? How else could I get all the stuff I wanted from life? I had to work. No one else was going to give me things that cost more than I needed to pay—and I figured that out right. If you ask others to give you what you want, you will owe them so much you cannot repay and end up resenting them, and the resentment kills that relationship, ad infinitum. But if you do your own work, you can have it all or you can reduce your wants like I did.

Now I am here in Merida and have this thing going on, but I don't exactly know what it is. I sort of move around and look at people and pay attention to some and not at all to others. If I look at one person intently, I can 'see' right through them. If I ignore them, I don't notice a thing. It's like they are not there. If you think it is easy to ignore people, you should try it on someone who bothers you and see for yourself. It is not easy. You really have to work at it.

When I work now, I do it differently than when I was on Wall Street. Now I sit and stare at the air and it appears or it does not. I see things or I hear the answers, but you know it is hard work if you ever tried it yourself. It is much harder than shuffling papers and chatting on the phone. You really have to concentrate!

When you decide to work on your own life, determine first if you are serious or not. You do not have to decide at all if you are prone to laziness or normally postpone all your decisions, but when your life ends you will have to come back again. What a waste of time!

When I was young and foolish, I tried to get into the mind of someone and see what he was doing or why he did something, but I never found out. Why? Who knows why anyone does anything? Only God. Of all the entities in the heavens, no one knows the heart of the fool—only God and the fool. But if you waste time on others and don't figure out your own life, then you're a fool and only God knows why.

What about this latest trigger-happy guy who caused the deaths of several people he probably didn't know? Why would he do that? He cannot be sane, but is he insane? I was never interested in such men, but when women began to kill indiscriminately, too, I became interested. Why? I guess I always figured women were too wise to commit such brutal acts. Apparently I was wrong or women are changing. Which?

Which is not why, but it ends up just as dead. You cannot figure out why people work their lives the way they do, and you cannot rely on why they say they do, either. If you listen, they either tell you some silly story about blame and guilt from the family of their youth or construct some grand image of what they intend to make of themselves in the future. You cannot put any stock in either illusion. You have to watch to see what they produce. If their work is stupid or foolish you know who they are, but if they do something brilliant, you might still be watching a fool at work, so it is wise not to watch others work. You learn nothing about them and their work is never yours.

Now is when you have to concentrate and start doing your own inner work or you will lose in the end. I found out the easy way, but you may not. If you cannot figure out why you are here and what you came to do, you have a long way to go before you can die, but then again, you may be doing your work—sub-consciously.

When I went to school, I took courses that passed themselves. I never studied too, too hard but did read all my books and attend every lecture. No one ever pushed me. I did a lot of extra credit work, but never burned the 'midnight oil' like the girls who crammed or waited to fail. I wonder how they are now? Probably not too good. But then again, it is their life and their choice. I cannot compare them to me or me to anyone else. Can you?

What about the guy who crept up on me in the jungle and the jaguar ate him? Isn't that weird? You think you are about to die and suddenly you are alive—and the one who threatened you is dead and you never lifted a finger. I wonder why?

Maybe I was supposed to be the victor? Maybe it was preordained that I would be there in the jungle and the jaguar would surrender its power and let me take over? Maybe I was the jaguar and it all happened in my mind? I don't know—and no one else is talking about it, either.

When you come to a strange land, you think they are strange, but when strangers visit you in your land, you think they are strange. Strange isn't it? We are so egotistical or ego-bound we cannot see we are all alien and strangers in our own land. What else could explain it?

Wherever I go now the children ask me to share something with them, but I seldom have anything to hand out. I want to give them chewing gum or candy, but never have any. I forget to buy it. I want to give them a treat, but have none. They all laugh and shout and give up on me after I show them I have nothing in my pockets, but each day it is the same routine.

When I get home, wherever that is, I am going to sit down every night and listen to the birds go to bed—that seems the best way to unwind. I am not going to drink or eat or talk, just listen to them. I bet the birds know everything. I bet all the birds and beasts know what is really going on now. Did you ever see a bird get lost? No. They figure out where they are going first. We are the only ones who do not. What is so beguiling about the birds compared to the beasts? Most animals eat birds if given the chance, and birds eat beasts but most don't, yet we tend to think of birds as being less threatening than animals. Ever wonder why?

Well, so much for philosophy. I have to go to town and see why the old women are not making room for me. They ignore me or say very little, and when I get too close they back away from me. Only the men and children observe me and let me approach them on the street. Wonder why?

There I go again. When will I ever learn to stop asking why?

Whatever you do, do it, or you enter limbo. If you sit and never move, the limbs go—limbo. You are not able to move if you do not know anything or do not want to go. I want to move now. I want to get going on something, but what is not known.

When I get lost in thought I often find myself in the same scene, but lately the scene is different from any I have ever seen before. The people all look like people but are less business-like in their dress and have fewer possessions. I seldom see cars and toys but do see a lot of people laughing and walking and talking. I wonder where I am then?

The future? It seems strange, but that is what I heard. I wonder when? Year 2000 isn't right, I can tell, but when is the *new age?* I want to be around then, but I can't tell if it is soon or late. I want to be sure and be there—but maybe I am scheduled to be gone by then. What could take so long anyway? Maybe we are not as advanced as we think we are. We have to adjust our minds to new things and it takes all of us thinking about it together to do it, but the world is ending and a new one is waiting to begin—of that I am sure.

Since no one wants to be responsible for drawing up the plans, it still looks a lot like this one—only no one is in charge. I hope it works, but usually you need an organizer to get you started. But on the other hand, organization is a product of this world and maybe it will not be needed anymore. Wonder if we can get along without a government? No, I don't think we can, either. I think we need to keep the workable systems and evolve into better individual lives. But how to let go of the old and let the new take root?

What if I just sit here in Mexico and dream of a new life? Would it happen? I think so. I am going to dream now and figure out what is going on down here with all these murders and people who don't seem to know I am back and find out why I am here.

Where can I go that will be safe enough to meditate and dream for days if necessary? Maybe my hotel room? No, the maids run in and out all day. I better rent something somewhere else, but there aren't many places for rent in

Merida that would provide me with the security and freedom from prying minds that I will need. I better move around the countryside and find a nice out-of-the-way place where I can fool people into believing I am not there when I am, to make sure no one bothers me.

What about Uxmal? I love it there. It is my place and time. I feel so different there, but peace is not what I crave now. I need privacy. Where can I find it?

Cancun! Why not? Everyone there is so Americanized I can rent a condo for a month and never have a maid or anyone come near the place. No one will care if I am there or not and no one there would ever think to include me in anything. Americans are extremely anti-social anymore—especially when they aren't on their own turf. Yes, Cancun is where it's at!! I can hide and never be touched. I'll pay my hotel bill here in advance like always so no one will know I am gone until I am gone. When I pay, I will mention I might go ruin hopping in Belize or Guatemala, that should throw anyone off my track if they come looking for me. I need time alone and the means to see what is happening in Europe and America.

What a way to get away! I will grab a couple pairs of shorts and tees and forget everything else until I get there. I can get a car from the rental agency across town, jump in, and drive toward Uxmal then double back and go to Cancun and rent a condo when I get there.

What you don't think of when you let your mind sit. You can discover who you are and where you should go, but your mind does get upset. My mind is rebelling now about leaving town and not telling anyone. I can feel the tension. But so what? I need time and my mind can take its time to adjust to the new order. I won't cause it even more confusion by changing my decision again.

What to do when you get so confused you do nothing? Do something—anything! Which is what I am doing now. I will drive and let the car take me wherever. If I end up somewhere different than Cancun, so what? No one is expecting me anywhere. That is freedom! You have to be free of all ties before you can know who you really are, but few want to be truly free. I wonder why?

Sorry, I can't stop asking why. Well, this is the time to be on my way—one place or another. I am beginning to feel restless and boredom does not become me. It won't be around me ever again, but the creeping willies will if I don't move soon. I feel them return every now and again. They are getting colder and damper, but not so fierce as I had expected, which is good since, like I said before, I'm not very courageous.

Let's get going! I can see this world is changing and I'm not. After today I better know what is happening or crawl back into the past and regroup again. Even if I can't figure out why I am here and what is happening, I still have to work out this life and it won't be easy if I never seek. Better learn some new tricks and jargon while I work until there is nothing left undone or I will have checked out of my old life for no good reason.

Whatever I do now has to be right. I did not think before. I let my higher self do all the work. If I trust in me—and I do, I can't be wrong.

Is Anybody Listening?

The time you are going through life is not now or then but the time you are—and the only time you have to either work or get stuck in time. You have to move! You cannot sit and stare and expect life to be there. You are, but life is when you are.

Why did I sit around and wait for Freddie or Jorge to appear? Conditioning! It's the way women are built today. We sit and wait for men to appear and then get mad at them for not being there. What a waste! I wonder if I will ever be free of it?

When I was a child and had no friend nearby, I played by myself, but my sister and brother would not. They either played with someone or played not at all. I wondered about it then, but I see I am like them now. I don't have the fun I want but do it to myself. That is why I am taking off by myself to see what happens. I am sure I can handle anything, but I better be a bit more prepared than I was the first time.

"Let's see. What do I need?"

Good, I'm talking out loud, which means I am rolling again. I never talk to myself when I am in a muddle over anything—just when I get it together. If it sounds relatively reasonable, I confirm my ideas, and do whatever.

"What should I wear?"

That is always my first question. Conditioning. What if I am dressed inappropriately? No, that would not be nice. The Maya are a formal race and do not look with pleasure at some of the outfits American women wear in public places, so I will not offend them. I want to blend in. Besides, I look better with more clothes on than off these days. When you are a sweet young thing you can get away with skimping on clothes, but sagging thighs and bulgy knees are not pleasing to the eye—at least not mine looking at me.

"What day should I go?"

No problem. I will go now. I'll pack up this stuff, stick it in a bag, and go and see if the rental agency has anything inconspicuous. If I wait another day, I might be snagged by someone or something that will prevent me from finding out everything I think I need to know now.

"Whatever happened to my bag?"

It was here, but now it isn't. What if someone took it? No, I am not going to get paranoiac again. I will go next door and buy another one on my way back from renting the car.

"Well, it looks like everything is okay."

Yes, I can move.

What if I drive over to Cancun and sit around all week in the sun and nothing happens? No, never! I find trouble in the middle of a sunny day. And in Cancun? Definitely, there is trouble there.

"What if I can't figure out what is going on?"

So what? You can do it there cheaper and easier than here if you cash out your room now.

"No, not a good idea."

Okay, here is what we will do. We will drive over to Cancun and sit all week in the sun on the patio of some secluded condo near the beach and eat in every day. No one will know we are there, and if someone does find us, then *I* will know they are trouble, too.

*   *   *   *   *   *

When I drive, I usually sit and stare at the trees ahead of me, but here all the trees are very short, almost like hedges edging the highways. You can see for miles over the jungle, but you can't see any activity—except occasional buzzards and small birds and, of course, the bees. Mayan bees have imbued their culture—probably the basis for its belief in hard work. They all work hard. No one stands around very long wherever they are, and they seem to love construction work best. I wonder if that is why they built so many pyramids? It was a lot of fun then—or more likely, they like construction work now because they have done it so many times before.

"What about this place is so familiar?"

Jorge and I drove through it, but we never went near Cancun—or so I thought. Maybe we did and I just didn't know it then. After all, how many places can you go in Yucatan? Well, technically Cancun isn't in Yucatan—but so what? It seems like it.

"What would force people to chase after *me?*"

Why would anyone be interested in a middle-aged, showing-the-signs-of-wear, woman from America—especially when she minds her own business?

"That's it!"

I *am* minding my own business! That is what Jorge was trying to tell me. I am here because I left things undone and now they are ready to be finished. I can do it, but someone or someones does not want me back. Maybe they are even Maya?

Wonder if I can zoom in on what is happening—once I settle down and meditate for maybe five or six hours? Probably not. But what if I keep at it until I am in constant meditation? I will be able to see what the universe has in store for me—if not everyone, then.

"Wonder why I am so confident of that?"

Yeah, I know. I have never meditated for even a day—let alone a week. But why not? I can. I just have to let the mind know everything is going to be okay; I am in no danger; and Cancun is the best place for us to be.

"What if I just sit and stare at the sea?"

No, that is not a great idea. People are always walking up and down the beach and would notice me within minutes and see me as a tourist in need of trinkets and blankets. No, I better confine myself to a house—hopefully, with a walled-in patio and maybe even a pool. No, a pool would cost too much. I can take a dip in the ocean before dark if I get too hot.

Wow! I have it all figured out and don't even know where I am going to sleep tonight. Sounds sane though. Doesn't it? And, I can always drive down the coast if nothing surfaces in Cancun. No, not a good idea. Lots of people would comment on a single woman living in a house far from others. Better not risk it.

* * * * * *

Funny how easy it was to get this place. Almost heaven sent—or was it? No, I am not going to look at anything like that again. What is to be gained? I scare myself—which is about as stupid as you can get. Why scare yourself when there are so many others who want to do it for you?

"What would it take to hide here for a week?"

The cold floors are great! The terra cotta tile won't have to be cleaned at all, so I don't need maid service. I can make up the bed—or not. Who will know? Oh yes, I will.

It's such a beautiful place—so Spanishy. It's hard to believe I got it so cheap. Just tell God what you need, how much you can pay and when you need it, and it's yours! It works every time! Since I never had any problems with it working before, why would it backfire this time?

"That's more like it."

Yes, we are going to like it here. I have to get some food and drinks and we are all set. I don't need anything else because the owner, whoever she is, thought out every detail without being pretentious. I really like it, but then I am a Mexican art freak.

"Wonder if anyone is living next door?"

I better watch myself. I'm talking out loud almost constantly now.

"So what? Who says you are crazy if you talk out loud instead of silently worrying like crazy? I don't."

Okay.

"Yes, I can do whatever I want. I'm Lady of the castle keep, and I can do whatever I want. Besides, who will hear me?"

Whatever happened to houses with bathrooms next to the living room? I hate running upstairs and down the hall just to go to the john.

"Oh, here's the bathroom. I didn't look far enough. Now I have everything!"

Almost. There is not another human being to talk to who would not want to make money off of you. So, let's just talk to ourselves.

"I wonder if the satellite dish on the roof is turned on?"

Don't even bother to find out.

"You're right. No sense tuning into a civilization that's decaying as you watch when you can watch a new one emerge. I'll eat out if I get too house-bound for comfort. In fact, I think I'll go out now. I won't go far and won't be long."

No, you don't. You just got here and there is nothing you need to go out for. Just settle down. You can handle isolation. It's normal. It is living in the midst of hoards of people that is abnormal.

"Yes, you are right. Got to settle down. This is the life and I am here for a reason and the reason may even save my present life."

Where did that come from? I'm not in danger—at least not mortal danger, I'm sure. But maybe I am in danger? Uh, uh, no worrying now. Everything is great. The house is beautiful, the day is divine, and the sun is beginning to peep into the patio where the hammock beckons.

This is the greatest feeling! Just lying here with the breeze stirring the palms occasionally. You can hear people talking far away but can't make out what they are saying.

Relax! You feel safe. No one knows you are here, but you know they are there and can even spy on them.

"Ridiculous! Why spy?"

I'm beginning to really babble a lot. I guess it will take a bit of getting used to sitting around all day doing nothing, but I think I can do it—maybe even like it. Wonder what the others think? I never told anyone I was leaving.

"Who is there to care? Only a bunch of weenies who hang around waiting for Happy Hour in the hotel lobby. They won't realize I am gone until I'm back. Their alcoholic haze is so dense they wouldn't know if their paycheck bounced."

Snide and ugly. That is no way to talk. If we talk, we talk nice.

"Okay. You're right. We'll talk philosophy. Okay?" Right. Like I'm some kind of Jean-Paul Sartre. "Maybe I am. I never tried. But why not? Who was he—or any other philosopher?"

Just a guy with an opinion on the way the universe operates. He never said it was right or wrong, but loved to argue, and it made a good case for keeping the populace down while he meddled or muddled in the depths of despair and disillusionment.

"I'm not cut out for gloom and doom, but I bet I can argue a good case for self pity—which is about the same thing. What happens when you get into yourself?"

You disappear. You do not actually disappear, per se, but you disappear from the reality of being you. You do not feel you are, so you are not. It is an easy concept since you only have to disappear, thus have no opinion.

"Great, I sound French already! But I wonder if I will ever write that book I keep telling myself to write? Probably not, but it makes for great daydreams. I can see it all now: local woman wins Pulitzer Prize for Literature while loafing in Cancun."

No, local woman takes all the prizes with her award-winning novel, The Grapes of Life.

"No, that is entirely too trite. I better write—rather talk, about something I know—Me. No, I don't want to hear another word about Me. I have Me'd me to death. I can think of a million other things I would rather talk about today. But it always comes back to Me. I can't avoid it. I am the world! I am not here because God sent me or because I want to do something for others. I came here to live and do things for ME. I am who counts to Me. Everyone else comes in second—or should, but sometimes I do leave my senses and put someone else before me—and regret it every time. Wonder if it is suppertime yet?

No! You are not hungry. You have all the fresh fruit you can eat sitting on the kitchen table and cold drinks in the refrigerator and lots of stuff in the cupboard. You do not need to eat—not right now, anyway.

"Wonder if it is going to be dark soon or should I just lay here and sleep? What a stupid remark, and you think I can philosophize?"

Yes, and do very well.

"Now, if I were the only one in the world, who would make me unhappy? Me. I don't need anyone—ever—to make me unhappy as long as I have Me along. I do it to me, just like everyone else."

Wonder what it is about Cancun that makes people so happy? Maybe it is just being in a foreign country while being totally American or whatever? I bet tourists think they are having great adventures when they come down here, yet it is as tame as noodle soup—no, tamer.

"Why did I come here to be alone? I have time to go anywhere in the world, yet I came to Cancun. Wonder why?"

You have to meet someone. You have to be here when he comes to see you.

"What? Who said that?'

I did. I know exactly what is happening. I am here inside and know exactly why you are and how you are and I still think you can make a difference. I love it here, but at times it is tedious. You never let me talk.

"Who are you?"

I AM, one of your Guides, but the one most responsible for You in this life. I traveled to Earth with you in order to help you leave Earth at the end of this life and not have to repeat the episode. I do not want to have to guide you again, so shape up and get into the flow of what is going on down here so we can end all this and be done with the world. You should be ready to ascend.

"Not too soon, I hope."

Of course, it will be soon.

"Oh, my god. You have brought me to Cancun to die!"

Now that is truly stupid, and you have said some really dumb things this life about you. I mean, there is not much time for this world and you will not be here when it ends if you get your act together now. You can live to be an old lady and not have to worry about the world ending, but if you return again, it would place you in mortal jeopardy.

"Why?"

You have to know by now that Earth is not breathing. You cannot possibly believe a society that rips out trees and plants houses and never replaces anything it takes would actually wise up and begin to conserve in order to save Earth and the human race. You are not dumb, even if you do talk too much.

"Talk too much? I haven't said anything for days. I mean not anything beyond the normal small talk that lubricates the wheels of conversation and business."

You all talk too much. No one listens—especially you! That is why I made you come here.

"You made me?"

Yes, you are now about to listen to the Higher Guides talk, but you are still in control.

WE ARE NOT HERE IN A COMMITTEE FOR NOTHING. WE ARE HERE TO HELP YOU BY BANDING OUR ENERGIES TOGETHER IN AN

ATTEMPT TO GET YOU TO CHANGE THINGS. WE WANT TO CLEAR UP THIS MESS NOW AND GET AS MANY PEOPLE AS WE CAN TO EXIT EARTH FOREVER WHEN THEY LEAVE EARTH THIS TIME. WE DO NOT WANT TO BE HERE WHEN THE EARTH SPINS OFF ITS AXIS OR COL-LIDES WITH SOMETHING BECAUSE IT CANNOT MAINTAIN ITS BAL-ANCE DUE TO ALL THE PILLAGING OF ITS RESOURCES.

"I'm listening now. I can hear you. Were you always so close?"

ALWAYS, BUT YOU WERE NOT OPEN TO US. WE HAVE A FEW THINGS TO DO, BUT WE WILL BE BACK LATER TO TALK. KEEP THE CHANNEL OPEN—AND NO TELEVISION. IT POLLUTES THE ATMOS-PHERE. RADIO IS BAD ENOUGH, BUT TELEVISION IS SO NEGATIVE WE CANNOT ENTER SOME HOMES—LET ALONE GET THROUGH TO THE CHILDREN LIKE WE ONCE COULD. WE CANNOT DO MUCH IF NO ONE LISTENS.

"So, you have been calling, and nobody was home!"

THAT ABOUT SUMS IT ALL UP.

There is Nothing
in the World

When you first see something, you think. You see it, but you think and then decide to do what you think. There is nothing in the world that will make you accept anything. You have to take what your mind can accept and tells you is okay to do or you do not do anything.

That is how I first realized my life was changing. I never saw it coming or thought about it, but there it was. I was sitting on the divan and a thought chased another one out of my mind and suddenly I saw myself in the middle of a jungle.

I was an old lady—not very good looking, but sort of handsome in an elderly kind of way. My hands were young, though. I had dark brown eyes set deep under a forehead not any different from my own now, except there were no horizontal lines and vertical furrows. I looked careful and wise and a trifle pleased as I listened to the proceedings of a meeting. I was not doing anything just sitting in the middle of a group. I did not speak—at least not much, but was definitely deferred to—though not the center of conversation. Nothing was required of me. I just sat there.

If you look at yourself in the mirror, do you ever see You? I don't think so. I think others might, but I don't think you do. I was sitting here looking at myself as an old lady and realized it was not me as an old lady in this life. How could it be? I am not Maya and there were a lot of Maya around me in the vision.

When you sit and stare at the place where you once lived or you visit a former playmate, do you ever see yourself as you were then? Maybe, but probably not. You could have been their friend or lived there, but it is a lot of hard work to remember.

Try this instead: Put your mind on my mind and let me transfuse this to you. While I talk, you think. I will listen to what you think, then you say what you think I heard. Okay? It is sort of complicated to explain, but it is what we do all the time. I tell you what I think, then you think about it and repeat it back to me, but you may not be aware of doing it now.

What I am about to say is shocking me, but you will be able to handle it. I think it is because I take the initial infusion and it lessens the impact on you. If you want to be shocked, you have to do the meditating and thinking first and transmit it to me, but let us continue as is.

I went into a room and a man was sitting there with a lot of feathers stuck in a leather bag. He fanned the fire with one feather after another while I idly watched. If he got too close to the fire, the smell of the singed feather was acrid and unpleasant and I warned him to back off, but he did not stop waving it back and forth. As he crouched beside me, he passed the feather over the fire a couple of times and then rocked back and forth on his heels and sang softly.

There is one thing you need to know in this life now. You have to sing to yourself. You cannot let the world get so close that the vibrations within you become a jumble. If you do, you get really nervous. I am only reminding you. You know it already, but we tend to forget our wisdom as we age.

He began to sway and I watched him grow dazed and confused, but not crazy in any way. I sat there and directed his swaying with the motion of my right index finger. If he moved too far in one direction, I seemed able to correct it and make him move in the other direction. It looked like I was conducting a band—a one-man band, but nevertheless a band.

When I stopped directing, he faded. He disappeared and never came back. I don't know what he did, but something strange happened. Feathers remained at the scene!! He took his bag and things but left the feathers behind. I hastily picked them up and shoved them into the pot sitting beside me in the center of the room.

Whatever move I made, I was sure of it. I did not seem to be concerned about a thing. I felt great! I knew exactly what to do, but no one else did. I was in charge!

Funny, in real life I hate being in charge. I hate being caught in the middle of a group. I try to keep from becoming too involved or being seen as too demonstrative or too into spiritual happenings, but there I was in the middle of a big group—in charge, and it felt good. I liked it and was totally respected!

I wonder why I hate to be respected? I mean, I wonder why I hate to be singled out for honors? I really do. I never go to ceremonies—like graduating from college or acceptance into Honor Societies or whatever. I don't show up due to some 'unforeseen event'.

You have to enjoy life, but this one has not made me happy. I liked making money, but it didn't help. It was just a pastime. I looked at what they had for sale on the stock market, then waited for someone to want it and someone always does. How successful can you be if you don't have to have any talent? And how smart do you have to be if you never risk your own money?

Anyway, when I saw what was going on in the meeting room, I thought at first it was now and I was sitting in this room daydreaming, but the scene wavered and I saw a clock on the wall. It was different. It was not at all like what we use now. It had a lot of numbers and things like messages on its face but projected the precise degree of the second—not just a dial with the time displayed in approximate segments.

When I looked back at the clock later, the time had advanced only a fraction of a second. It went so slow it could not have been anymore than a speck in the eye. You could not blink that fast, yet could see it move.

Whatever I do, I think of all the things I still have to do. I have always worried over what has to be done next; but when I do have time, I usually waste it. Wonder why?

There is a kind of timer in the corner of this vision. If I look at it, I cannot do anything. I lose perspective. I forget everything, but I can see the time moving. My lesson? I have to leave time. I have to let it be.

When you concentrate on time, you cannot live. You may look like you are moving somewhere, but your mind is always on the time. Let time go!! Don't worry, you won't be late. Just say: 'I need to be wherever by whatever time', and there you are—on time. You don't have to think about it again. It just happens.

Think of all the times you were late. You were there on time, but everyone else wanted you there earlier. Actually, you did not want to go. I was never late for anything I really wanted to enjoy completely. In fact, I am always early. I waste time in order to go and sit and be totally ready for whatever, and in that way I do not have to transcend anything to accomplish the deed. I am there and everyone enters my auric field—not the reverse. I experience no stress that way.

When you are not able to 'see', you think you could do much better than now if you knew what was coming your way, but if you could you would not do anything. You would wait for it to happen or worry about it, but either way, you would loaf and do nothing. So why know? You still have to work at life and *know* you deserve it before you can accomplish much. For example, some of my worst moments in this life were when I decided I had it made.

What is there about this room that makes me digress so much?

I keep talking to myself about Me, but it does not change You and it would if I said you were the one I was talking about. It would! You would listen if it was about you.

When I think about all the things I know, I know I know almost nothing, but I reassure myself that this is the greatest life and I deserve it. Why? I know I am not doing enough. I know I am not working, so I tell myself how good I am.

What if you and I decided to go into business together? Would you? No, you would sink your funds into your business and I would do the same, but we would not be doing the same thing. I would be trying to do my thing while you would be doing yours, but we could not do the same thing at the same time.

What if I asked you to be my manager? Would you? No, you would be your own manager and think about my stuff after yours was all taken care of. You would! No one cares about someone else's life. It is only human to care about yourself only.

Your life is confusing to me, but you see through it easily now. I wonder why, but you don't. I think if you had to sit here and look at the space behind your forehead for hours you would see things, too, but you don't like to meditate. You keep telling me that like you think I do.

Work is work—and meditation is my work. I think a lot now, but it is not as hard as not thinking. You get so tired of chasing out the blues and the blahs, which are not half as bad as the demons of the mind you have to chase away after the first day or two—or go crawling back to reality.

When you have the time I want you to try this, but don't do it until you have enough time—which is never, you say. Try to think of nothing. Just try it. You can't. You have to think. You have to process energy and do the work. You can't stop thinking.

What if I eased into your mind and erased all your work? Can't be done! I can't enter you in any way, shape, or form. You have to change. You do your own changing, but most likely blame everyone else.

What if I lean on you and depend on you? You would grow to hate me. I know. I would, too, but you have to support me. Right? No, you do not, but your mind accepted the burden. I think you have it now. You will know if you accepted all this when your mind says it is okay, but if I try to even infringe one inch into your reasoning, you will drop me so fast I will not be able to see it coming.

What if I talk about this vision I had? Would it make sense to you? Not likely, since you did not share it with me. How can we share if you want one thing and I want something else?

We cannot merge or marry or join a club or form a partnership and see anything the same; so why do I think you will know? You will. I will accept it as the truth and go forward and you will see it works for you.

Now that I'm all set, I'll let you square away the things you have to do, but don't waste time. I have to get back.

Your life is like mine but totally different and a lot harder. I know. I see you the same way, so we have a common background. Just listen to me talk and I will nod if you should answer. I don't want you to get bored.

What if I sing and talk at the same time? You don't get it? Okay, I will write and you read, then if I get too boring you can drop it or turn the page to find something more interesting.

I know when you read this you will believe you are in a different time than when I wrote it, but you will be in the same one as I am in right now.

That really stopped you cold. Now that I have your total attention, I want to write. I want to talk to you about time. I want to let you see me, but I cannot. I do not have a mind or body. I am in spirit only. You are not exactly in spirit, but you are. You will find you can spin a yarn like this one, too, but why bother. It takes time, and you are too busy.

When you get busy, you do not see yourself—you forget yourself, which serves time best. You will be okay. I will not take much longer. I can tell the entire story in a sentence. Yes, I can, but it would not satisfy your mind. You have been following along forever—not able to figure out why She is not in the jungle and why She isn't able to end this seminar. You haven't figured out the plot yet and want to know how it all turns out before you let it all flow from you and go.

What plot? You watched a frantic woman in New York move to the quietude of Merida in the Yucatan with no agenda and then she went to Cancun to sort out her life. See! It's easy and straight forward. You think up all the complications, I don't.

What if you stop reading now and sit there with your eyes closed? Can you see me? I think you can. Now I know you can, but what you see is not what is me. I am a woman sitting on a green sofa with a glass of iced tea and a few things spread out around me. I am holding a feather and a stone etched with a picture of a funny little bird and my bare feet are crossed under me.

There, now I think you can see me better, but if I told you what color my hair was or is, you would begin to erase your picture and recreate me. I want you to keep me just like you have me pictured now. Do not change. See? You can't do it!. You had to change. You cannot stay the same, but you keep saying you do not want to change. Why not stop the conflict? I can. Yes, I can stop conflict within myself, but not within you.

What do you think of when you sleep? I bet you don't sleep. I bet you go from mind to mind looking for anything amiss. If one of your lives is not moving in the right direction, you merge with it and do its work. You don't worry about being in someone else because you know you are many people within one now.

When you think of me, do you see me? No, but you think you do. If you ever conjure up an image of me, then expect me to call. I will. I will either phone or be there in person, but you did it. I merely answered your call.

Why not sit and just think? Why bother to conjure anything? You do not need anyone. You do not even like most people, but you think you have to do something all the time with others—and you are right. That is why you came to Earth!

What if I slip out of the way now and you visualize or conjure up someone? Can you do that? Listen. Do you hear anything? You will. You will know if you accomplished this simple task or not and don't be too pleased with yourself when it happens. It's no big deal! You have always known how to do it, but simply forgot.

What you know now is not nearly as necessary to survive as it is to succeed. You have to succeed or be returned to Earth. You know your success is not mine, but you will judge me based on yours anyway. I cannot get through to you, but you will pick me apart and criticize me for doing what you cannot do—that way you do not think you have to do it, but you are wrong. I can see through that ploy and so can everyone else, so don't cut down anyone when you are a mess yourself.

What if you lay down on the couch beside me? Would you get aroused? I never think like that, but I picked up right away on what one reader had in mind today. What do you think you are doing now? Do you think others cannot tell what you are thinking? Don't be silly.

You know what you mean, but others will take it and misconstrue it if it's in their own best interests to do so. If you're popular and easy to know, most will not believe you. But if you are like me—a mystic, you have to watch what you say and watch what they say about you because no one ever knows You at all, but will try to say they knew you well on another day.

What if I let you lie here while we all sit and talk about you? You would like that, but no one will do it—no one. Psychiatrists let you talk and never talk back because they do not know you and seldom listen. They want you to tell them about you and figure out why you are not happy. They are not into you. You will not let them in. You have to be in charge, but right now I would like you to lay there and let me tell you what I know about you.

"You are bright. You have a lot of sense. You do not think of anyone as being mean but know of a lot who are—you are not, but can protect yourself. You know of a few who take advantage of the weak, but you do not. You have never hated anyone, but know there are some who hate you."

There is only so much I can say out loud without laughing. I have only to think and I get excited. I want you to understand you are the same as everyone else while you are here, yet cannot be the same—all souls are totally different.

What if you sit there and stare at this page and don't see me or anyone? If you see only a page with print on it, you are a very literal person. You have little imagination or cannot use what you have, but you have intelligence or you would not be obeying my instructions.

What if you are not told a thing? You would be dead. You would never survive. You have to learn and develop a set of principles that help you stay away from Earth's demolition crew. If you do not know a thing about soul survival, you are lost. You got sucked up into the vacuum during the early years of this life and were not able to see or develop much beyond the ninth or tenth grade, regardless of how many years you stayed in school—yet you would think you were smart.

It's that way everywhere. You could live in China and know exactly what you need to know in the United States or live in the United States and never be able to survive beyond your own family. You cannot succeed if you do not study or learn from others. If you stick only to your own kind, you are in danger. What to do? Learn what you need to know. Go about and listen to people or talk to them, but they cannot be at all like you if you want to learn from them.

I was so mad at a Klu Klux Klansman. I shouted at him. Why? He did not see things as I did. I was mad at him for being different. I hated his indifference to my views. I was intolerant and said he was. I hated me right then. I know it now, but then I was sure he was wrong and I was right. You have to live to learn what is right for you.

What if you let everyone else decide if I am telling you the truth? You can. I bet someone will be glad to tell you what I mean. You have to fight the tendency to adjust to the viewpoint of others, but you can. You can try to stay the same, but the tension is so severe you cannot. You might as well get used to being changed by what other people say and accept it. It happens!

Where you are now is where I was when I left New York, but you are further along because you learned from my story. You either take my way and escape or head for the next bus and go home. You decide. Your life is your own decision and no one else's, ever. You keep trying to convince us you are not responsible, but we are not listening to words, we believe what we see—YOU.

You have to believe me when I say I had a long rest in Cancun and experienced a lot, but I will not tell you what I saw. You have to figure it out. You have to imagine how much time I spent on my 'vision quest' and why I thought I needed one, but I know and you know you were there beside me all the time.

The Time is Not Why

If you begin to think about it you never have time, but you do. You can do whatever you want to do and when you finally do, you say you never before had time to do it. Why? It makes no sense to me, either.

When I left Cancun to return to Merida, I thought I had plenty of time to make it there before nightfall but was still on the road as the sun set and the moon came out. I could not figure out why since I had left early enough, but one thing after the other delayed me.

What I need now is a precise bearing on my life. I do not want any crude approximation of how much time I have left. If I knew exactly how long I had to live on Earth, I think I would take a more careful approach to life here. I would do things better or have more fun, but this way I do not know what to do.

I guess if I knew when, I would worry myself to death—literally. This way I get up every day and do what I have to do and whatever else I want to do and then go to bed to get up tomorrow and do the same thing over and over again—and it works. But maybe I should be doing more?

It was nine-thirty when I arrived in Merida. It was dark and gloomy—not bright and noisy as usual. In fact, there were so few people around I thought maybe the vacation exodus was in progress. You see, in August, all of Merida goes to the beach at Progresso.

After checking in with the desk clerk at the hotel, I went directly to my room. I was sure nobody saw me come back, but once I lay down in bed trying to sleep, I saw a shadow on the wall. It was of a man leaning against the wall of the patio below smoking a cigarette. I could smell his smoke. Strange, but I never noticed cooking odors ascending from below—let alone a single cigarette, and I never thought I could see a shadow on my wall coming from that direction, either. Perhaps the light was never this bright before. I knew the man lit one cigarette from another, so he could not be one of the kitchen help taking a break. Reaching that conclusion caused me to crawl out of bed and sneak to the window to see who was down below.

It was Freddie! I didn't know he smoked. He is so clean-cut and young— and intelligent, but there he is—smoking. I might as well go back to bed. I feel calmer and more secure knowing he is on guard down there.

At seven, I got up and shuffled around the room unpacking everything and stowing it in the closet. It did not take much time, but I did buy some strange things—now that I look at them. I cannot remember why, but they pleased me then.

There was a shoe box crammed full of plants and herbs and stuff I found at the big Indian market where I prowled for hours—like I knew what I wanted and nothing else would do. It cost next to nothing, and everyone seemed to know why I wanted it. I don't. But I have it anyway. Why the colorful basket full of paper and things to give to children? There were big jars and bowls which, I guess, can be used for flower arrangements or whatever, but I have never seen anything like this pottery in my travels—quite ceremonial and rather ancient in appearance, but no one would sell antiquities in the market-place. Would they?

I decided to go out later and look for Freddie downstairs or near the University where he is a student, and wondered again why I had never seen him around the area since my return. Where would Jorge hang out if he came to Merida? I have had him on my mind almost constantly, but he has not materialized. I never thought of Freddie at all while in Cancun, yet he is here. Makes me wonder about the universal laws of manifestation, but I guess they know what they are doing. I can wait. I know Jorge is somewhere around here now, but I can wait for him to reappear, too.

Glancing out the window one last time before leaving my room for breakfast, I saw Jorge in the spot where Freddie had stood the night before and he, too, was smoking. Weird!

"Speak of the devil and you smell his smoke!" A giggle welled up in my throat and I felt warmth spread from my face down my throat and beyond and instantly decided to creep downstairs, go around to the back of the patio, and surprise him!

"Howdy! How is life treating you?"

Jorge was definitely surprised. I could tell by the way he threw the cigarette down and ground it out with his heel.

"Why, hello, Amanda. How are you? I have been waiting here for days to see you. Where have you been?"

"Oh, come on, Jorge, you have to know."

"Well, I do not. I have never professed to have the means to keep track of anyone who does not want others to know where they are, and you certainly did not. We could not pick up a clue on you. You really disappeared! Put our whole network in a dither—which was sort of nice. We have grown rather complacent, thought we had you all figured out, but you are obviously ready to teach us all a few new tricks again."

"Tricks? Is that what you think I used?" I could not stop laughing for some reason, but managed to say between giggles, "Visa is the only magic I used. I took off like anyone can, but left no forwarding address. You will have to guess where I went."

"Seriously, we were not able to pick up on you. You stopped transmitting and we could not pick up anything until around nine last night. Where were you, and what were you doing? Sleeping?"

"Oh, come on, you know when I'm sleeping. No, I flew back to New York." I cannot resist tormenting men who act like they are superior, but are sort of cute anyway.

"Oh, no, you did not go back to New York. We would have known."

That's weird. How could they? I kept my thoughts to myself and said, "Yes? How is that?"

"You know."

"No, I don't know." At least not consciously.

"Aw, come on now, you are not going to try to give me—your oldest friend, a hard time about this. Are you?" Jorge sounded unlike himself in some odd way.

"I told you before. I don't know what goes on here half the time. Why would I know how you keep tabs on me and know if and when I am in New York or anywhere else?"

"Okay, assuming you are serious—you transmit your location."

"What? I find that hard to believe. How do I do it and how do you pick it up?"

"Mandy, everyone does it, but not everyone wants to work hard enough to listen. We do—you and I. We work. We meditate. We strive to learn what is in the world and what is not, but most people are content to know nothing. In fact, the worst offenders today are the scientists who believe they know every-thing. We shamen get no credit while they do, but they are lost and we are not. Which would you rather be?"

"Obviously, I prefer to know where I am and where I am going, but I don't."

"Oh, yes, you do. You know exactly where you are, and you control it by concentrating on being here now. If you let your concentration falter or choose to alter it, you can go into other times and other places; but if you do, you lose the purpose for which you entered this realm. You came to Earth to be you and do whatever you came here to do. But if you go back and forth from one dimension or time to another, when do you get your work done? Maybe never. So you concentrate, and when you do, we can read your whereabouts—and you were not in this world! We know that much, but we don't know where you were."

"And I am not telling you."

Jorge said in a restrained manner, "That is fair. We really have no business in that area of your life. We are merely here to make sure you are safe."

What is he talking about? Is he trying to manipulate me into doing something weird by scaring me? "What do you mean by 'safe'? I am as safe as you are."

"That is my point, Mandy. I am not safe, either. We both know too much."

"You sound like the mob is out to get us."

"In a way."

Now he is not making any sense at all, but maybe if I play along with him, he will. "Why hang around here, if you are in danger?"

"Usually, I do not. But you are here, and I am here to reunite with you and take you where you will be safe—but you knew that!"

"I don't. I don't know why I am here and don't know why I left this place to go to Cancun. Yes, I was in Cancun! Don't look so surprised. You can seek asylum in Sodom and Gomorra. It's what you make of it. Right?"

"Right! I was not putting Cancun down. It merely seemed an unlikely place for a pilgrimage."

"Yes, I guess it was a pilgrimage, but I never thought of it that way. Wonder why I had to go there for my little hiatus?"

"You did live in that region—surrounded by snakes—and were feared by everyone because you casually walked anywhere and were never bitten. It was an awesome sight."

"Really? Up until two years ago, I was terrified of snakes. In fact, I decided to practice behavioral psychology on me and conditioned myself by looking at pictures of snakes, then going to the zoo, and finally actually petting one at a circus. Thinking about it now, I wonder why I had to do all that? I always thought I was scared of snakes because my family killed them every time they found one. At one point I even imagined I had been killed by a snake in a previous life! But that flies in the face of what you've just said."

"Come to think of it, Mandy, at that time one of our enemies did use a snake to kill you. It was not real in the everyday sense. He conjured a snake and it attacked you and you fell backwards into the sacred cistern. You actually died of drowning but the snake appeared to bite you, and we all killed the villain. But it was too late. You were drowned."

"Wow!" Even if this is all nonsense, it really makes me feel good. I don't know why, but it does.

"You are a well-educated woman in this life and have learned many things that when combined with the ancient ways will make you the greatest healer and wise woman of our race, so we are all anxious for you to get started."

"I'm anxious myself. I want out of this place. I used to like Merida, but now it feels alien—the people are strangers to me. I don't feel right. I want to go."

"Okay. We will have someone come back later and remove your things. Act like you are taking the rental car back, but head out of town and leave it at my friend's place for him to return tomorrow."

"Sounds like we are being watched."

"We are—constantly. You are not welcome here. You are no ordinary American tourist down here on a lark—or to visit the shrines. You are too much for the local authorities. They don't want to be responsible for you. You are not here permanently—or so they think, but you are, and we have to make you disappear now."

"It's starting to sound really interesting. Where are we going?"

"Can't risk saying now. They may already be watching and listening to us. You can't be too careful. They have been on our backs for a while now, but so far today, we have eluded everyone. Better act like we just met—like I bumped into you."

We walked into the hotel lobby and I grabbed his arm while saying, "Oh, Jorge! I can't believe my luck! How wonderful to bump into you like this. Why don't you come with me to breakfast. I found a really nice place on the other side of town. Come on!"

"It sounds great, Amanda, but I have only an hour or so before I have to go to the airport."

"No problem. I only have to return my rental car and the restaurant is on the way there."

"Sounds too good to turn down. How are you anyway? You look great! Have you been in Merida long?"

"About a month or so. I decided to relocate and—"

"Relocate? Why? What would ever possess you to do that?"

"Oh, it's a long story and not that interesting—trust me."

"I am not complaining, I am happy to see you here. We have to meet again when I get back in town."

Once inside the car we continued to act like old friends as I drove the little Geo over the rough streets, but he was unlike the man I had met on my previous trip. He was extremely tense and vigilant.

"What is wrong? You keep shaking out like you are easing your mind, but you are still tense. Why?"

"Someone is onto us. I know it, but I cannot see who it is. It is not my imagination, but maybe it's not in flesh."

"Huh? Are you serious, Jorge?"

"Always! I never joke—or haven't you noticed. It is an occupational hazard. We try to guard against it, but usually lose our sense of humor around the third or fourth round."

"Well, I still find most of life absurd."

"You would. You have always been wiser than me, but then again I am always the one who has to rescue you. So, how wise can you be?"

Checking his face out in the rear-view mirror left me with no clue as to what we were really doing.

"Wait a minute, Jorge! You don't throw something like that at me and then retreat into silence. I have to know. When have you ever had to rescue me?"

"I, or should I say, we—have been continually rescuing you since New York."

"I don't believe you. I went back and sold everything. It all fell into place so easily you would have to know it was meant to be."

"That is true, but we had to get you out of New York—the first time. You never had any idea of all the close calls you had. You thought muggers abounded, but you were being watched and the intensity of their surveillance increased when you began identifying the other time warps within this one. They knew you were awake then and started moving, so we had to rescue you."

"I don't believe it."

"You will."

His rigid mouth and the firmness in his jaw indicated I might as well stop and save my breath. He was not about to reveal anything else—at least not now. What about all this rings true?

He was not in New York, but he knew about the close calls I had had over the last six weeks I was there. In fact, the nervous tension caused by those encounters is what prompted me to fly away forever. I decided on Merida as though it were the same as Paris or Rome or any other worldly capital, yet was surprised when everybody else was shocked at my choice.

Maybe that last would-be mugger was not an ordinary scum bag, but the guy who came out of the shadows and rescued me was an angel as far as I'm concerned and deserves my gratitude. But if Jorge is right, all those angel sightings were his guys in disguise. No, that is too weird!

"You had so many close encounters with foreign emissaries that we had to ask for help above. You were assigned to the detachment in New York, but they could not be everywhere—you do get around. So, angels watched over you—and even they complained. You do not watch out for yourself very much."

"Are you serious? Yes, I can see you are. But angels complained about watching over me? That is too far out even for me to believe."

"Oh, yes, the angels can complain—and they did. They are not here to protect you, but to help us. We are trying to keep evil at bay until you can help us free all the souls here, and if the angels can help us, they do—but you were too indiscreet. You walked down streets without looking around and you used dark alleyways to save time, but they were always there."

"Are you saying my need for speed makes me or made me a pain in the butt?"

"Exactly! Remember, we Mexicans do not like to rush."

"Well, well, Jorge. You have just made a joke—a very little one, but a joke. We might be able to get along after all."

He jerked his head around to look at me, then his voice dropped as he said mildly, "Get along? Of course, we get along. We always have. We always will."

"Don't be so sure of yourself, Jorge. I just might find another guide."

"No way. I'm it. I am the one you married. That is why I am so annoyed. I would think you could at least remember that much some of the time."

If we had not been getting out of the car and checking to see if anyone was watching, I would have laughed out loud, but Jorge did not look amused.

The Ways to Be

There is nothing so rare as rain in the Yucatan in winter, but this winter there is so much rain you can see it coming and going and still not realize it is over. Daily you decide if you want to change your clothes after the rains or just let them dry on you. Another view: if you work up a sweat, you can pretend it is rain and not change. Whatever you do, you will be forgiven. The Maya may not believe it, but they are the most forgiving of all races. You must know that to be able to take what they will give you one day.

Whatever your day, you can be happy or sad. You have the time to do whatever you want to do. Some people shirk their duty and say, 'I don't have time'—but why bother with them? I would rather walk in the dark than sit in the light of a dim person.

Wow! That really sent me. I like it. It's a wonder some of the things I say! But why would *I* be surprised?

You have to wonder about your life, too. Nothing worries me now. I let it all go. If I can figure out what is going wrong, I do. If I can't, why worry? Life is simpler this way and I have more time—and a lot more fun.

When you worry, you stop. You do not do a thing. You sit and stare and do nothing, but think you are thinking. You are not. You are stalled. You have to start up the whole process of initiating a thought once more. You cannot sit and do nothing without hurting the entire process.

What happened with Jorge was such a shock that I put it away until today, but nothing changed. It is still there—hanging in the air. I am Jorge's wife! I am his equal in all things! I am not crazy, but I am not real either. I am sort of here and maybe there, yet alive. What kind of life is this? You tell me!

When you decide who you will be, you figure you will marry and have kids or you will never marry or have kids, or you will have a big job and no career, or a little job and no career, or have a real job doing what you love—which is a career, but you really cannot see into the future. You cannot see yourself not being you or not having a thing to do. You cannot see yourself as being in two different time frames, either, but it can happen.

When I first arrived here I was sure I was a New York investment coun- selor, but left knowing I had lived many lives as a Maya and would return again this lifetime. What could have happened to change me? Nothing, but I did. No one asked me to change my mind or make a decision or do any- thing—I just did!

What if you had the same experience? Would you be able to accept it? I do now. I know it is true. I believe I am here now and was here before to prepare me for this time, and now that I am living in Mayaland I will do whatever I have to do to save my people—as was prophesied.

Whether you agree or not, you have to admire my respect for what I cannot figure out but truly believe exists. I can't figure out who you are either but think I have me sorted out—at last. It took this last transition for me to realize life is not at all easy if you believe you exist only once and at one time. You cannot make it all come out right. It does not match up. You have nothing to control. You do not know. It is too limited, too mysterious.

When you decide to let go of all the 'real' world's mumbo-jumbo, you are disoriented for a day or so, but you find it again. It does not disappear. You do, but the life is still there. I want you to figure out how you can disappear, too, yet not be out of the picture, but you are getting worried now and that is stop- ping us all. We all have to move or the continent will shift. We cannot just stop. If all the universe stopped to think, we would all stop the universe—and then where would it be?

When I go out, I think, 'What are you doing?' When I return, I say, 'Where have you been?' I do this because in reality I never left. I may have looked like it, but I stayed here and the world left.

See how I get? I sort of blend my orientation, then slur over the bits and pieces and pretty soon it all makes sense—to me. Can you follow? You may never have figured on it happening, but now you understand quantum physics, even if you say you are confused.

You should see how much money I have saved since I moved down here. I don't buy anything. I see what is on the plate and eat it, but don't cook or pre- pare it. I still shop, but it is not the same as before when I would say to myself: 'I like that dress.' Now I see myself in the dress and agree it is nice, ergo, no need to buy. I like it this way. No problems ever.

You get into problems when you have too many choices. After all, you have to decide everything in life! You can't let time be. You have to drink or eat, do this or that, go here or there or be in the opposite place. I intend to shorten the time I waste, but don't want to throw it away. I will sort out what you can use, then let you digest it later. Don't get too bogged down now trying to understand me.

What if I sit and think about you and you think about me? You would be in me and I would be in you, but who would be in who? I mean, who would be in whom? Are you able to continue? If you aren't, just skip it. If you can follow, let me teach you.

There is nothing in the world that exists for no reason at all, but if you do not know about it or do not use it, it might as well not exist. When you decide to use it or learn about it, you see it everywhere and everybody talks about it. Was it always there and you never knew or did you need to know to create it?

What you need to do to gain access to the inner workings of your mind is a microscope, but you use a telescope. You do not realize how small your mind is! You think so little when you know it all. It sounds confusing to use only a portion of the world to know it all, but it is the truth.

What if I said you had nothing on and you thought you did? Would I be lying to you or you lying to you? I don't know what to say, but if you tell me, we will both know.

I go on and on like this until I find a connection and open to you and you accept. You will. You want to know. You do not like to be upset but hate not knowing even more, so if the mind shuts down, you ignore it and go into the work yourself. Whatever you do now, let the mind absorb what it can and keep going. You cannot afford to let it stop. If you do, you will be forever locked in this time.

When time stops, it stops! You think of yourself as lost but the space is not. The space is there and you are not. You think of things you have in your mind, but you do not have a mind. You only have things.

You can see now that when I decide to rationalize, I can, and you cannot resist trying to follow me. I was doing a job on my mind and pretty soon you were, too. Why?

The time is now, but you have it all and think it is not now. Why?

My work is not going well down here and they all think it is because I am not able to absorb the primary reason I am here, but I am. I am able to absorb the life I have here and why I am here, but the Spirit does not understand that this mind is not equipped to do the work. I have to train it.

When you decide to train yourself, you have a huge task before you that will reward you immensely—if you can take it. I meant to tinker with only one small area of my consciousness and not bother with the rest, but it does not work that way. I had to stop and reuse the old ideas to find ones that still work. It is hard to be totally original. You cannot explain it.

Any explanation for the time you have wasted is not very appealing, and if you do not accept it, you cannot figure out why you have no luck. You blame luck for everything if you have any, but cannot blame it if you never had any. You figure it out—but it is absolute.

Whatever you believe you do not have now, you had to have had at least once. For example: If you say, "I don't believe in God," you have to have believed at least once or it would not make any sense to disbelieve.

Whatever you really want, you get but you might believe you wanted what appeared, although you never asked for it. Why? You rationalize everything or nothing. You cannot be half-way about anything. You are the way you are. The way you are is the way you will be. You cannot change. You cannot be different. You have to be the same, which prohibits change, so work on being exactly the same—then you will change! The change occurs when energy is used to move or maintain whatever. If you exert energy, you are and cannot doubt that you change.

What if you and I decide to enter the work of others and remove all that is not of love? Would we be able to do it? Of course, we can—but their work would remain. It would not collapse. Love is not energy. Love is there in the filament, but it is nonexistent. You have only the idea.

The idea of being in love is not enough to make you love, but some are convinced now that love is the answer to all their problems. Why? They are tired of working on themselves and prefer to blame another. You can, if you are attached to someone. You can blame them for all that does not work. No one will believe you, but you can blame them.

There are two different people in me now. One of them is still in a stage of denial saying it cannot be, and the other one is trying to say I am. I want to be, but I cannot accept it. I will, but I can't. I have accepted, but I do not know. It mutates and grows into the blubbering idea that you are not able to be you. You get in over your head and feel like you are drowning, but instead bubbles rise to the top and carry you with them. I like the idea. . . .You have to let power rise.

Rising in the waves of the ocean of the mind is an idea or an ideal you alone produce, but you may not believe it. You may want others to believe you have great power, but you do not if you need others. You may want others to decide for you what is going on here, but you have to decide why you are doing it. When you know, you go.

The leaving behind of dead issues is the toughest idea yet, but if you follow now, you can end all the troubles you have ever had. All trouble comes from the past. It never exists at the moment. You have trouble because you did not take the right road or made the wrong choice, but you were right at the time you made the decision.

Whatever you think now, you will find out later if it works. You cannot be sure now. You do it, and if it works, you have to remember what you did. We either go forward—straight and narrow and not lose the path or go into the alleyways and risk losing the train of our own motives and thoughts. It is always our decision, but one is easier to live with in the future than another.

Really old people often lose their way while still on Earth and erupt into strange behavior which no one else enjoys, but the truth is they know and can go, so they slow. Do you want to wander around seeking help when you get old or do you want to know? I bet you, too, will know and let others think you do not—that way they will leave you alone. I know I will always know. I cannot forget just because I am done working here.

Your past is no assurance that you are now okay, but it can tell you what you chose. If it was bad for you—it causes sadness. The past is usually full of bad ideas and not-so-hot people who came and went—what a concept, and you have to decide why and who you are now, which can be confusing to you. If you get too confused, you get depressed. That is not what we need.

We want energy and light, not dispirited people who are dim and not able to linger. You cannot linger if your light is going out. You will have to rush to find the end.

What if you die when you are still in your teens? Would you want to come back? I bet you would. I bet you figure it was easy and you 'just didn't have the right parents this time!' I know. I remember how arrogant we are in our teens this life, but today's teenagers are still babies. You are not here to know anything; you are here to remember what you always knew; there cannot be a difference. But at the teenage level of development, you are not able to concentrate or know much. You think about yourself so much you do believe that you alone exist or that teenagers are the only ones who matter. It takes time to become wise, but teenagers are wise when they just let it happen.

When you do not let life happen, you end up being made. You cannot be made if you do it yourself, then you are the creator. I want you and me to create, but it is too hard to work together. I think I will tell Jorge about all this stuff and see if he wants to continue as a couple and go nowhere or if he wants to uncouple and go forward.

I bet he already knows. He is such a nice guy, but arrogant. Most men are—at least with women, but they cannot be that confident or they would be better off. The average man never has much until he marries and even then he may not succeed if he does not marry wisely.

You think of all this and you wonder, 'What is it all about?' But if you do not think, it all makes sense. I want to make sense, but I do not know how to stop thinking. I want you to be able to understand me, but you can't stop thinking, either. Let's just forget we even tried and go on together.

This is the End

I started out to say I had nothing left in my mind to think about, then Jorge showed up and all I did was think. Weird. You have to be loose or you will crack. You have to be able to fall and be shatter-proof if you want to make it back.

When you are old and gray like I am getting to be, you will know why you did most of what you have done, but never figure out all of it. So, why wonder now?

We were going to leave Merida and never return, but I had a few things which had to be done first—even though Jorge thought nothing of them. They were important and he was wrong, but never mention it when the other person errs. It makes for messiness if you do.

I went into my bank and offered to take out a CD or some other kind of certificate to invest my money, which seemed silly to him. Why would I need money? I have never seen money as clearly as right then. It had a life of its own and I had to do something or it would die, so I asked them to change the name on my account. It was simple. Anyway, I ceased to exist—financially.

When we drove out of the bank's parking lot, I felt eyes on me but decided to say nothing. Whoever or whomever might be able to pick up on us and I did not want to tell anyone anything until I knew where we were headed.

Whatever you do, do not let the world know you are going to do it until you are ready to do it, or the troops will be marshaled about to prevent you from doing what you want. The world seldom comes to your rescue, but the universe will. I know it sounds like the same thing, but it isn't.

The universe is all that is and God is the supreme, but in this world you and I and every other comedian can arrange it to suit ourselves. If you plan on doing something not kosher as far as I am concerned, I can stop or delay you—

so do not let the world know too much too soon if you wish to move forward. Just say your little prayers out loud in the privacy of your own space so the universe knows what you need or want. Do not talk to others about your plans if you want to avoid static.

You will have to figure out how I embarked on a trip with Jorge—as his wife, yet never remembered marrying him. It's no big deal to figure out, but the mind likes puzzles and this one will keep you busy later.

I like to be enigmatic because it causes others to drop you and not mess in your life. If you are patient and kind and forgiving and sad and foolish and helpful and decidedly undecided, everyone comes into your aura and tries to help you or do whatever to you, and it is a waste of time and energy. If you keep to yourself, nobody will bother you, but they will start rumors. If you are dramatic or puzzling or unpredictable, you may cause some to try to figure you out, but if you are all of these put together, they give up rather quickly and leave you alone. It is easier to be that way.

Why not sit and stare and think yourself into another time? Because you have to do time there, too. You cannot just move in and out and do nothing. You have to see yourself there, then do it. But you can walk in for a time, leave, and come back again if you just want to check it out. That is permitted.

You seem surprised. Why? The universe has rules which cannot be broken. You can try, but you will not succeed. Always remember the universal laws and forget Earth's decrees only if you are out of touch with the way your world works. If you forget Earth's laws, you may end up sacrificed to the economy or the nature of people, so do not forget to obey your own laws, after all you made them. The universal ones are all included in your basic rights, but some of the weird constrictive ones are anything but of God. You wrote them, so get rid of them or pay your fines.

Whatever we do down here is not the same as in the States, but it is. You have to remember that the people are poorer here, thus obey more laws and do less to attract the notice of others, particularly the police or the government. Nevertheless, they are still human and there are millions of them. You will not find them at all any different from you—unless they are Maya.

The Maya are not the only ones in Mexico, but they are the most true to the memory or traits of the ancients, thus, get the most attention today. I doubt we would remember them if they had not remained pious, but some want to think the old ways died out. Why? It would seem to prove that it does not matter how God-fearing you are, you will end up dead forever anyway. Man may rationalize that way to make up for evil ways, but it is not true.

The Maya are here. They are not anywhere else, but they are here and there and around and about by the simple means of being able to transcend the universe and gain access to the upper planes and then descend. You do not understand? Let me try to explain.

You do the same thing every time you climb the stairs in a house to get to another floor. You are still in the same building, but on a different level. Once upstairs, you either stay there or go downstairs. It is your choice. But if you do not know there are steps or you are not allowed to climb them, you think you cannot enter the upper level.

Here is another example: If you had a broken leg and had no means of climbing steps, you would be handicapped like us. We have this broken leg we call a mind and it refuses to let us enter anything we do not know or understand, so we take time to learn all the steps required in order to freely ascend. Hope that helps you, but it is hard to talk about something you 'just know'. Know what I mean?

Whatever you do, you think about it first and decide if you can follow or not. Then you either do it or you do not. You cannot just leap, because you have to land and are very much aware of it all the time.

What if you did just jump? You would regret it. You would be sorry you did not think it out first. The mind gets upset every time you take a shortcut and do not study enough. You leap and think but cannot do two things well if you have not done enough work before-hand in both areas.

When you learn rapidly how to accomplish something that normally takes weeks or months to learn, you just have a talent for it. Right? No, you did it before—at some time. When? Maybe this life, maybe another. What is surprising about that? You live. You die. You live. You enter the next plane, and so on, but in reality you never die. You merely cut back and regroup from time to time.

If this life requires you to know how to play the piano and you never played it before, you will get opportunities early in life to learn. You may not have the ability to finger the keys well but without much effort you will be advanced beyond others of your own age. It is no big deal! If you want to play the piano and never get the chance, it is because you do not need to know it in this life to advance but like it because you played once or twice before.

When you sort out all the ways you make sense, you realize you are not ever an irrational being thrust into an irrational space and time, but the place within it and the world you create are seldom rational. Why? You design your place in the world and then help build that world around you.

You are not able to change the world? Nonsense! You help maintain it every time you speak and obey. You obey the land and the laws because you chose to be here and do your work here, but you may not want to work now. That is probably why so many are not happy today. They are here to work out a life they asked to do on Earth, but got sidetracked—which is how to become a miserable failure while appearing to be a huge success.

When you are very wealthy and successful, you may be as happy as possible and others say you are not, but you know. If someone is wealthy and not happy, it is because they are not at the stage in their development where they can accept the fruits of their labor or they are not there at all. Money does not make you happy. It just is.

The money I left in the bank is going to feed an entire village over in the Guatemalan highlands, but what I did is of no use if they have already given up. If they can hold out until I get it to them, they will be okay; but if they lose faith and run to the city, they will be lost and so will the money.

When you give up ownership to money it takes a few days or weeks to accept you have nothing. Why? You chose to do something you had no clue as to how you would feel when it is done. But, it does feel good now!

I like the feeling of not having to concern myself about the stock market, interest rates, or the maximum rate of return on certificates. I feel light and free and have no remorse.

What if I do regret it later? I can always go back and rebuild it again—but what would I gain? I am not here to live. I am here to be in this life until I can ascend to the next one. But if I died rich, what would I get from the money? Not much, but my heirs would be busy becoming greedy or overwhelmed with the responsibility—depending upon their nature.

What I did was not a big deal, but the people in the highlands are up and about now. They will be able to stay. I will be able to live. I will be able to go there and be immediately accepted by them—even though they will not know the money came from me, but I digress.

When I went to the bank, the eyes of a thief and a would-be robber were upon me, but I left with no money and they knew it. How? The presence of money in your pocket is an aspect of the mind that reveals itself. Thieves can see it. They merely have to watch for the signs.

When I left the bank penniless, the thief was obviously annoyed and the would-be robber had no further use for me. How can they appear to be the same, yet not act alike? You are two different people, too. You think and act another way, but you are the way you are. The thief is curious and steals for the way it makes him feel, but the robber is there to take and may or may not repeat it once he has what he wants.

What you take from the universe is not going to be returned. The universe has enough, but you have the need to take. You will never take once you find out your needs are what hold you here. You hold up your own soul's progress. We could all leave Earth now, but our needs here and now hold up our progress. When the attachment to goods is gone, you will still feel attachment to people. You have to learn that your goods are not you, but the people you love are. This is not easy to explain.

Let's go back to the dead man in the jungle, Regis Fawley, maybe it will help you understand. You did not stop thinking about him, but I did. I had little curiosity because I knew the man and did not like him. You are still curious because you were introduced and never had a chance to judge whether or not he deserved to be murdered. When you know all the details, you usually lose interest and are less curious about the outcome. As a bystander, you need to know why. You want to know if it could have been prevented, could it have happened to you, and would you be capable of the crime, but it is not important. The victim is no longer on Earth. He is not here and does not exist. You are here and exist. Your life is less or more from having known about him, but you cannot be aware of why that is until the mind figures out why he was murdered and who did it. If you want to backtrack, you can, but I prefer to just enter the picture and go forward.

When I left the crime scene I was absorbed in watching Jorge fade from the crowd and disappear. I wondered where he was and how he left the scene. He was there, yet he was not. You can do the same thing, but it takes a long time to master. You practice by withdrawing your attention as people talk to you and then withdrawing your energy from them, and if you are adept at this, your body fades away. No big deal if you master the universe, but definitely not something for beginners to attempt.

Jorge knew who committed the crime. He 'saw' it all, then withdrew his attention because his curiosity was not attached to the moment. He knew, therefore was no longer curious and lost his insight immediately.

If you cannot figure out who did a crime, you become preoccupied and nervous. But if you 'know' how it was done, why it was done, and who did it, you are not likely to remain attached to it. Remember your own preoccupation over OJ's trial? You either were simply astonished and could not get on with *your* life or knew it was the way it was and lost interest. That is one way to learn to be yourself.

You cannot give up your energy and life to somebody else—particularly someone whom you have never met. You cannot expect them to care. You do, but they cannot. They do not know you. Then why bother to invest your time and reality in them? Your mind is not busy enough.

Whatever you do, you will do well only if you want to do it. We are not bothering about all the details of the murder and why it happened because my mind is busy with things more interesting to me. You can flesh it all out, but better not. It is not wise to devote time to negative activities—and the taking of a life is definitely not a positive action.

If you enter the press corps, you have already decided to enter the race against time and people. You cannot sit still until the story is produced and because you know everything, you feel powerful. You may even feel so powerful you do not report the news—then you become the news.

What you have to do to discover who committed the crime is not worth the trouble, but you do deserve an explanation. We want you to feel your life is complete; but how can it be, if you have to finish my story and never find out for sure why Regis Fawley was murdered?

Well, it is a long story about a man as feeble-minded as anyone you will ever meet in your daily rounds, who also was so greedy he wanted it all. He wanted his own life *and* the life of everyone around him, and to achieve that end he became a bully who would talk and drain the life out of everyone near him, but he never thought of himself as a success.

Word got to Regis that hidden in the jungle was a beautiful idol capable of curing the sick, healing the mental illness of the heart, and even clearing up acne, so he had to have it—if only because others valued it.

Only two people in this world collect things—the collector of the past and the collector of the future. You either collect to stock up on what will be valuable some day or you stock up on what you love and want to preserve. Regis was neither. He was just an arrogant and evil man who wanted what another possessed. Being just as angry as he was arrogant, when someone told him he could not have the sacred image, he inconvenienced himself to come to Merida and impeach or break the spirit of the owner or whomever he thought had it.

Suddenly finding himself all alone in the jungle, he realized evil forces had surrounded him and he died—mostly of fright. He was distraught and could not remember where he was or how to escape. Furthermore, he was so upset that his mental and nervous disposition entrapped him in the snare of those who remained calm and cool, although equally as diligent in seeking what was not theirs—namely his money.

When Regis went to the shrouded area of the parking lot, he attracted the attention of several different people and none of them were there to meet him. They picked up his intent ethereally and suspected he had come to rob the Uxmal site, so they watched him carefully and even radioed the police for backup. However, Regis never noticed a thing. Having no respect for the locals, he never noticed them as he became totally absorbed in trying to find a path through the brush.

When he finally found this path and entered it, he did not take time to fold back the bushes the way pirates would but left the trail wide open for anyone to follow him. His heart apparently so heavy with greed that he could not sense anyone around him, he went straight to the center of the clearing and did not see the trap until it was too late.

His money came from his mouth only—he had no real cash. He tried to bargain—said he wanted to see the idol first. Refused to answer their questions about the money, and adamantly questioned them about the value of the religious relic. When he saw they did not have the statue with them, he threatened to arraign them for thievery and that was the end of him. He entered the outer realms of this plane instantly with the first deep thrust of a sharp machete. The psychological trauma was so severe his brain never registered pain. He never felt it, but his bulging eyes divulged his shock.

What you need now is time to remember why you got nervous. I was not nervous, as I told you, but I was curious about why you have to know who did it, why you have to know things about people you do not know, and why you have to solve the mysteries of this life. Don't you see? It is all part of the reason why you came to Earth, but some of you get so odd and weird that you believe anything that is odd and weird and ignore the basics of reality.

What if I had told you some witch caused this man's death by sucking the air from his lungs or he merely died of dehydration? You would say it was okay for this story but could not have happened in real life and would be upset with me for having wasted your time; but now that you know it was due to obvious motives, you are still not happy. You prefer bizarre mysteries with twisted motives, but they can only occur in like lives. You want to be in touch with the supernatural or upper realm's work and all I offer you is mundane explanations. That is because you have to master the mundane before you can get to the upper realm. You cannot be less than you are. What you need now is a break from the tension, but I have to show you something else before you snap.

Remember the man and woman in Merida with Chip? I was there but sort of out of it. You paid attention while I sat in a trance. You have to remember why I was there, so I don't. When I saw Chip talking to the two Mexicans, the third level of my mind absorbed his intent. I could have listened or channeled everything Chip said, but why bother? The intent is all that matters. You can do whatever you want, but the final outcome is what counts. You may possess an original, but if it is reproduced, it is no longer an original—even if you say the others are copies.

There were several different people on that corner, but I was there to observe Chip and find out what he was up to, so by concentrating on him alone, the other two people faded from my awareness. I did not pay attention to any one else, but if I had, I would have noticed the way some people watched Chip yet took care not to be seen by him. I was not interested or involved enough to pick up on all of the details then, but I did later.

When you totally rehash something mentally, your version may be less distinct or a bit blurred unless it is really important to you to remember every detail. Since I figured it was important to you to know why Chip's death by a jaguar at Chichen Itza was never reported in the news, I meditated upon it during my time in Cancun and came up with a story that satisfies me, but maybe not you.

Chip was a reporter! He always had to know what was going on—especially if he could get a by-line on it. He prided himself on being on top of all the current issues concerning the Maya revolutionaries and why they were not winning the war, and he also saw himself as a great environmental crusader—if he was paid enough.

He must have been in on the entire fabrication of the war—certainly involved in maintaining it so his newspaper chain would pay for his expenses while he lived well doing nothing at all. We know he had no story, but others thought he did. We know he had no real insight into the issues surrounding the unhappiness of the Maya, but he implied he had put his career on the line in order to help the revolutionaries. They entrusted him with taking their message to the world—but he never did.

When it became apparent back home that his information was skewed by his lack of personal and professional ethics, the syndicated news corps refused to pay him to further pursue guerrilla or government leaders. He was too self absorbed to see that you and I do not care about war anymore. We want peace. We do not want any more bad news from good places about the same old stuff. We are all tired of it.

When his resources dwindled, he shifted his concentration and saw a profit could be made in stolen Mayan artifacts. This is what signed his death warrant on this life. He could not get near enough to betray again the guerrillas who had initially helped him as payment to get their message out, and he could not work with the government, so he figured out how to get others to steal and rob for him. Unfortunately for him, they expected to be paid. When he met two of his principals in the city, he was sure he could pick up the goods while avoiding payment; but being of the same mind, they had nothing with them, either.

It was a reenactment of the preliminaries leading up to the Regis Fawley murder, but the villain in Chip's case was his own sloth and unwillingness to work. He was not killed by a man, but by his need to cover his fanny while attacking whomever might appear to be stopping him from having it all.

When we met that day in Chichen Itza, he feared I was trying to block him, and his instinctive desire to eliminate the threat—me, caused him to die. The jaguar just as instinctively reacted to his blood-thirsty thoughts. Both are gone now. The jaguar was tracked down and shot since it posed a threat to the public, or so a rich American hunter said later on the evening news. Reportedly, the pelt is on loan to the Museum of Anthropology in Merida, but will not be displayed publicly, but I can 'see' it tacked on the wall of the hunter's mansion.

What you do when you are in pain is exactly what you are. Others may never know you until then, but you know. I want you to be without pain as much as I am now. I want you to fly from this room and get your own life. I want you to put aside this story and never think of it again, but your mind will. Why? You have entered data into it that is puzzling and enigmatic and has to be sorted out—but really, it is not important!

You are who counts! You are the only one listening to my story. I know you can duplicate it, but you won't. I want you to be sure you have it all down pat, but you do not have to rewrite it to know it. Your life is in this life, but it is not as neat as a novel. Why? When life is neat and tidy, you start thinking you are on top of everything and somebody is going to mess it up—and so it is. As you think—you are. Personally, I like it neat and tidy so I can take off when I have to or want to go.

Before you go, I want to let you know Jorge is no longer my husband. It was easy! I merely had to make him do a few things around the house he hates to do and nag him about his faults the better part of two days and he left.

No one wants to change, even if it is for the better. So if you have changed while you walked down this path with me, do not try to change anyone else— they might leave you. Where would that leave you? God alone knows, but you would still be YOU!

A Day is Never Done

Now the only day left is the day I end this one and go into the next, but to end one day is not the same as going into the future and having a lot of people want you to stay in the past. I did that most of this life, but now I want to move and go into the future while all around me are trying to tell me I am here to end the past.

What if you were here and had so much to do and so many people trying to make you do it? Would you do what they say or would you resist? If you think it is easier to do nothing, then let's see what happens when you resist.

First of all, you have to go into the center of the room and declare they are all crazy, then you have to tell all the shamen you have met that their belief in God is false and you are not in the world to help them. This is easy?

Now, what if you decide to just do it? I tried, but when it got down to the point where I had to totally submerge my personality into an old woman and begin to see things in *every* thing, I got miffed. I am not old. I am tired of acting like I am wise, and I am tired of not knowing what is going on when I talk. How can I enjoy being me? I tried. I really tried. But what a disaster for the ego!

When you totally give up the world, there are a few things you have to do that most people never dream of or even consider. For example: You have to do your own work! You do not have anyone to come in and tidy up and take care of little details for you. You have to enter every conversation as a wise woman—with no sense of humor or you end up without clients—or whatever you call these people who want to become dependent upon you.

When I entered this field I thought it would be for only a short time then I would be able to return to business as usual, but now they have me going to their homes for fiestas and feasts and doing religious ceremonies and all sorts of things that are fun but a bit tedious after the first few. I really do not enjoy them as much as I did at first, but I have to go if I previously went to one of their family or friend's affairs.

Yes, jealousy has no boundaries! You cannot run away from it even in the jungle of Yucatan. It exists. It has a life of its own. I tried to understand why all the people in town were growing desperate, and now that I am out here in the sticks, I find they are too. It is contagious.

Whenever a woman is a shaman she has to contend with the men being jealous of her profession and women being jealous that the men are jealous. It's not easy. You should have seen what the youngest shaman did to try and unhinge me. He set up a test and almost succeeded in trapping me into saying I was a shaman and had power, but I managed to sidestep it—which greatly annoyed him.

Several people down here are trying to help but most are in the way of progress or growth. Why? I guess no one really wants anything to change because if enough does change, everyone will have to learn new dialogue—if not new roles.

When you are down here like I am, you will see how the air gets sticky and hot and water seemingly hangs suspended in the atmosphere—which is not atmosphere but air that is hot. You can cut it up in chunks and move it like building blocks, which makes it easy to construct a new world That is why I think the world will begin to rebuild here. The atmosphere above and beyond Earth is not easy to cut, but it is here. Earth is not too dense or light, but the air is being depleted of so many chemicals—and oxygen is fast depleting all the universe of its components in order to provide humans with enough to live. You have to wonder who set it all in motion and why.

As I sit here with this book on my lap and a ball-point pen in my left hand in order to make sure I am connected to my own source rather than the universal one, I see you have time to do your life. But whenever you get too crowded— like Earth is now—you can't breathe, so you gasp and pant and try to free yourself. That is why I think we have to hurry. Sit beside me in your mind and watch the aura of the Earth. You can see Earth gasping and panting. Doesn't it sort of rise and fall under you? When I have a bad day I lie on the Earth and watch it. But lately, every time I do this I see the Earth shrinking—yes, actually shrinking from my touch.

What we have here is a classic case of the good dying young. The Earth is one of the youngest planets in the universe and we arrived shortly after it was created by a dynamic infusion of gases and started raiding it and taking things it needed for itself before it had a chance to settle down. We attacked our host right from the start!

You may have heard we tried to inhabit another planet once and it was so inhospitable we all returned, but that was not the way it was at all. We were so inhospitable to others from another planet that they had to go.

Wow! That really caught my eye. How about you? I never even contemplated that idea before. I have never considered the possibility of aliens—other than us—being on Earth. I accepted that we grew from amoebic plasma, determined to grasp what we could and thereby control our destiny—which became the human race. But this makes you wonder. Did we come from another planet as full-blown humans?

Yes, it is hard to believe that this Earth's slime could evolve into a race of giants among animals who would be able to submit to no one but God—and seldom doing even that. I guess I find the idea of an alien-being founding Earth as a satellite rather interesting, but not particularly compatible with my present thinking. It takes time to destroy old ideas, but even longer to build a whole new mindset. I am not sure I want to do it or have the time. You have to decide, too.

What if we just sit now and not say a word?

There, I sat for an hour and said nothing. It is an hour! I said it was. Why would it be more or less? It all depends upon you and what you believe, and I believe I spent an hour in meditation. What do you believe?

This morning is going by so fast that if I explore the possibility of space I will do nothing else, but the people around me will not let me take that much time. Why do we let others intrude upon us? Guilty of ego. That's it! I am so into being human I can't let up trying to help. I have to help every one I meet. It's not even occupational. I try to help the butcher, the baker, the candymaker, and even try to help friends if I am on my way to the post office or whatever—often delaying my own work.

When you decide to end your life in the 'real world', you won't have it nearly as tough as me. You can just rent an apartment somewhere nearby and not go out again and no one will care until you die, but down here they expect you to mingle—and I mean mingle!

In the States when you go to a social event you can stand around with a dinky little wine glass in your right hand signaling you don't wish to shake hands, or let your eyes rove over the crowd to indicate to anyone approaching that you don't wish to talk to them, but down here you have to talk. These people are honest, sincere, and very patient, so if you say nothing, they stand beside you for hours—literally, until you say whatever it is they are there to find out. I love it.

When you love being where you are, you have an entirely different attitude from those around you who are there under duress. The atmosphere is full of you. The new You. The new One! The totally different, special being you came here to be. I love this one, but the old one wasn't so bad, either. However, I do not remember much about her anymore. I want no part of her old life, but she was a nice person. I remember that much, but why she lived in New York or any of those other big cities is now a mystery to me.

What to do about living in your own space—yet having none? I tried, but it caught up with me and stabbed me so deep in the gut I had to exercise my will to exorcise the spirits of people forever trying to manipulate others to get to their purses. I threw it all away, but you do not have to do that ever. It is better not to do it, but if you do, come and visit me first. Don't rashly rush into selling off the condo and getting on a plane to Timbuktu.

Your love of adventure helps if you plan to leave anything, but it won't last. If you live in an exotic place for more than a week, it becomes home. You then have to go somewhere else for leisure and adventure. So, use the place you have to explore the rest of the world and then if you still want to live here among the Maya, you will have to work, believe me, but you are always welcome.

The Maya are not going to feed and clothe you. You are not going to be given handouts and facelifts and other sorts of deals to make you feel less out of the popular spirit. You have to hang on here and do it well or you fail, and you can't rush in and say, "Give me some of the $2 spread and I'll give you a $5 piece of baloney." Does that even make sense? I guess I am getting silly.

You have to understand—these people are not poor, but most have little money. You automatically think money is where it's at if you are an American, but down here you would be disfavored by all for such a belief. You are measured, of course everyone is, but you are not measured by wealth or tolerance or any of the means used in the world called America.

America was a dream of the past that crystallized a few years ago and now is being destroyed in order to rebuild another world, but the few who have any idea of what it should be are not being heard and the many voices who are heard are trying to make a profit—so it is going the way of Rome. So what? It will not last a day.

There is nothing you can take from that world into this one that will help you, but you will want a few niceties at first and even have them shipped to you upon occasion, but within a few months, you will forget. You will not remember your close attachment to indoor plumbing and beds. You will see for yourself that love is better than a bathroom.

What you need here is a hot tub and a bathing suit and a few other amenities? You could have them, but why? You don't have time. You have only a few moments in this life to prepare for the next and to waste them sitting in a Jacuzzi with a dumb person who is trying to be nice is a total absence of mind. Just try to meditate or carry on a deep, meaningful conversation in any pool with a lovely person in a swimming suit and I will show you the consummate act or lie.

Three times I have tried to end and go on to the next area of my life, but three times is all you have. If you cannot get it together then, you are out.

I tried to do it all at one time but got caught the last life and had to come back to renew a few old acquaintances and deliver a few sermons on the rights of women before I was free to live again, but I avoided it. This time I tried so many different things with my body. For example, I tried skiing and biking and horses and stuff everyone does, but it was all too tame and did nothing for me; then I tried the beauty routine and had manicures and pedicures and different things aimed at pampering the body, but none of it did much for the inner me. In fact, I became cranky and started to act like a spoiled cat.

'You have to design your own life' is what they all said, but when I tried, it was never what anyone else wanted. I would say, 'I'm going to teach kids how to live' and everyone would reply, 'how nice,' then turn their back on me. But if I said I planned to run off with a traveling salesman, they all wanted to know *everything* about it. Why?

Gossip is not as bad down here. It exists wherever there are two people trying to find a common ground, but down here they know who you are and need to only update from time to time to see if you are staying or straying from your own line, which only takes a minute or so to pass the news. You do not have to talk for hours to find out why they called or why they pulled you aside that day.

I try to help out the world from time to time, but I go into it seldom. I usually sit outside my door on a small stool-like chair and look like I am awake, then they arrive. I don't know where they all come from, but they arrive and stay most of the day.

My work begins in the morning and straggles on into the afternoon when I usually eat, but a lot more times than not I don't. I do not seem to need to eat much. I eat so seldom that my body is now almost half the size it was, but much stronger.

What you have on now is half of what you need, but you wear or carry it everywhere. I used to dress like I was headed for the arctic if it looked like snow, but down here I just drop a shift over my head and say, "I look nice" and walk out to my chair and never bother to look at me again that day. It is so much easier that way.

If you are still hung up on your outward appearance, you don't have to worry about removing it, it just goes. Instead, work on the inner spiritual beauty for an hour or so and you glow. You can take either approach, but the slow one lasts.

I want you to visit, but you have to decide when. I can't. I cannot work and tell time. If I try to figure out who is coming to see me or when, I waste energy better used to heal or serve. I do not wear time and don't even care what day it is. But I guess if I had to catch people and drag them to see me in order to get them to work on themselves like doctors and dentists in America and Europe, I would probably wear a watch, too—but what a waste of time.

What you need to do to prepare for your end is the same thing I am doing now. Wrap up any loose ends, portray your life in a single sentence or a simple monologue, then let it flow and go from you time and time again. You do not have to wait or work for anyone. You just let go like I am leaving you now.

End Notes

The author resides in the United States and travels much. Her favorite destination is Mexico.

If you have just begun to work on Time or have been at it for a long time and wish to share your experience with Ruth Lee, you may contact her at LeeWay Publishing.

This work is not done—more to come...